The Trap

by

Jonas Saul

PUBLISHED BY:

Imagine Press Inc.
Ebook ISBN: 978-1-927404-55-3
Paperback ISBN: 978-1-998047-64-2
Hardcover ISBN: 978-1-998047-65-9

The Trap

The Sarah Roberts Series

Dark Visions (One)
The Warning (Two)
The Crypt (Three)
The Hostage (Four)
The Victim (Five)
The Enigma (Six)
The Vigilante (Seven)
The Rogue (Eight)
Killing Sarah (Nine)
The Antagonist (Ten)
The Redeemed (Eleven)
The Haunted (Twelve)
The Unlucky (Thirteen)
The Abandoned (Fourteen)
The Cartel (Fifteen)
Losing Sarah (Sixteen)
The Pact (Seventeen)
The Terror (Eighteen)
The Chase (Nineteen)
The Betrayal (Twenty)
Sarah's Return (Twenty-One)
The Hunt (Twenty-Two)
The Delivery (Twenty-Three)
The Trap (Twenty-Four)
The Ultimatum (Twenty-Five)
The Depraved (Twenty-Six)
The Condemned (Twenty-Seven)
Payback (Twenty-Eight)
The Unknown (Twenty-Nine)
Wrath (Thirty)
The Damned (Thirty-One)

The Game (Thirty-Two)
The Decoy (Thirty-Three)
The Disappearance (Thirty-Four)
The Whole Truth (Thirty-Five)
Alex (Thirty-Six)
Parkman (Thirty-Seven)
Darwin (Thirty-Eight)
Aaron (Thirty-Nine)
Remains To Be Seen (Forty)

The Jake Wood Novels

The Immortal Gene (Book One)
The Immortal Target (Book Two)

Standalone Novels

'Til Death Do Us Part
The Drowning
The Woman in the Woods
The Threat
The Specter
The Mafia Trilogy
A Murder in Time
Frequency of the Dead

Co-Authored Novels

Collision Course (Written with Gary Ponzo)
There Will Be Blood (Written with Rania Stone)
The Soulless (Written with Rania Stone)

Short Story Collections

Twisted Fate (Tales of Horror)
Twists of Fate (Tales of Hope)

The Trap

Chapter 1

"I DON'T LIKE THIS," Sarah whispered, leaning over the table to grasp Aaron's hand.

Aaron set his fork down, glanced around the dining room, and then focused on her eyes.

"Don't like what?"

Sarah released his hand, her stomach roiling, food untouched, and leaned back in her chair to study his face.

"Something is wrong. I can feel it."

Aaron wiped his mouth with the cloth napkin that had rested on his lap. "Wrong, how?"

She crossed her arms, doubting Aaron was back—*fully* back with her.

"Vivian said something about bigger things being in play than her and me."

Aaron waited a moment, then nodded for her to continue

as he lifted his wine glass and sipped.

After glancing around the restaurant to ensure no one was listening, Sarah said, "And she told me something about walking into a trap. I have no idea what she means, but it's been bothering me ever since she said it about a month ago."

"Did she tell you more about this trap?"

Sarah shook her head.

"All she said was a trap was coming?" Aaron asked.

Sarah nodded.

"So, on a scale of one to ten, this trap is probably one or a two."

Sarah leaned forward again, unlocking her arms to rest them on the table. "Why would you say that?"

Aaron shrugged. "Because if it were serious, like life-threatening serious, Vivian would tell you more. Leaving you in the dark means it's no big deal."

"That's not true. There have been times when she withheld information, which caused me more trouble."

"Fair enough, but you're still here."

"Meaning?"

"Everything will be fine." He picked up his fork and resumed working on his mushroom pasta dish.

Sarah stared down at her Greek salad. "I'm not comfortable with *fine* anymore," she whispered. When she glanced back up, he was staring at her. "There's a baby inside me, and I will do everything to keep him or her safe. If Vivian doesn't want to explain things better, then fuck it, I'm done."

Aaron took a bite, swallowed, and then washed it down with more wine. "Okay, be done. But done might not work in the event of a trap. You could walk right into it."

"You're not helping." She glared at him.

"Look, I don't know what you want me to say. If you just want me to listen, that's cool. But all I'm saying is, Vivian knows you're pregnant and how you feel about your baby's health—"

"Our baby's health."

"Exactly, our baby's health. Your sister won't be a part of another miscarriage. Vivian isn't stupid. She'd lose you forever. So, I'm convinced she will ensure you know all you need to know if something bad is coming."

Sarah placed a hand on her stomach and glanced downward so Aaron wouldn't see the tear that formed in her eye. Was she being too emotional? Was she overreacting? As a natural-born protector, she had challenged so many people over the years to stand up for the underdog, the abused, and the misused. And now, with a child in her womb, she would protect her own baby with everything she had. That also meant she would protect her unborn child from her own sister if Vivian weren't willing to leave them alone. And if something needed to be handled, Vivian would need to be more forthcoming, or Sarah wouldn't deal with it.

Sarah had never been selfish, never looked out for herself in this way. But being a mother changed things, and Vivian would need to learn the new dynamic.

"Sarah?" Aaron whispered in a soft voice. "You okay?"

She wiped her eyes and raised her head. "I'm not being emotional. I'm not being irrational. Vivian isn't talking, and I'm worried. We aren't doing enough. I feel it. Something's wrong, and we aren't doing enough. For all we know, being here tonight might be a trap. And your scale of one to ten is fucked. This trap thing is not a one or a two. It's likely a nine, but probably a ten. And when we're done here …" Her voice trailed off when she realized how loud she had gotten.

Aaron waved his hands in a calm-down gesture.

She glared back at several diners watching her. Even one of the waiters by the door to the kitchen stared at them. He had a worried look on his face. After offering everyone a snide grin, she turned her attention back to Aaron.

"We need to leave."

"Why? We're not finished eating."

"Too many people listening to our conversation," she said, loud enough to be heard by some nearby tables. "I'm finished, and I'm getting pissed off."

"Why?" Aaron asked, irritation evident in his voice. "Just calm down, eat some of your salad, and we'll leave." He held his wine glass up and then sipped.

She glared at him a moment. He drank wine while she ordered water. Normally, that didn't bother her, but everything bothered her tonight. After what happened last month with that sick vigilante delivering them body parts in boxes, Aaron had done the right thing regarding them and their future. He had committed to the betterment of the relationship in all things, spoke about marriage, and spent considerable time massaging her while discussing the future. With the trap closing—whatever that meant—getting information from Vivian was difficult at the best of times, which caused Sarah's concerns to increase. And not just for herself. Her sister had alluded to this trap thing involving all of them, but who were *all of them*? Did that include Darwin, too? How about Bruno? Her parents?

"Aaron," she said, keeping her voice lower this time. "I'm worried, and it feels like you're brushing me off."

"Brushing you off—" He shook his head, his eyes swimming from the alcohol. "I'm merely taking you out to dinner and conversing with you over the meal. When we're done, we can continue talking at home." He shrugged. "What's wrong with that? I'm not brushing you off. I would never brush you off."

"Well, whatever's coming might happen tonight, and we're out on a date like nothing's going on. That's what's wrong with that." She got up from her chair and dropped the napkin beside her untouched salad. The waiter by the kitchen door started their way. "I'll be in the car. You deal with the bill."

When she heard the cluck of his tongue, she fought the urge to slap him. Instead, she stomped out of the restaurant like she hadn't gotten her way in an argument and hated herself for it.

She didn't want to mistreat Aaron. He didn't deserve it. But she was pregnant, and her sister hadn't reached out in weeks. The trap was coming for all of them, and no one was worried, least of all for her. Once in the car, she remembered that Aaron had the only key.

Sarah wrapped her arms around herself in the late fall chill and waited, leaning on the trunk of their car.

After a moment, she pulled out her phone and tapped in a text to Parkman.

IS EVERYTHING OKAY? ARE YOU SAFE?

After sending it, she copied and pasted the same message

to Daniel, Benjamin, and Alex.

She peered up at the restaurant door and shivered again.

"C'mon, Aaron," she whispered.

An idea came to her, and she made a snap decision. Once WhatsApp was open, she dialed Darwin's number. He answered on the second ring as it was morning in Italy.

"Sarah?" he said, concern always in his voice when she called out of the blue. "Everything okay?"

"Not really."

"What's wrong?"

"Not sure yet, but something is coming."

"Can you be more specific?"

"No, not on the phone."

"I can encrypt the hell out of this line."

"It's okay," she said, the cold making her voice quiver. "How fast can you come to Toronto? I'll pay for it."

"Sarah, why are you shaking? I hear it in your voice."

"Because it's chilly outside, and I'm waiting for Aaron by the car."

"He left you outside in the cold?" Darwin's voice rose a notch.

"No, I stormed out of the restaurant. He's paying the bill."

"Oh." Darwin cleared his throat. "Stormed out? You guys fought?"

"Not exactly. We just don't see eye to eye on this trap thing."

"When have you two ever seen eye to eye on what Vivian tells you?"

"Ha, true enough." For some reason, this still made her

heart sink further.

"How about tonight?" Darwin asked.

Sarah frowned, watching the front of the restaurant as a well-dressed couple entered, the man holding the door for his date. "What about tonight?"

"I can take the train to Rome and catch a flight to Toronto out of Fiumicino tonight. I'll be in Toronto by tomorrow afternoon."

"Really? You'd come that fast?"

"Sarah, if you need me faster, I can look into chartering a plane, but that'll get pricey."

"No, no, it's fine. I just feel exposed and paranoid."

"About what?"

"I'll explain more when you get here. I'll cover the flight costs, too. It'll be safer if we're all together." Her phone buzzed in her ear. One of the boys had responded to her safety message. "Something's happening, and I'm more nervous than I've ever been before. This trap thing makes me feel vulnerable. I have a feeling whatever it is doesn't include you, meaning we may need your help in getting out of whatever trouble's coming."

"No issue on the costs, Sarah. I've missed you guys. And I think Disco is still in Toronto. I'll see if he can pick me up at the airport. See you soon, Sarah."

She clicked off and whispered, "I sure hope so."

More people entered the restaurant. A couple exited, laughing about something, then headed toward a lone Cadillac.

Her phone vibrated again.

Parkman and Alex had responded that they were fine.

She checked Benjamin and Daniel's messages, but both were still unread.

Then Parkman asked if she was okay. She would respond when they got in the car as the cool October air was making her shake too much now.

After another moment, she strode toward the front of the restaurant and stepped inside.

What was taking Aaron so long?

The table they had sat at was empty.

The waiter who had watched them by the kitchen door was clearing their table. He was easily recognizable because of the stripe of gray in his hair on the right side.

Where the hell was Aaron?

She jogged over to the table. "Where did he go?" she asked. "The man I was sitting with. Did you see where he went?"

The waiter shrugged. "I'm sorry, ma'am. The bill was paid, and he left." The waiter went back to wiping the table.

Sarah glared at him a moment longer, then spun in a full circle, studying the faces of everyone in the restaurant. Not willing to wait for another unhelpful answer, she strode toward the men's room and banged the door open. Two men stood at the urinals, but the stalls were empty.

"Excuse me," one man said. "Wrong bathroom—"

"Mind your business," she snapped, then exited the bathroom and ran for the double doors that led into the kitchen, passing half a dozen tables with people still eating, chatting quietly.

Once inside the kitchen, with the smell of meat cooking and the bustle of food prep, she counted six men.

Two cooks stopped what they were doing to stare at her. The others hadn't noticed her yet.

"Did a man come through here?" she asked, her stomach dropping with the realization that they would tell her they hadn't seen Aaron.

The men exchanged a glance, then looked back at her and shook their heads.

Sarah lifted her phone to see if Aaron had texted anything.

He hadn't.

There was no way in hell he would have just left her there.

No way in hell.

"I need to see your manager," she said, loud enough to be heard over the fryer where another man had just dropped a tray of something breaded.

"I'm the manager," a man's voice bellowed to her right.

Sarah spun that way and stared at a short, plump man with glasses. He held a calculator in one hand. Behind him, a large window looked in on an office, a desk covered in paperwork. He must've seen her barge in and got up to see what she needed.

"I'm Dennis," he said, wiping his hand on his leg and holding it out to her. "How can I help you?"

Without shaking his hand, she quickly explained. "My boyfriend and I were having dinner. I went to wait by the car. He didn't show, and now I have no idea where he is. Have you got cameras in here?"

The man frowned. "He left without you? He stood you up?"

She shook her head, already exasperated as her patience was running thin. "No, he was paying the bill and didn't come out to the parking lot. He wouldn't stand me up. Even our waiter said he paid the bill."

"And who was your waiter? How about we talk with him?"

"The man was just cleaning our table. He's the one with the gray streak in his hair."

The manager frowned, stepped over to the double doors, opened them slightly, and peeked into the restaurant. After a brief moment, he closed the door and met Sarah's gaze.

"I don't have a waiter with gray hair."

She wasn't trembling from the cold anymore. This shiver was a mix of fear and anger. *Oh, Vivian, this had better not be the fucking trap, or I swear I'll find a way to hurt you.*

"My boyfriend is missing," Sarah declared, her voice back in control, her demeanor focused. "Collect all your waiters, and I will point out the one who served us."

"I don't think that's necessary, Miss—"

"Collect your fucking waiters"—she leaned in close to Dennis's face—"or I will burn this restaurant to the ground." Her hands clenched at her sides. "Do. Not. Test. Me."

To his credit, the manager only hesitated a few seconds. Within one minute, four waiters stood in front of his office window.

"The man on the left was on a break," Dennis said. "The other three have tables to serve. Make this quick."

Sarah didn't recognize any of them, but the young man on the far right with the buzz cut. He had taken their order.

"Our waiter isn't here."

That frown again. It was like the manager was permanently confused. "Well, these are the only waiters on staff this evening."

"The one on the far right took our order and brought the food, but the waiter with the gray streak in his hair brought our wine."

The buzz-cut waiter stepped forward. "I'm new here, but I remember you two. You guys had an argument. You didn't eat any of your salad."

Sarah moved toward him. "Where did my boyfriend go?"

He shrugged. "I'm sorry," he said, genuine concern on his face. "I didn't see him leave."

"And where's the other waiter?"

"Ma'am, there is no other waiter," the manager reiterated.

Sarah spun around and glared at him. "Yes, there was."

"Oh, the man with the wild streak of gray?" Another waiter asked.

Sarah lost her balance momentarily when she spun back around too fast. "Yes. Where is he?"

The man shook his head. "No idea. I thought he was from head office, you know, watching us."

"He was standing by the kitchen door a lot," Sarah added.

The man nodded. "I saw that, too."

And yet another frown from the manager. "What man was standing by the kitchen door?"

"This is maddening," Sarah whispered, her teeth clenched.

She checked her phone.

Calling the police was out of the question. Not only would they not be interested in helping her, but Aaron was also only gone ten minutes. And one of the waiters saw them arguing. How would that look to the authorities?

There was no text from Aaron, no phone call, and nothing from Daniel or Benjamin yet.

Vivian, what the hell is going on?

"Look, ma'am, I think it's better if you wait outside," the manager was saying. "I'm sure your boyfriend is in the bathroom, or he's—"

The fire alarm sounded a shrill wail. Sarah jumped nearly a foot off the floor. Her hand tightened on her cell phone to avoid dropping it.

The sprinklers above activated, and water began streaming down on top of them all. The din in the restaurant increased as diners protested their dinner and clothes were ruined.

Sarah pulled her phone close to her stomach and leaned forward to protect it from the moisture as she ran for the back door.

Outside, sirens were already en route, yet she couldn't see a visible cause for the alarm. There was no fire in the kitchen, the most likely spot in the entire building.

Restaurant goers piled outside from the front doors and one side exit, some heading for their cars. An SUV braked before hitting a four-door sedan. A green delivery truck labeled ACME Carpets eased away from the building and drove to the outskirts of the parking lot, no doubt making room so the emergency vehicles could get in close.

Sarah moved around the side of the building until she

could see their car.

It was parked in the same spot, still empty.

Aaron wasn't standing beside it, nor was he inside the car.

Aaron was gone.

Sarah leaned into the building to hold herself up.

She had never felt weaker and more out of control.

What the fuck is going on, Vivian? Tell me, has one of the traps been sprung?

Has someone taken Aaron?

Chapter 2

Parkman switched off the TV and stared at his phone. Why was Sarah messaging him to ask if he was okay and then not responding?

He got up and moved to the window to look out over the city at night. This autumn was cooler than he was used to, but it was Toronto—sometimes, they even got a dusting of snow in October. It was rare, but it could happen.

He checked his phone again.

Nothing. No response.

Usually, he didn't get nervous when thinking about Sarah, but her text had unnerved him, and now she wasn't responding.

He tapped the phone several times to dial out and placed the phone at his ear.

Sarah answered on the second ring.

"Sarah?" he said, relieved to catch her. "What's going on?"

"Aaron's gone," she gasped.

"Gone?" He stared at nothing, trying to process what she'd said. "Gone, as in gone, gone?"

"I don't know where he is."

"Have you tried calling him—wait, weren't you guys going out tonight?"

"We did, and he disappeared at the restaurant."

"Disappeared at the restaurant? How the hell is that possible?"

Sarah went on to explain what had happened.

"And no one knows this waiter with the gray streak in his hair?"

"No," she gasped.

"Are those sirens I hear in the background?"

"Yes."

"What happened? You call every cop and fire department to find Aaron?"

"Someone pulled the fire alarm or used a lighter on those water suppression systems in the ceiling."

Parkman spun away from the window and paced in his living room. "Wait a second. Let me get this straight. You and Aaron had an argument, then you went out to the car, and he didn't show. When you go back into the restaurant, the waiter disappears, and the fire alarm goes off."

"There's something else." Sarah's voice was unmistakably upset. She was taking this hard as if she had personally caused Aaron's disappearance.

"What else, Sarah?"

He detected her moving at a good clip as her breathing in the phone was a rapid pant.

"The waiter no one knows served our wine bottle."

"And?"

"I didn't drink any because of the baby. Aaron was on his second glass by the time the food arrived."

"What, you think the wine was laced with something?"

"Quite possibly. He can handle his booze. It was only his second glass, and his eyes were already swimming."

"Okay, that doesn't add up."

"And I can't get ahold of Benjamin or Daniel. You and Alex were the only two to respond to my messages."

"I hope nothing happened to them, too. Did Vivian say anything about this?"

"No," Sarah shouted. "My sister isn't around again. She showed up to tell me about some trap that was coming but didn't bother to fill me in on any of the details."

"Sarah," Parkman said, his tone heavy. "You know what that means, right?"

"Yeah, that everything's fucked, and we have no idea how bad."

"No, it means everything will be okay."

There was a pause on the other end. Parkman stopped pacing to listen. Sarah had been walking, but he couldn't hear her footsteps anymore.

"Sarah," Parkman continued. "You know as well as I do that when there's serious danger, Vivian is there. If she's not around, then whatever this trap thing is, everything will work itself out."

"As much as I'd like to believe that, I'd be more

convinced with Aaron at my side."

"Look, I'll call Benjamin and Daniel. Don't worry about them. They can take care of themselves. Where are you now? Do you need me to come and get you?"

"I'm in Mississauga, a few blocks from the restaurant on Dundas."

"Okay, I'm ten minutes from there." Parkman strode to the apartment door and slipped into his shoes. "I'll come and get you, and we'll find Aaron together."

"Parkman, please hurry. I'm soaked and freezing out here."

He reached for the door, then stopped. "You need me to bring you a jacket?"

"Yeah."

"Okay, I'll get you one." He grabbed a leather jacket out of the closet.

"I'll be outside the Super 5 Inn. Wait, no, I'll be in the lobby. Warmer there."

"Okay, give me a few minutes—"

Someone knocked on his door three times.

"What was that?" Sarah asked.

"Someone's at my door. One sec." He leaned forward to check through the peephole.

"Parkman," Sarah shouted in the phone. "Don't answer it."

Two uniformed police officers stood outside his door.

"Sarah, it's the cops. I have to answer it."

"Parkman." Her voice caught on emotion. "I have a bad feeling about this. They may not be cops."

Parkman stepped back from the door as the officers

knocked again.

"Police," one of the men said. "Open up."

"Is that gut instinct, Sarah, or is Vivian telling you something?" For the first time in a long time, hair stood on his forearms as his body tingled in the anticipation of danger.

"Parkman." Her voice came through strong and clear. "All I'm saying is, there's something wrong tonight. I can feel it in my gut. This feeling is the strongest bit of intuition I've ever had without Vivian leading me. Those men aren't cops. I can't lose you tonight, too."

"But, Sarah—" They knocked again, cutting him off. "What else can I do? I'm on the eleventh floor. I can't jump, and they heard my voice."

"Open up," they shouted.

"Are you armed?" Sarah asked him.

"Seriously?"

"Parkman, take a photo of them with your phone and text it to me when you open the door. Slip the phone in a pocket while I'm still on the line. If there's trouble, I'll call 911 right away and supply the pictures to the cops."

"Okay, pulling the phone away from my ear now to open the camera app."

Sarah said something else, but he missed it. The cops knocked again.

"I'm coming," Parkman shouted through the door. "One second."

Camera ready, he clicked off the lock and pulled the door open. Both men moved inward, crowding the door.

"Hey," Parkman said, stepping back. "Take it easy, guys. I didn't invite you inside. What the fuck is this?"

"You're Parkman?" The guy on the right asked.

He held up his phone and was able to click both their faces in one shot. When he lowered it to send the photos to Sarah, the cell phone was knocked from his hand. He jerked back at the sudden violence and braced himself.

"What the fuck was that for?" he shouted, already regretting his decision of opening the door. He should've listened to Sarah and kept the door closed.

"It's him," the guy on the right said, nodding slightly.

The cop on the left raised his hands. A weapon materialized like some magician trick.

Parkman reacted instantly, his police training from years ago still in his blood. The spare jacket he would take to Sarah swung in a wide arc as he attempted to knock the weapon from the man's grasp.

Something struck his neck, and then one of the men shot out a foot and pushed his chest.

Parkman fell backward, landing hard on his ass. He rolled to the side even as he hit the floor, preparing to push up and get to his feet, but something wasn't right.

One of the men landed on him, pinning his arms to the apartment floor.

"I don't think so," the man said, lying flat on Parkman, holding him down with weight alone.

Parkman struggled, rolling left and right, but his strength diminished quickly.

What had they shot into his neck? A tranquilizer? Was that safe to use on humans? If not, did these guys care?

His vision blurred slightly. He had to get up, get away. There was no time left. It was now or never.

He rolled onto his stomach and placed his hands flat on the floor. When he shoved upward to get off the floor, he didn't go anywhere. The baseboard at the bottom of the wall hadn't moved—it was still in his direct line of vision. His strength had disappeared too quickly.

What the hell did they hit him with? Why couldn't he get up? What was wrong with his arms?

When keeping his eyes open became too much of a chore, they closed on their own.

Consciousness went with the darkness, and Parkman went under.

Chapter 3

SARAH SCREAMED INTO THE phone until her voice grew hoarse. The line had died, and when she redialed Parkman, it went directly to voicemail.

After a moment, she stared up at the dark sky and shouted at Vivian, who was still strangely absent. It was no surprise Sarah didn't get an answer.

"So, what, tell us about a trap, then say there's nothing we can do about it and abandon us? Fuck, why does our relationship feel so toxic?"

No longer cold, heated through with anger at the moment, she glanced around and stopped to look at a man on the sidewalk who was gawking at her.

"You okay, miss?" he asked.

"Yeah," Sarah said, fighting the urge to tell him to mind his own business. Anger had a way of bringing out her worst.

She turned around and dialed Darwin again.

"Calling back so soon?" he asked. "Everything okay?"

"Is Disco still in Toronto?"

"You need him?" Darwin's tone turned serious.

"Aaron's gone, and two cops just jumped Parkman—or guys dressed as cops—at his door. This is escalating out of control by the hour." She quickly explained their plan of Parkman texting a picture to her, but he didn't have the time, and now her calls are going to voicemail. "I need to get picked up. And we have to get to Daniel, Benjamin, and Alex before this spirals into someone dying. Darwin, we are being taken out one by one."

"Holy fuck, Sarah, it sounds like it's already out of control. Where are you? I'll have someone pick you up."

"Dundas Street, Mississauga. By the Super 5 Inn."

"Okay, Disco will be there to pick you up within the hour. Get inside. Do not stay visible to the street."

Sarah started for the lobby.

"I'm sorry, Darwin," she whispered. "I had a feeling something was going to happen tonight."

"*You* had a feeling? This sounds like something new. It's usually Vivian who tells you all the shit."

"I know, but this was different somehow."

"Okay, look, we can talk more later. I've booked my flight. I'll call when I land tomorrow. In the meantime, stay with Disco. He'll protect you with his life, or he'll have to answer to Bruno, and no one wants that."

"Got it, but we're not staying in hiding."

"What do you mean?"

"We're going to pick up the others."

"Okay, I'll tell him. Just stay with him until I get there. He'll bring his own backup."

Sarah entered the lobby, the door giving off a loud chime twice. "I'm inside now, off the street."

"Gotta go make some calls," Darwin said. "Get your boys ready for pick up."

"Will do."

Outside the motel, a cruiser with its lights flashing eased by the entrance on Dundas. It braked, then backed up and turned into the parking area.

"Darwin," she said, covering her mouth with her hand. "A cruiser just pulled into the parking lot, lights on."

"So, get out of there. Hide in the back somewhere, rent a room, run outside, but don't let them take you."

Sarah turned to see the clerk watching her. "I'll just go to my room," she said into the phone loud enough for the clerk to hear as she skirted by the desk and headed down the hall toward the back.

Halfway down the corridor, the front door chimed twice as the cop opened it.

"Darwin, I have to go. Cops are in the lobby." She killed the call, slipped the phone in her pocket, and ran the length of the hallway.

"Hey," a man shouted behind her.

At the end of the corridor, she glanced back to see a uniformed officer already chasing her.

She shouldered into the back door, smacked it open, and jumped outside.

Another cop was already standing five feet from the rear door of the motel, but there was no police cruiser in sight.

"I don't think so, Sarah Roberts," the man said. He spoke into a cell phone he had cradled in his hand, his eyes never leaving her. "We got her, boss. Bringing her in now." Then he slipped the phone into a pocket on his Kevlar vest and stepped forward. "Thought you could get away from the restaurant, huh?"

There was no way she was going anywhere with this guy. No fucking way.

Especially not after what just happened to Parkman.

With no interest in debating or formulating a response, she lunged at the man standing in front of her in a police uniform. As her hand attached itself to his throat, her thumb pressing inward at the base of his neckline, the man grabbed for something at his belt line.

Whatever he had reached for was a waste of his time. Sarah's thumb had choked off his air supply and instantly sent him into spasms of gasping for air.

She spun sideways, unclipped his holster, and seized the butt of his weapon before shoving him away from her. The man stumbled sideways, both hands clinging to his throat as he struggled to breathe, his eyes wide.

Sarah raised the weapon at the door she'd just exited from, finger inside the trigger guard, and waited.

The door smashed open, and the cop who had bolted down the corridor after her stepped outside.

"Don't fucking move," Sarah shouted, spittle shooting from her mouth.

The second guy spotted his colleague, who had now dropped to his knees, still struggling for air, then faced Sarah, a defiant smile raising the left half of his mouth.

"Nifty trick," he whispered. "You'll have to tell me how you did that."

"Why are you following me?"

"Threats of burning down the restaurant, then setting off the fire extinguisher to get out of paying the bill can lead to charges. The owner said you ran toward this motel." The cop shrugged. "Just trying to pick up a thief, a dine-and-dasher."

Sarah blinked, her hand wavering. Were these guys real cops? Did the manager, that Dennis guy, actually think they started shit to get out of the bill? But the waiter with the gray streak in his hair said Aaron had paid the bill. It didn't make sense.

Unless the waiter with the gray streak took their money.

"Then why did that guy," she pointed at the man on the ground, "just say into his cell phone that he had got me and was bringing me in? He used the term, *boss*."

The cop looked from the man on his knees to Sarah, then back to the other cop. "I have no idea who he is or what force he works for, but that uniform isn't regulation—"

A weapon fired beside her, cutting off the cop mid-sentence.

Sarah's body jerked with the sudden noise, her finger tightening on the trigger in her hand. Something clattered to the concrete beside her.

In that moment of surprise and the seconds it took to get her bearings, she realized that the man gasping for breath on his knees had pulled another weapon from somewhere. The cop in front of her dropped to the ground, his face a mask of blood and bone.

The man on his knees pivoted toward Sarah when she

adjusted her aim and fired. She fired again, then again.

Anything to save her baby and, by extension, herself.

The look of surprise on the man's face was enough to tell her she'd hit him with all three bullets. The range wasn't more than four feet, and each bullet cleaved a hole in his flesh, with one going through the vest.

Through the vest? How was that possible?

Unless it was a slash vest, which was built for knives and not bullets, Kevlar was so much more money.

Both men shot, both men in uniform. She moved quickly, slipping the weapon into the back of her pants and kicking the gun out of the other guy's grip. Then she grabbed him as he slipped to the ground.

More sirens wailed in the distance.

Help was arriving in minutes. She needed to get lost and fast.

"Who sent you?" She spat into the guy's face, dragging him upward by the collar. "Who hired you? What do you want with me?"

Even as blood slipped from the edges of his lips, the man smiled.

His confidence in the face of death startled her. Did he have a grenade or something on him?

She glanced down at his hands, but they dragged uselessly on the ground on either side of him.

The sirens roared into the parking lot out front. Tires screeched.

"Who are you? Where have you taken Aaron?"

"You're all finished," he gasped, coughing blood onto her shirt.

Car doors slammed out front.

She was out of time.

"Finished? What are you talking about?"

"When the job is done, you're all dead. Not even your precious"—he coughed, his eyes squeezing shut in pain, then he collected one large breath—"your precious Alex can save you this time."

Someone shouted close by.

Real cops were coming. Too many of them.

Sarah dropped the man to the ground as his eyes rolled back in his head. She stuffed her weapon in the cop's hand, stole his gun, and ran for the bushes behind the motel.

The back door whipped open, but she hadn't made it to the bushes yet.

When she glanced over her shoulder, the cop who had come through the door first was leaning against the wall, a hand over his mouth while staring down at the two bodies.

She leaped into the bushes as the cop vomited beside the crime scene.

Confident he didn't see her, but needing to get as far away from the area as possible, she ran through the darkened brush, hopped a fence, and then skirted the back parking lot of a short strip mall.

Slowing a moment to catch her breath, she checked her back.

No one was in pursuit. She was alone—for the moment.

She had to tell Darwin so Disco could pick her up somewhere else.

She reached for her phone, but it wasn't there.

She stopped and stared down at her pants, slapping all

the pockets.

Glancing up, staring at nothing, she recalled being startled by the fake cop's gun going off. She'd jumped. Something had dropped near her.

It had to be her phone. Maybe she didn't stuff it deep enough into her pocket.

Whatever had happened, she didn't have a phone now.

"Shit," she said, slapping one hand into the palm of the other. "Now what?"

She had to get out of the area. Without any way to contact Darwin, an extraction was out of the question. She was on her own now.

Putting one foot in front of the other, she thought about what had happened over the past hour. Aaron was gone. Parkman was gone. Fake cops nabbed Parkman, and they just about got her.

And now, with a real cop lying dead at the back of the motel after searching for Sarah and her phone left within a few feet of his body, the resulting manhunt for her would be enormous.

She'd done nothing wrong. They came after her.

And she'd never shoot a cop—well, unless her life was in danger and they were assholes about it. Real cops, acting properly, didn't deserve disrespect of any sort.

And even though she should go to the nearest police station to explain everything, she knew she couldn't. They'd never take her word for it. And whoever was coming after them was going to kill them all anyway.

Not even your precious Alex can save you this time, the guy had said.

What did that mean?

Going to the authorities to report a missing person was out of the question now, too.

How the hell did things get so fucked up so fast?

Revolving lights flashed across the wall of the building up ahead. The cops were out searching for her. They would probably bring in a K9 unit, too.

Sarah pivoted to her right and ran for the bushes again.

It was time to get clear of the area as fast as possible.

Extract herself—Disco wouldn't find her now.

Get out of the area.

At all costs.

Chapter 4

Daniel elbowed Benjamin as they exited the theater.

"That wasn't so bad."

Benjamin elbowed him back. "What do you mean, wasn't so bad? Jason Statham did great. Even Bruce Willis couldn't keep up with him this time."

"Yeah, but did you see those super-human stunts they tried to pull off?"

"Hollywood always takes martial arts to another level. It's dramatic theater."

"At least they didn't have people flying around like that crouching dragon movie thing."

"Alex didn't tell you?"

Daniel glanced over at him as he fished out his car keys. "Tell me what?"

"He coached them on that movie."

Daniel momentarily stopped at his car door, staring over the roof at Benjamin.

"You know, I could believe that. The way Alex flits around, I'm surprised he's not the next Jet Li."

Benjamin shrugged. "Maybe he'll be discovered. But until he makes it in Hollywood, you think you could unlock my door?"

"Oh, right."

Daniel opened his door and slipped in behind the wheel.

Benjamin banged on the window, bending down to glance inside the car.

"Hey," he called, his voice somewhat muted by the closed window.

"No problem," Daniel shouted back. "One second."

He started the car.

"Hey," Benjamin yelled, a notch of irritation in his voice. "Drive away, and you're paying for the taxi."

Daniel put the car in gear, eased forward a foot, and then unlocked the door.

Benjamin jerked it open, and Daniel released the brake, the car rolling forward again.

Benjamin clung to the open door, mumbled something about balance, then deftly dropped into the passenger seat and slammed the door.

Daniel continued forward, turned right, and headed for the exit.

"Asshole," Benjamin grumbled.

"Just thought after watching a martial arts movie, you'd want to practice some balance."

"Hit the dojo, and I'll practice balance all over your

face."

Daniel snuck a glance over at him as he slowed at a red light. "That a challenge or a threat?"

"It's a statement. You take it any way you like." Benjamin pulled out his phone, and the screen lit up. "Oh, hey, I got a text from Sarah while we were in the theater."

"What's it say?"

"She asked if everything was okay and if I was safe." Benjamin tapped a reply on his phone.

"What are you saying?"

"Asking her why she would ask that."

"Maybe it's because we're all friends, and she's just checking in." Daniel let out a short laugh. "Dude, you can chill. Everything's cool."

Benjamin set the phone down and stared out the windshield. "But didn't she talk about some trap thing last month when Detective Ricigliano threw us a party?"

"Shit." Daniel crept along The Queensway, staying in the right lane to exit and hop on the Gardiner. "You think something happened?"

Benjamin shrugged. "Who knows?" He stared at his phone. "She isn't reading the message."

"Call her then."

Benjamin dialed out. "I'll set it on speaker."

As Daniel turned south to access the Gardiner, Sarah's phone rang five times. Benjamin's thumb hovered over the phone, about to kill the call, when it stopped ringing.

Someone had answered it.

Daniel shot a glance at Benjamin, who was staring down at the phone.

"Hello?" Benjamin said. "Sarah?"

"Who am I speaking with?" a man asked.

Benjamin offered Daniel a worried look. "My name is Benjamin. Put Sarah on the phone."

"I'm afraid I can't do that, Benjamin. Can you tell me about your relationship with Sarah?"

Daniel leaned closer to the phone. "That's none of your business," he said sternly. "Where's Sarah?"

"That's what we're trying to determine at this moment."

"Who's we?" Benjamin asked.

"I'm Officer Dreyfus with Toronto police. There's been an incident, and we feel Sarah may have information—"

"Then why do you have her phone?" Daniel cut in.

"Who else is with you, Benjamin?" Dreyfus asked.

"Look," Daniel said. "My name isn't important. But what is important is you telling us how you have Sarah's phone."

"It was left at the scene of a crime. And since Sarah is well-known to the authorities here in Toronto, we're willing to listen to her side before jumping to conclusions, but it isn't looking good for her, Benjamin."

"How so?"

"I can't tell you more over the phone, but I'm going to have to assume that's either Parkman or Daniel with you."

Daniel merged into traffic on the Gardiner, then gawked at Benjamin. They really were well known to the authorities in Toronto now.

"Your lack of response tells me I'm correct. So, here's what we need. Reach out to Sarah and get her to come in on her own, or we'll see her reluctance as guilt. She doesn't want us coming after her. One could never tell what will happen during an arrest, especially if she were to resist."

"Hey, wait up," Daniel shouted. "Are you threatening Sarah?"

"Not at all." The officer sounded like he was walking now. "Let's just say …" he paused, then there was a rustling on the speaker. "We have two dead cops," he whispered. Believing he was speaking with Sarah's friends, evidently, he had decided to tell them the truth. "Both men were shot. Sarah's cell phone was found by the bodies. Our officer radioed for backup when he saw Sarah through the window of the motel lobby. We suspect her prints will be on the weapon. Guys, find a way to get her to come to explain this, and I'm sure we'll work something out. People can't go around shooting cops and then running. That doesn't look good."

"It's a trap," Benjamin mumbled.

"What was that?" the cop asked.

"It has something to do with the trap."

"What trap?"

Daniel leaned over. "Don't worry about it. We'll find her and reach out." He nodded at the phone and mouthed the words, *end it*, motioning to kill the call.

"Guys, this is serious. Who will tell this cop's wife and kids that he's not coming home tonight, and who will—"

Benjamin ended the call.

They rode in silence for a few moments.

"What the fuck, man?" Benjamin whispered.

"Something big happened for sure. This bites."

"Weren't they supposed to go for dinner in Mississauga tonight?"

Daniel nodded. "Last I heard."

"So, dinner with Aaron turns into two dead cops and Sarah on the run?" Benjamin stared down at his phone. "How the fuck does this shit happen?"

"Call Aaron. See what he says."

Benjamin dialed out and put it on speaker. This time, it went straight to voicemail.

"Try Parkman. He'll know what's going on."

Benjamin dialed again. Back on speaker, Daniel listened as it rang several times, then switched to voicemail.

"I don't like this, man." Benjamin's voice lowered in genuine concern.

"Me neither." Daniel gripped the steering wheel tighter. "Where is everyone?"

"I'll try Alex."

"Good idea."

Once again on speaker, the phone rang twice, then Alex picked up.

"Oh, thank God you answered," Benjamin muttered.

"What?" Alex said. "This about Sarah's text?"

"Sarah texted you, too?" Daniel asked.

"Yes. Asked if I was safe."

"She texted me as well," Benjamin said.

"Shit, I didn't check my phone." Daniel squeezed his fingers in his pocket and withdrew his cell phone. After he lit up the screen, he said, "Yup, I got texted, too."

"Since we're all good, what's up?" Alex asked. "Vivian prompting this?"

"See, that's the thing. We're not all good."

"Tell me."

"There are two dead cops near some motel, and they have Sarah pegged for it."

There was a short gasp over the line. "How so?"

Even though Alex was an overly sensitive young man, he was all business in these kinds of moments. Those two words sounded like an emotionless hitman waiting for instructions on his next kill. He was truly an enigma to Daniel.

"We called Sarah's phone, and a cop answered."

"And?"

"He told us they were looking for Sarah."

"If she killed them, she had a reason." Alex adjusted something on his end of the line. It clanged through their speaker.

"What was that?"

"I was planking with weights on my back. Rolled them off. Getting ready now."

"Getting ready?" Daniel asked. "For what?"

"To fight."

"Who?"

"Whoever tries to hurt Sarah."

Daniel and Benjamin exchanged a glance.

"Okay, well …" Daniel swallowed, his mouth dry. "Let's slow down a notch. We don't even know what happened."

More shuffling on Alex's end of the line.

"What are you doing now?" Benjamin asked, a perplexed look on his face.

"Prepping. Don't worry about it. What does Aaron say? They were out tonight."

"Aaron isn't picking up his phone."

The movement on Alex's side stopped.

"Parkman?"

"Same story. No answer."

"Have you tried Darwin?"

"In Italy?"

"He tracks us. Darwin might know something."

"Good idea. We'll call him."

"Meet me." Alex's trademark one- and two-word sentences always seemed to make the most sense to Daniel, but only Alex could pull it off. The fact that he was talking this much was a huge change from years past.

"The dojo?" Daniel suggested, trying Alex's way to communicate.

"One hour."

"Done."

The line died.

Benjamin eased the phone onto his lap. "Now what?"

"Call Darwin."

"Oh, right." Benjamin tapped a few buttons. "Sorry, dazed out for a second."

Daniel increased his speed as they passed through downtown Toronto on the elevated highway. The dojo was twenty minutes away for them. Plenty of time to make calls and try to figure shit out before Alex got there.

The line connected. "Darwin here."

"Darwin, it's Benjamin and Daniel."

"I was wondering when I'd hear from you guys. Trouble's brewing."

"Seems that way." Benjamin was shaking his head. "How do you know?"

"Sarah called me." Darwin briefed them on everything he

knew so far.

Daniel listened, shocked at what he heard, while Benjamin held the phone up between them.

"Shit," Daniel shouted. "So Sarah was on the run after fake cops nabbed Parkman?"

"That makes more sense," Benjamin said. "How do we even know that a cop answered Sarah's phone?"

Between them, Daniel and Benjamin filled Darwin in on what they had learned and how they were meeting Alex at the dojo in an hour.

"I'll get Disco to scout the area of the Super 5 Inn. Sarah knows him and his Hummer. If he can't find her, I'll get him to head to the dojo. I'll be there in twenty-four hours to help."

"I'm sure we could use the help." Daniel stared at the road. Then added, "If anything happens to Parkman or Aaron, Sarah will be pissed. But if anyone threatens her baby, she'll murder everyone involved and fuck the consequences."

"I know," Darwin said, an element of panic in his voice. "We need to keep Sarah safe so the public stays safe."

"That's not too far from the truth," Benjamin whispered.

"Look, guys, let me call Disco, and then I'm leaving. Rosina is packing my shit for me and making food to go. She'll monitor things from this end. I have to go as my train to Rome leaves soon."

"Okay, what time do you land tomorrow?"

"In Toronto shortly after six in the evening—18:10 to be exact."

"Okay, thanks, Darwin. See you soon." Benjamin killed the call.

Daniel exited the Gardiner and stopped at a red light before turning left, now only minutes from the dojo.

"Someone set a trap," Benjamin said. "Sarah warned us it was coming."

"She's about four months pregnant, too."

"I know. That's what worries me."

"It worries us all."

"Whoever is doing this will face severe wrath."

"Wrath?" He glanced over at Benjamin. "What are you, Shakespeare, now?"

Benjamin faced him. "What would you call it then?"

"Hell. Whoever is doing this will face a fate worse than Hell."

"Wasn't it Shakespeare who said, 'Hell is empty, and all the devils are here,' or something?"

"That couldn't be more true. I fear we will see much more Hell before the week ends."

"That's what I'm afraid of."

Chapter 5

Silvio Rossi checked the time. The coordinated attacks had started on time and were all supposed to be finished by now. But plans had a way of having to be modified.

Sarah and Aaron were out for dinner.

Parkman was at home.

Both were easy targets for his men. But somehow, they'd missed Sarah. Luckily, Claudio caught up with her and was able to nab her outside that motel.

Silvio stared at the clock for several seconds. According to his estimation, Claudio would be at the warehouse with Sarah within fifteen minutes.

Then there were Daniel and Benjamin. No one expected them to go to the movie theater on The Queensway at the last minute. His men had to improvise and were now following Daniel and Benjamin as they approached their dojo.

Alex was the last one to be taken. He would prove to be their hardest target.

But Silvio accounted for that and decided not to assign a single man to Alex for fear of losing that man.

Alex wouldn't be abducted like the others anyway. He would come willingly to Silvio. And with one phone call, too.

The warehouse door beeped and began to rise.

The first members of his team had arrived with their cargo.

Domenic Bianco eased his vehicle inside. The second the rear of the truck cleared the doorframe, the door began its slow descent, closing behind him.

Silvio checked the time again, then watched as Domenic drove by him, leaving room for the others to park inside the warehouse.

After Silvio adjusted his suit, he strode slowly toward Dom's truck.

The man got out and nodded at Silvio, then proceeded to the back and opened the double doors.

"Got Aaron," he said. "Sarah was another matter."

"I heard. Claudio has her now."

Dom glanced at him, then shrugged. "How could we know she wouldn't drink the wine?"

"It's fine. Claudio followed her and picked her up by the motel. He should be here in ten to fifteen minutes."

"How are the others doing?"

Silvio leaned past Dom and peeked inside the back of the truck. Aaron Stevens was sleeping in the rear, the drugs having taken full effect. Blood coated his face from a cut on his forehead. Silvio looked closer and saw blood had pooled and smeared on the floor of the truck.

"What happened to him?" Silvio pulled back and addressed Domenic. "Why is he bleeding?"

Dom shrugged again. "Took a couple of corners too quickly, I guess."

Silvio assessed the man before him. Dom was quick to violence. He'd always enjoyed being the first in a fight and had scars on top of scars on his knuckles to prove it.

"And taking corners too quick with a kidnapped man in the rear of the truck didn't strike you as attention-grabbing?"

"Attention-grabbing?"

Domenic must've been hit in the head too often as well. He was known for being slow on the uptake.

"The police, you idiot."

Domenic smiled and showed crooked teeth. "No, don't do that."

"What?" Silvio frowned.

"Don't call me names."

Silvio suppressed a laugh. Were they back in grade school? "You take corners so fast that Aaron's bleeding, which could have led to the police pulling you over, and you don't think that's an idiotic move considering what we're doing here?"

"The fire department and cops were coming," Domenic said, throwing up his hands. "I had to move the truck, get it out of the way. I hit the gas hard, turned too fast, and parked to wait for Claudio. When I looked back, Aaron was bleeding."

Silvio felt lost. None of this was the plan. How did they

deviate so much?

"Why were emergency vehicles coming again?"

"Because the plan got fucked up, and Sarah was looking for me."

Silvio's eyes widened. "Why was she looking for you?"

"Who's stupid now?" Domenic asked as he glanced around. "Where is everyone?"

"Bringing the rest of Sarah's team here." Silvio rolled a hand in circles. "Please, tell me why she was looking for you."

"She figured out I wasn't a waiter and was looking for Aaron. Claudio and I had met Aaron at the front when he went to pay for their dinner, and then he passed out, and we slipped out the side exit, placing him in the truck."

"And where was Sarah?"

"Out by their car, but since she didn't drink the wine and she was too visible, Claudio suggested I clean their table and wait for her to return."

"Did she?"

Dom nodded. "But then she called the manager and started looking for me, so I hid in the truck until I heard the sirens."

"Who called the cops?"

Dom shrugged. "No idea, but the fire alarm was going off inside the restaurant. My guess was Claudio pulled it."

Silvio rubbed his chin in thought. "Probably. Anyway, doesn't matter now. Claudio called. He got Sarah and is coming here."

"Great." Dom slapped his hands. "Almost payday."

"Not yet. The payday's when the job's finished."

"But it is finished."

Silvio laughed, fighting the urge to call Domenic an idiot again. There was a reason Silvio was in charge, and Domenic wasn't.

"The job is complete when Alex comes in and agrees to our terms."

"Yeah, and that'll be tonight. So, payday."

"Don't be too enthusiastic. Even though he agrees, everything else still has to play out the way we need it to."

"What? Once he agrees, we kill everyone anyway, so what does it matter?" Domenic gestured at Aaron. "Aren't these guys fighters or something?"

"Yeah, something like that."

"Well, later, when it's time to kill them, you think I could fight a couple of them, you know, kill them with my hands?" Domenic held up his hands, flipping them around, then back again.

"I don't think that's a good idea. They're apparently pretty good."

Domenic gave him a hard stare. "Another insult, eh?"

This time, Silvio laughed. "How is that an insult?"

"By saying they're good fighters and that I shouldn't fight them means I'm not as good as them. It can look like a compliment to them, but actually, you're insulting me."

"Well, that wasn't my intention." Silvio stepped away from Domenic and checked the time on his phone.

"You don't even know the street fights I've gotten myself into. These amateurs wouldn't last a minute in the ring with me."

"I believe that," Silvio said, barely paying attention.

Domenic was a last-minute addition to the team. And only because he was working with Claudio did he allow him to be on the Aaron/Sarah team. He'd used Domenic several times in the past, but only on rough jobs where a scrapper was needed. Domenic pulled his own weight each time. With this being a more delicate job, Claudio promised to keep Dom in check.

Whereas Claudio and Silvio went back to the years when they were both running a gang in their early twenties on the streets of Vancouver. If it weren't for the Asian gangs, they'd still be in Vancouver, still making a hundred grand a year while mules did all the work.

At least in Toronto, there was always someone who needed a job done, a warning sent, a man beat up, hospitalized, or killed.

Murder wasn't an issue for either man as long as it paid well enough. And guys like Domenic were great to have in your corner because most jobs they took were rough.

"Eric and Nestor should be here any second with that guy, Parkman—"

The garage door beeped and began to rise.

"Speak of the devil."

Eric's headlights shone inside the garage as he drove through the door and parked behind Domenic's truck.

Both men got out, evidently happy with themselves, smiling like they knew a secret. They were still dressed in their police costumes, with Eric wearing the tranquilizer gun in his holster.

"Everything work out well?" Silvio asked.

"Too well," Eric said.

"How can it be *too well*?" Silvio asked.

"Parkman was easy," Nestor said. "We knocked, shouted the word police, he opened the door, Eric shot him, and we held him down until the Midazolam kicked in."

"Was the dosage good for a man his size?"

Eric nodded. "He was out within a minute, maybe a minute and a half."

"The mixture worked perfectly," Nestor added.

Eric snapped his fingers and pointed at the trunk. "He's in there."

"Okay, guys. Bring them out of the vehicles and line them up on that couch over there." Silvio pointed at the area set up for the phone call to Alex they would be placing soon.

His men got to work as Silvio called Claudio's number. The man had Sarah and would be there soon enough, but why wasn't he picking up the phone?

"Hey, where's Claudio?" Eric asked.

"I'm trying him right now."

"What about the other guys?"

"Randy and Joe?"

Eric nodded as he grabbed Parkman's arms and heaved him out of the trunk.

"They're grabbing Daniel and Benjamin as we speak."

"You think they need help?"

Silvio shook his head. "No, they got it covered."

At least, he hoped they did. Sarah might be a problem, but Claudio said he'd handle her.

She was only a woman. How hard could she be?

He dialed Claudio's number again.

Now, he was starting to worry.

Chapter 6

Daniel parked across the street from the dojo. Without a word to each other, Benjamin and Daniel got out and hustled to the front door, where Daniel used his keys to unlock the martial arts gym.

Once inside, still without a word to each other, they scoured the gym, checking the small kitchen area, the bathroom, and the back room, turning lights on and off as they searched.

"Find anything?" Daniel whispered.

Benjamin shook his head. "Clear. The back door is still locked, too. No one's been here."

"Shit."

"What? You wanted someone here?"

Daniel nodded. "Yeah, like Aaron or Sarah hiding out. Maybe Parkman."

Benjamin placed a hand on Daniel's shoulder. "We'll find them."

Daniel looked at the floor for a moment. "I know." He raised his head. "If one of us were in mortal danger, Vivian would've said something, right?"

Benjamin nodded.

Daniel rarely felt the need to be reassured—in fact, he was usually the one doing the reassuring—but for some reason, this bothered him more than normal. How could they get picked off one by one? Who was that powerful to be able to get to each of them? That also begged the question, who would want to challenge Sarah when she had Vivian to cover her ass? No one had an ear for the other side like Sarah.

Or had that changed recently? Wasn't Vivian's communication less and less on each issue they dealt with? And if that was true, then why was she backing off?

It had to be the baby.

Maybe now that Sarah would be a mother, and Vivian knew Sarah would ease back into raising her baby, Vivian would play a less active role.

But if so, that left them high and dry when they needed her the most.

Benjamin's hand lowered from Daniel's shoulder as he stepped away and moved toward the kitchen. Daniel followed him.

"Brainstorm with me here," Daniel said.

Benjamin opened the fridge, snagged a water bottle off the door, uncapped it, and drank. "Brainstorm what?"

"Who would come after us at this level?"

"How should I know?"

"What I mean is, who would have the resources?"

"Who knows?" Benjamin shrugged, then dropped into a seat at the table.

"C'mon, help me here. Think about it. The manpower it would take, the expertise. If they know who we are, they'd know we wouldn't go easy."

Benjamin drank more, then set the bottle on the table. "Are you thinking mafia? Something like that?"

"Biker gang, street gang, mafia, organized crime, Cosa Nostra, the bratva, who knows."

"Bratva?"

"The brotherhood."

"Brotherhood? What the fuck is that? Illuminati shit?"

"No, the Russian mafia."

"And what was that house one? Casa something."

Daniel frowned. "Dude, you should read more."

"Not knowing something doesn't make someone stupid or uneducated. Just tell me, dickhead."

"Cosa Nostra is the Italian mafia."

"What's with all the fancy names? Mafia is mafia is mafia. Be done with it."

"The names tell us where they are from. Like MS-13, they're from El Salvador."

"How the hell would you know that?"

"I read. Also, Sarah dealt with some MS-13 members several years back. Remember?"

Benjamin shook his head. "Daniel, if the mafia came calling and the man's name was Igor or Viktor, I'd know it was the Russian mafia. If his name were Valentino or Vincenzo, I'd know it was the Italians. End of story."

"Fair enough, but it's not that simple." He leaned back against the wall and crossed his arms. "Besides, the bad guys rarely walk up and tell us their names. And also, bickering about this shit isn't getting us anywhere. Who could orchestrate an attack on all of us simultaneously? They have to be big, well-financed, and ballsy."

Benjamin stared at the wall for a minute, his eyes seemingly focused on nothing. Then he blinked and refocused his attention on Daniel.

"Whoever it is will regret it. That much is true. We've got Darwin and Disco."

"Darwin and Disco sound like a couple of cartoon characters. Here comes Darwin and his sidekick, Disco," Daniel said dramatically, "as they swoop in on their horses made of paper mâché."

Benjamin frowned. "Not funny."

Something made a thumping noise in the main area of the dojo.

Their eyes locked on one another a moment, and then Benjamin was up from his seat so fast that the backs of his knees bumped the chair over, tipping it back. It hit the floor with a loud clatter.

Each man moved to the door of the kitchen, where they stopped. Daniel held up three fingers, lowered one, waited a heartbeat, lowered the second, waited once more, then dropped the third finger.

Daniel first, Benjamin following, they slipped out of the kitchen and into the darkened gym area. The light from the kitchen spilled out onto the mats but left several corners of the gym in the dark.

Benjamin moved right, and Daniel took his cue to move to the left. As a unit, without a word, they moved along the wall toward the front. The glint of a streetlight reflected off the bottle of water Benjamin still held.

How was he supposed to fight if the need arose with that in his hand?

At the front window, Daniel peered out into the street.

Nothing seemed off or wrong. No one was on the street near their business, and only a random car eased by on Queen Street.

"Hey," Benjamin whispered.

Daniel shot a look his way.

"Did you leave this open?" Benjamin pointed at the door.

It sat open several inches.

Daniel shook his head.

They both turned around and stared down the length of the dojo. Darkness enveloped the back beyond the dim light spilling from the kitchen.

Without weapons, should they run or just leave the place? Then what? Call the cops? For what? Did two martial artists get spooked at their own dojo? Also, Alex was coming in thirty minutes or so. Disco might show up, too, whether he found Sarah or not.

No, they trained for years for moments like this. They were the weapon.

But what if their opponents had guns?

Daniel stayed close to the wall as he started back toward the kitchen.

"Hey," Benjamin said, moving across the mats to him. "Where are you going?"

"To hurt whoever's in here."

"Okay, but …" Benjamin hesitated.

Daniel stopped and faced him. "But what?"

He pointed over his shoulder. "Let me at least lock the door."

Daniel nodded and started toward the back again. The light spilling out of the kitchen was five steps away when a man materialized from the darkness, a weapon in his hand.

Daniel stopped.

The weapon spit something. Then it jerked in the man's hand again.

Whatever the man shot tugged at Daniel's shirt like an angry hornet.

Bullet or not, breaking in and coming after them pissed him off, so he did what he thought was right at the moment and ran toward the man.

Benjamin shouted something behind him, but Daniel was already dropping, sliding in low in a foot sweep. He hit the guy in the left ankle before he could get another shot off and then thrust a fist up into the guy's crotch when he began to drop from the impact.

Daniel ended up behind him when the man fell. He pushed off the floor, got halfway up to his feet, and shoved himself toward the man like he was diving for a fumbled football. The second he landed on him, the man was already curling into the fetal position because of the pain in his groin. Daniel hammered several strong punches to the man's face, aiming for the cartilage of his nose. He learned years ago that nose injuries ended fights rather quickly as the opponent's eyes watered profusely at the slightest provocation to the nose, crumbling the opponent's chance at a reprisal due to lack of vision.

The man covered his face with his arms, shouting for someone named Joe to help.

Daniel spun around, the dojo wavering in his vision.

A shoe met his face, and he dropped like a heavy bag of sand, the strength leaving him in waves. What the hell was happening? Why couldn't he get up?

He'd landed half on, half off the guy he'd pummeled. The way he was bent, he could see the wound in his stomach.

A dart?

Drugs? Tranquilizer? What the fuck?

Benjamin yelled something, and Daniel averted his eyes upward with enormous struggle.

The man who had kicked him down—probably the Joe the other guy called for—raised his weapon and aimed it at the front of the dojo.

He fired, but it sounded too late as the front door slammed shut.

Benjamin had gotten away.

The man below him grunted louder as he shoved and kicked until Daniel slid off him.

The front door banged again as Joe ran after Benjamin.

Daniel couldn't hold his eyes open any longer.

Then something connected with his head, and he was powerless to see it or attempt to stop it as consciousness faded and he experienced the sensation of falling.

Pain rose as he fell, and he was certain something knocked into his head again, but now he was too deep even to feel the pain.

Somewhere in the depths of consciousness, before he faded completely, he was grateful for whatever was in those darts as it blocked out the pain.

His head jerked again, but it was more of a knowledge thing—like he knew his head was moving but not why or how.

Then his awareness faded to depths that blocked everything, even light.

Chapter 7

Benjamin ran for their car, praying Daniel didn't lock it but knowing he did.

Was it wrong to run? Daniel needed him, but they had guns, and Daniel was already down. Wasn't he? Besides, it was always Benjamin who got shot. Guns had created a phobia in him that previously wasn't there. Sure, they all joked around with him, but the truth was, he'd been shot more than any of them, and he was sick of it. The surgeries, the bandages, the physical therapy—it all sucked. Grateful that none of the bullets had cost him anything more than scarring, he was convinced the odds of him getting shot again were low. Hadn't he filled an average life's quota by now?

Truly, it had been a while, but when he saw the gun in the man's hand, he fought the urge to bolt with everything he had. And he'd stepped forward to help as Daniel fought the guy on the mats. Daniel wouldn't need help from one opponent, especially one who had already dropped and was losing quickly.

But then that other guy stepped in and kicked Daniel in the face.

And pointed a gun at Benjamin.

When he saw the gun, he ran. And now shame ran with him.

He dodged a slow-moving minivan as he crossed the street, then got to their car and tried the doors.

Locked.

He smacked the roof and cursed under his breath.

It was in these moments when he wished he also carried a gun. That or had Alex beside him. Alex ran at guns and was able to anticipate the shooter's aim and when they'd fire. He'd done it several times and only got nicked once. Lucky bastard.

"Benjamin," a man called.

He spun around. The guy from the dojo was across the street, hands in the pockets of his jacket, no doubt concealing the gun in his right pocket.

Another man walked slowly, half a block up. From this distance, he couldn't be sure, but it looked like John Slade, one of their students who lived just down the street.

"Come back to the gym. Daniel wants to tell you something."

"Dojo."

"What?"

"It's not a gym, it's a dojo."

From where he was standing, he saw the look of

confusion on the man's face.

"Who cares, asshole? Grapefruits and lemons. Both circular. Tastes different."

"Don't you mean apples and oranges?"

Benjamin couldn't believe they were having this discussion from each side of Queen Street an hour short of midnight on a Saturday evening.

The man eased his right hand out of his pocket to show Benjamin the weapon in his hand.

"Come back now, or Daniel might not make it."

That stirred a wave of anguish and anger in him. He wanted to cry and pummel the man to death in the same instant. He even stepped toward the man, then stopped as a car honked and swerved around him. The driver shouted something but continued up Queen Street without stopping.

"Come get me," Benjamin said, leaning back on their car and crossing his arms.

The man stepped forward, slipped sideways between two cars, then waited for a cube van to pass.

Their eyes met as he crossed the street to Benjamin.

The weapon came out of his pocket. The man held it down close to his thigh.

"You going to shoot me out here in front of everyone?"

The man shook his head. "We don't want to kill you." He stopped four feet from Benjamin. "We have orders to deliver you and Daniel to a secure site." He lifted the weapon for Benjamin to see. "This is a dart gun. It won't kill you, but it'll put you to sleep."

"Why knock us out?" Benjamin remained where he was, arms crossed, leaning back against his car. He was like a pent-up wire of energy, waiting for the man to move one foot closer before smacking the dart gun from his grasp and then going back inside the dojo to save Daniel.

John Slade was farther up the block now and not available for help.

"How else would we be expected to take Sarah's team without killing them? We have to put you all to sleep. You guys are all fighters and shit." He pointed at the dojo as a large truck passed them. "Daniel got two darts and still almost hospitalized Randy back there." He shook his head. "No way, man. The pay for this job is good, but not hospital good. Just come with me, and we'll both live."

"Thought you said that's a dart gun, something to knock us out."

"It is."

"Then what's this about us both living?"

"If you don't come, tomorrow's team will set a trap to execute you. Today, we're playing nicey nice."

Benjamin pushed off the car, unfolded his arms, and placed them at the ready by his hips.

"Nicely nice, eh?"

A Brinks truck was coming along Queen Street at a good clip. The armored vehicle would be perfect. And even if he got shot with a tranquilizer of some sort, he'd still have time for what he was planning before being knocked out.

"Who hired you?" Benjamin asked. "What's this all about? Tell me that, and I'll go with you willingly."

The Brinks truck was one hundred yards out.

"It's just a job, man. No hard feelings."

Benjamin stepped closer. "No hard feelings? After what

you guys just did to my friend?" Fifty yards away now and closing fast. "You'll all pay for what you've done." Thirty yards.

The man raised the gun. "That's close enough."

"Shoot me, then."

Ten yards.

The man lowered his weapon to aim at Benjamin's stomach area, and Benjamin leaped.

He spun in a circle—something Alex would've been proud to see—and brought his hand around to smack at the dart gun. Even though he heard it fire, he felt no impact, and then the weapon was out of the guy's hand.

While still in a spin, which he needed to create enough torque to shove the guy several feet, he grabbed the man's arm and upper chest and leaned into a strong shove toward the middle of the street, right in front of the moving vehicle.

The armored truck was upon them, the massive grill four feet from Benjamin's head, when he stopped his forward motion and jerked back to get out of the way.

But he didn't get far.

Like trying to shove the man into a pool, he had grabbed at Benjamin's sleeves and locked him in a death grip, the absolute shock and fear painted on his face as the Brink's truck bore down on him.

Benjamin couldn't get out of the way in time.

The impact accompanied the screech of brakes.

The saving grace was the man hit the grill and the truck's bumper first, so when the forward motion of the vehicle got to Benjamin a tenth of a second later, his impact was softened by the man's body.

Benjamin heard things crack and snap, but he wasn't sure if it was the other man or pieces of the truck's grill.

And then he was airborne.

Cars scurried by beneath him before he realized they were parked, and he had been launched over them.

He blinked—or closed his eyes—and endured the impact when he hit the ground. That felt harder than the truck's initial contact for some unknown reason.

Unable to breathe, the wind knocked out of him, and Benjamin gasped for air.

Then, the pain came in a tsunami, overwhelming him.

That snapping sound he'd heard had been him, after all.

But what broke? An arm? A few ribs? His neck?

Air wasn't coming in the normal way. Panic caused him further stress.

The stars moved above him as car doors slammed nearby. Someone shouted something about numbers. Ones and nines or something.

The word emergency was called out twice.

The stars above were moving so fast, they were swimming now.

He still couldn't breathe.

Something heavy smacked his chest.

As his eyes closed, he saw a man in uniform pressing on his chest, and a strange thought raced through his mind.

Dude, I can't breathe. Get off me.

Then the pain died, and the stars winked out.

Somewhere in his consciousness, he smiled because it all felt better.

Like a wisp of smoke blown from a strong wind, that

thought broke away and dissipated, and Benjamin was under.

Chapter 8

THE DOJO TO ALEX'S house was no more than a twenty-minute walk. Since he said he'd be there in an hour, that would place him at the dojo at 23:30, but he wanted to be early. If danger was lurking around every corner and traps had been set, whatever that meant, all of them had to be more diligent and aware.

One block from the dojo, he slowed his step.

Flashing lights bounced off neighboring buildings.

He picked up his pace, and after a moment, he was running.

Bent forward slightly as he rounded the corner running, he came upon a group of emergency vehicles parked in the middle of Queen Street.

Alex kept running, and as he neared the dojo, the fire truck and ambulance were parked directly in front. Police tape had already been strung up, blocking the entrance to their place of business. At this hour, nothing was open, but that didn't stop Alex.

Daniel and Benjamin were supposed to meet him there. Could something have happened to either of them while he dawdled, thinking they wouldn't meet him until the full hour had passed?

"Hey," a man said beside him.

Alex lowered his center of gravity, spun around, and placed his hands in the most likely spot where someone would touch him, which in this case was the arm.

A cop in uniform had been standing behind the side of the firetruck. When Alex spun around, that cop was an inch from grabbing his upper arm. Because Alex lowered himself, an instinctive move for him, the man's hand clamped down on air an inch above Alex's shoulder.

He kept his hands rising and grasped the cop's wrist, then secured it by yanking it inward and twisting the hand back.

All this happened in seconds.

Before the cop could speak again, he uttered a short cry of pain.

"Don't touch me," Alex said, releasing the cop's hand.

The man stepped back and regarded Alex with crazed eyes as he looked from his reddened wrist to Alex's face.

"You just assaulted me," the cop said, his voice raised an octave.

"What happened here?"

"I should arrest you."

Alex glared at him. "You could try."

The cop stepped in front of Alex in a threatening posture.

"Grabbing at me from a hiding place." Alex gestured at where the man was standing. "You startled me, and I defended myself. You had not been identified at that time. When I saw the uniform, I released my attacker." Expressionless, Alex stared at the man a moment longer. "Now, what happened here?"

"You with this place?" The cop jerked his head at the sign for Aaron's dojo as he rubbed his wrist.

Alex nodded. "I work here."

"Yeah, but are you family?"

"Of course I am. We're all brothers." That was mostly true.

"Coming to work at this hour? Our witness said the gym is usually closed at this hour. What brings you out?"

"I was supposed to meet the other teachers. Late-night training session. Unscheduled."

"Well, two guys got hit by that armored vehicle." The cop pointed.

Alex stared at the Brinks truck. Even in the dark, he saw the blood on the grill. To the far left, a stretcher was being loaded into the back of an ambulance. The paramedics didn't seem in a hurry, even though the stretcher had a body on it. A white sheet covered the body completely.

Alex took a step in that direction.

"There's nothing you can do for him now."

Alex fought back the emotions. Who had died? Daniel or Benjamin? Was this the trap Sarah was talking about? And if so, how was texting them good enough? From one text to a phone call, this Saturday night had become a nightmare.

The cop was talking again. "Our witness down the street

said the two guys came out of the gym here and walked over to that car."

The cop pointed at Daniel's car, which was parked on the other side of Queen Street. Alex turned farther and saw the witness the cop was referring to.

John Slade was a regular class member. He joined when they first opened this location because he lived half a block down. If John said he saw Daniel and Benjamin, then that's who he saw.

"What about—" Emotion choked off his vocal cords. He inhaled, tightened his fists, then exhaled and released his fists. "What about the other guy?"

"Banged up pretty bad. The other ambulance took him first. Chest compressions, blood, broken bones, the whole lot. Those armored trucks are blocks of steel. Not a good idea to run in front of them."

Alex glanced up at the cop with water-covered eyes. "Run in front of them?"

"Yeah, two witnesses, plus the driver of the truck, said they jumped in front of him after standing by that car there and arguing. The guy who lives over there"—he pointed at Slade again—"said he even saw them park minutes before and go inside the gym. Thought it was odd for this hour." The cop leaned in close to Alex. "I hope you're okay, buddy. I only told you this because you said you were affiliated with the gym, that they were your brothers." The cop rubbed his wrist once more. "Now I know why you responded the way you did. I'm willing to let it slide and give you a break. That way, you can head to the hospital and see how your brother is doing."

Alex nodded his thanks, then stepped backward into the doorway of the dojo. He withdrew his key but didn't need it as the door was sitting ajar. He pushed it open all the way and took in the interior.

Nothing looked out of the ordinary except for a water bottle that had been dropped a few feet from the door. Its contents had spilled out onto the carpet.

He hit the switch to his left, illuminating the entire dojo except for the back area, which was accessed by another switch. With no interest in having police protection in case someone was still inside, which he doubted, Alex started toward the back, withdrawing his cell phone to check for messages.

There were none. No phone calls and no messages.

The light was on in the kitchen. He slowed and glanced inside, but it was empty. Staying close to the wall on the right, he edged closer to the back, hit the switch to turn on the lights, and took in the rear of the dojo. Completely empty. Once he checked the back door and saw that it was unlocked, he scanned the immediate area outside and then secured the door. Why was it unlocked? Had someone left through the back?

After killing the lights, Alex returned to the front of the kitchen, where he stood and stared at the rest of the dojo. Something about the back door bothered him. Why had the front been sitting ajar? What happened here in the past thirty to forty minutes?

Out front, the light from the emergency vehicles flashed across the walls of the interior of the martial arts studio. The cop was just outside the front window, watching him.

Behind the cop, one of the fire trucks eased away and disappeared from sight.

The scene out front was clearing, the accident was over, and the victims were taken care of.

But something wasn't right inside the dojo.

He inhaled deeply, his eyes closed.

Someone had been here recently. Multiple someones.

A quick scan of the area brought his eyes to a smudge on the carpet a few feet in front of him. He lowered to his haunches and edged closer. It looked like whoever dropped their water bottle spilled some here first.

Or was that water?

He leaned closer until his nose was less than an inch from the darkened smudge, then inhaled.

That wasn't water.

A quick dab of his thumb came away with a dark red liquid.

Someone had fought here recently and drew blood.

His stomach twisted at the mystery of what was happening tonight. He'd never been in charge or ran any sort of crusade. It had always been what Sarah needed. Or Alex responding to what Aaron asked of him. Sometimes, he'd taken it upon himself to advance on a target or leave an area on his terms, but that was because he was such an extreme introvert. The least amount of people, the better. Unless it was martial arts, teaching a class was never an issue. He remained alone at the front of the room with the students focused on his moves, what they were learning, and not him per se.

He gathered himself and started toward the front of the

dojo.

It was time to speak with John Slade to hear what he witnessed.

If something happened to Sarah, Aaron, or any of the rest of them, there was no stopping what he would do to whoever it was that brought this to their doorstep.

He flicked off the lights, then turned back.

The kitchen light was still on.

No bother. He'd leave it on for when they returned later.

There would be a later, wouldn't there?

Alex was overwhelmed by a deep sadness when he slipped the key in the door to lock it. Even his posture was stooped, his chin trembling. When had that started? For a man so in touch with his muscles, his training, to have an uncontrolled tremor concerned him. Not for the muscle group but for how much emotion he felt at the loss of his friends and the uncertainty of the state of the others.

Heavy-footed, body suddenly cold, he secured the door and faced the street.

Only two police cars remained on the scene. The cop who spoke with him was lumbering along between the two police cars now, tapping on a cell phone. Another man in civilian clothes was taking pictures of the front of the Brinks truck, the road blocked off and down to a single small lane.

He refused to believe one of his friends died tonight, absolutely refused to believe it.

Yet, with the life they had chosen for themselves, being on Sarah's team, one of them—or more—would die one day. They weren't superhuman or invulnerable.

Sure, Vivian kept them relatively safe, and Darwin

backed them all up with trained mercenaries, yet in the end, they were all flesh and blood and could be killed with something as simple as a slit of the carotid artery.

It appeared today might be the day that one of them could be lost.

When he glanced to his right, John Slade was gone. He was probably back in his apartment.

Which was fine with Alex. He wasn't in the mood to talk. The grief he was feeling had an immobilizing factor to it. Like grief and pain seized his heart, his muscles tightened their grip until it paralyzed his every move, his every thought.

He lowered to his knees and hugged himself. Just one moment, he needed one moment alone to breathe, to recharge, to collect himself.

Then he'd call someone, maybe Darwin, maybe someone else.

But for now, he just needed a meditative moment.

Alex lowered his head to the concrete sidewalk, setting his forehead down, a pebble pushing inward on his skin.

The slight pain was welcomed. It offered him a point to focus on. This was where he relaxed, where he breathed, in and out, in and out.

After ten breaths, he gritted his teeth, pushed up off the pavement, and landed on his feet in a small, tight stance. He was ready. Whatever was coming, he would endure, deal with it, and move on. He could do this. Of that, there was no doubt.

He yanked out his phone and started walking along the sidewalk.

After scrolling through his contacts, he stopped on Darwin's phone number, his thumb hovering above the button.

What time was it in Italy?

Before he tapped the call button, the phone vibrated in his hand. An incoming text, then another.

Someone was sending him pictures.

He opened the app and glanced at the first picture.

Bile rose in his throat, and he had to cover his mouth. His entire body broke out in a sweat. He moved the hand over his mouth to the back of his neck. Even his knees were shaking now, which wasn't his normal reaction to trauma of any sort. Fear never stopped him. Fear pushed him to fight.

Pain, like when he saw what happened to his parents all those years ago, paralyzed him.

The picture of Aaron and Parkman, dead or unconscious, on a couch in the photo scared the shit out of him.

He scrolled unwillingly to the next photo that came through.

It was a close-up of Daniel's bruised face.

The shock and sadness dissipated as anger took over. Even his stride lengthened as he trudged along the sidewalk with no destination in mind.

He was about to reply to the texts when his phone rang.

He stopped walking, answered the call, and placed it at his ear.

"Good evening, Alex. Have I got your attention, you piece of shit? Or should I send another photo? A dead Sarah? A dead Benjamin? How about it, Alex? Another photo, or are you prepared to listen?"

Alex's jaw locked in anger. He would kill them. He would kill them all. The pain they'd endure would be a pleasure. Anyone and everyone involved would regret their decision to hurt his family, his people, for the short time they still drew breath.

But he had to do it right. He had to get close to them.

He had to listen to their demands, observe their behavior, take it all in, feel it, decide on a course of action, and plan their deaths.

All that relied on finding them, and Toronto was a big place.

To already have Daniel in their presence told him how close they were because the accident had just happened out front of the dojo. He had spoken with Daniel and Benjamin about an hour ago.

He would find them. And he would kill them. They had set traps, as Sarah had suspected, but all they did was snare themselves.

"Alex? You still there?"

He struggled to open his mouth. Then he found his voice.

"I'm listening."

Chapter 9

Silvio studied the three kidnapped men. "How fucking hard is it to tranquilize people and bring sleeping human beings to a warehouse?"

He glanced at his assembled crew.

"This was supposed to be an easy fucking job," he shouted, his voice reverberating throughout the warehouse, echoing back to him.

"Now I can't get ahold of Claudio after he called and said he had Sarah and was bringing her in. My contact on the police force said Sarah is on the run after killing two cops, and we just lost Joe."

"We don't know that, boss," Randy said, his voice nasally. He held a bag of ice on his face at the bridge of his nose. "I got beat up. By the time I heard the sirens and checked out the front, Joe and Benjamin were surrounded by a small group of people." He swallowed audibly, a loud gulping sound as he kept his mouth open. His bottom lip was bleeding, too. "That fucker got shot with two darts and still broke my face. I had to carry him out their back door, hide him behind a dumpster, and then drive back around to pick him up."

"Well, it looks like that Benjamin asshole took care of Joe, doesn't it?"

"When this is over, I get to kill Daniel," Randy whispered. "And, boss, we don't know if Joe died for sure."

"Yeah, well, one of them died, is what I hear, and the other was rushed to the hospital fighting for his life." Silvio suppressed the urge to punch something. "We were supposed to bring them all here, then call Alex and convince him to take the job. Easy peasy. Once the job is done on Monday, kill them all, dump their bodies, get paid the rest of the cash, and leave town for a while. Fuckin' simple." He raised a finger in the air. "Actually, this is one of the simplest jobs we've ever had."

He kicked at Aaron's foot, knocking it to the side. All three men were set up for the photos—two on the couch, with Daniel on the floor.

"Sarah's on the run, and Benjamin is either dead or on life support." He thumped his chest twice, then screamed, "They're all supposed to be here. Especially that bitch, Sarah. Without her, I can't guarantee Alex will be compliant."

"He'll do what's required of him," Domenic said.

"And how do you know that you fuckin' idiot," Randy spurted.

Domenic shot a hand out so fast, it was a blur. At the end

of his arm was a gun, and it was pointed at Randy.

"Call me an idiot one more time. Please, I really need to kill someone tonight."

Silvio took two wide steps to Domenic and drove a fist into the side of his face, knocking the man off the couch's armrest. The gun flew from his hand and landed with a metallic clang on the concrete floor of the warehouse.

He needed to jump on Domenic and beat the shit out of the man but held back. He may need him later. At least he got that punch he needed to get out of his system.

"Stop your fucking high school whining about being called names," he shouted in Domenic's face. The man rubbed his cheek where he lay on the floor. "How old are you? Get up and act like a man and stop threatening the rest of my fucking team because of a fucking name."

"I'll fuckin' kill him if he pulls a gun on me again," Randy whispered. With the bag of ice on the bridge of his nose, he glared at Domenic on the floor.

Silvio felt ready to burst an artery. "Okay, that's it. If you all don't fuck off and shut up, I'll kill you all myself."

"You could try," Domenic whispered, gathering himself off the floor. He leaned down and retrieved his weapon, then slipped it away, a defiant look on his face.

Domenic would have to be handled at the end of this job. The guy was an idiot through and through, unstable and unprofessional.

This was Domenic's last job with Silvio.

It was his last job ever.

Silvio pulled out his cell phone and snapped several photos of their prisoners. Then he moved away from the group to stare out at the street from one of the windows while he set up the text to Alex. After picking the two pictures he'd text, he sent them one after the other.

He waited a few heartbeats, then called Alex's number. It was answered quickly, but no one spoke on the other end.

"Good evening, Alex. Have I got your attention, you piece of shit? Or should I send another photo? A dead Sarah? A dead Benjamin? How about it, Alex? Another photo, or are you prepared to listen?"

Silvio listened to Alex's breathing on the other end. Two cars eased by on Queen Street outside the warehouse they had rented for the week. It was close to the dojo, as they had suspected they'd catch them all there. But that hadn't worked out well at all. He'd listened to Domenic's plan to assign men to pick up each of Sarah's team, and so far, that hadn't turned out well, either.

At least they had three of the five they wanted. And Claudio would bring Sarah in soon. At least, Silvio hoped he would.

That had to be enough for Alex.

"Alex? You still there?"

After a moment, Alex whispered, "I'm listening."

"We have your friends."

Silvio waited. Alex remained silent.

"You saw the pictures?" Silvio asked.

He waited again but was only rewarded with a steady breathing on the line.

"Speak to me and answer me when I address you," Silvio said, losing his patience.

"Small talk."

"What does that mean?" Silvio said. "Small talk?"

"No small talk. Just tell me what you want." Alex sounded like he was breathing out the words, his tone heavy.

"My kind of guy. Straight to business. I like that." Silvio glanced over his shoulder. The men were loading their captives into the ACME carpet truck as planned.

"What do you want?" Alex and his word breathing again.

"I want to meet you."

"Where?"

"We're in a warehouse. A few blocks from you."

"Address?"

"Alex, my man, you don't talk much, do you?"

"I'm not your man."

"On the contrary," Silvio said, allowing himself the pleasure of laughing at Alex. "You are totally my *man*."

"How so?"

"Because these maggots you work with are mine now. So, you will do as you're told."

"What am I to do?"

"Meet me and find out."

"Where?"

"Several blocks from the dojo. On Queen Street, just past Coxwell Avenue. The warehouse on the right. I've left a light on at the front door."

"When?"

"Now. We have a lot to discuss. I'll wait an hour. After that, we leave, and you won't ever see Sarah Roberts, Parkman, Daniel, or Aaron again. Benjamin's already dead or in the hospital on life support, but I can tell you with utmost certainty that he won't make it, either."

"Why?"

Silvio detected the first sign of emotion in Alex's voice.

"Why what?"

"Why are you doing this?"

"Does it matter, my man? I *am* doing it. In your realm of understanding, I feel that's all you need to know."

"I'm on my way."

"Good. One hour. That's all you've got. After that, I'll text you a few more pictures. Ones that'll haunt you for the rest of the week."

"The week?"

"That's the projected time it'll take my team to hunt you down and kill you for not doing what you were told."

Silvio waited a heartbeat. Alex didn't respond.

"One hour, my man, one hour."

Silvio killed the call and turned to his assembled men. Randy was lifting Daniel into the back of the truck. He dropped him hard enough that Daniel's head bounced once.

"Easy," Silvio shouted at Randy. "You kill them now, and Alex might not listen. This entire operation depends on those assholes being alive until the deal is done, and we're paid on Monday."

"He's fine," Randy shouted back, his voice sounding worse as the swelling around his nose bulged larger. "Another couple of bumps on the guy's head won't matter squat."

"Okay, we all know the drill. Randy, take the truck to the barn. Wrap at least ten rolls of duct tape around their wrists and ankles. Ensure it's so thick they can't bite or cut through it. Then wait for us there. Eric, Nestor, and I will deal with

Alex." Silvio addressed Domenic. "I want you to find out where Claudio is. He called and said he had Sarah. If he stopped somewhere with a tranquilized Sarah to feel her up or something, I'll fucking kill him. When Alex demands proof of life, we have to be able to give it to him."

"Where would Claudio be?" Domenic asked, frowning and staring down at his cell phone.

"That's why I'm asking you to find him. We don't know."

"What?" Domenic glanced up and met his gaze.

Silvio wondered why he included Domenic in this job in the first place. He recalled thinking that the more men he had, the better he felt. The pay was solid and easily split seven ways. Yet, at that moment, he wanted to pull his weapon and shoot Domenic.

"Dom, I'm asking you to find Claudio. Please don't ask me where he will be. That's the point. I want you to answer that question."

"Oh, okay." Domenic nodded and slipped his phone away, getting to his feet. "But, how would I know where he is if you don't?"

Silvio clenched his hands into fists. Eric and Nestor covered their mouths and turned away. Even Randy was laughing.

"Domenic, just call his cell phone, go to his house, and drive by where he was last seen. I don't really care. Just focus on finding him while we deal with Alex. Can you do that, please?"

"Sure, but I want to *deal* with Alex. He should know who's in charge."

Now, Domenic was testing Silvio's patience at an entirely new level. "He will know who is in charge, Dom, because we'll tell him. Now, you were working with Claudio to snatch Sarah and Aaron, and you brought me Aaron. Leave now and get me Sarah and bring Claudio in."

Silvio strode past him to check on the door where Alex would enter. He was by far the one they worried about the most. After reading up on Sarah and her group of vigilantes, Silvio's team had steered clear of them, kept quiet, and operated on contracts that were easy but paid well.

Until now.

This arrangement paid extremely well, and only someone with Alex's unique skillset could pull it off. When they discussed how to persuade Alex to do the job for them, they could only come up with their current plan. One by one, take his friends off the street and offer him a deal. One job for his friends' lives.

Other than a few setbacks, they had accomplished their goal. With Claudio missing and Joe likely dead, they were down to five men. Domenic would be dead at the end of this gig, so the few million they were getting would be divided four ways.

Silvio smiled to himself. That was more money than he'd made in the past four years combined. Who knows, maybe another one of his team will find a way to die before the weekend is over, and the money will be split into larger portions.

The idea seemed even better when he thought of the extra cash that gave him.

Wasn't this job tougher than usual, more dangerous?

Didn't he deserve a million dollars for himself?

A million meant vacation time. Perhaps Cuba for a year or Mexico. With that kind of money, he could afford bitches, booze, and blow for a year or more.

"A fuckin' year," he whispered.

"What?" Domenic asked.

Silvio turned to him. "What are you still doing here?"

"Helping you set up for Alex."

Silvio fought the anger rising in him. He couldn't believe Domenic was that fucked in the head. This final act convinced Silvio should've never brought Domenic in to help with this job. "I thought I told you to go find Claudio."

Domenic shrugged from two feet away. "I have no idea where to look, so it would be a waste of time."

Eric and Nestor watched them. Silvio smiled at everyone in the warehouse.

Domenic the asshole, Domenic the idiot. The man just confirmed his uselessness.

Silvio placed a hand on the man's shoulder. "Fair enough, Dom. You're right." He nodded to the left. "Help me with the rope over there."

Domenic glanced over his shoulder.

Silvio withdrew his weapon from behind his back and placed it at Dom's temple.

"Fucking idiot."

He pulled the trigger before the man could turn back around.

The shot reverberated throughout the warehouse, the echo lasting as long as it took Domenic's limp body to crumple to the floor.

Silvio stared down at Dom a moment, then slipped his weapon away. Surprisingly, he felt nothing. He had taken a life so often that this was just work to him, a job. Removing Domenic from the team felt good. The man was an idiot and had pissed him off one too many times.

When he turned to his assembled team, Eric, Nestor, and Randy were standing side by side now, watching him.

"We ready?" Silvio asked as if nothing had happened.

Nestor nodded, looking from Domenic to Silvio, then back to Domenic. "We are ready."

Eric seemed more in control. He pointed at Dom. "What are we going to do with him?"

"Leave him. It'll be good for Alex to see the body. At least then he'll know how serious we are."

Randy gestured at the truck. "If that's what you need, Alex, to see bodies, then can I kill Daniel now?"

Silvio stared at him for a moment, wondering where criminals were born. Was there a directory under a listing titled Criminals Anonymous or Idiots for Hire?

"No, you cannot kill Daniel. A dead body sends Alex a message that we mean business. His friends—alive for now —keeps him under our control. Sending a message and controlling a machine like Alex are two entirely separate things."

Randy nodded. "Okay, but after this is over—"

"You'll get your chance. Now, take your hiding places and be ready. Alex will be like a raging bull. It'll be hard to contain him if he loses his shit."

Randy clucked his tongue. "He's just one man. This trap thing we're doing will hold him. I'm not worried."

"Let's hope so. Now, leave before he gets here. If he knows his friends are in the building, he'll kill us all and take them out of here."

Randy snorted. "You give this guy too much credit. We can fight, too, man."

"Yeah, okay. When this is all done, before we kill Alex, you can have a go at him."

"I didn't mean that," Randy said as he jumped up into the ACME Carpet truck and turned it on. Moments later, he exited the warehouse and was gone with Alex's friends.

Silvio moved off to the alcove several feet to the right of the main door to wait.

Alex was coming, and they were prepared.

Phase one was complete, and their payday increased.

Things were looking up already.

The last hurdle was getting Alex to comply and agree to do as they asked him.

And no matter how good of a martial artist he was, fuckin' Jet Li or Bruce Lee, it didn't matter. Bullets won every time.

And his team were all excellent shots.

Alex would agree to their terms, or he would die in half an hour, along with all his friends.

That still left Silvio time to complete the job if he had to do it himself. He just didn't want to get his hands dirty on this one.

Threatening the life of the Chief of Police for the Toronto Police Services was a serious deal. He'd be surrounded by hundreds of fellow officers, too.

But it was something Alex could do without even being

seen. Or Alex would forfeit his life and the lives of his friends.

They would all die anyway, but Alex didn't need to know that yet.

Silvio smiled, feeling so much better that Domenic was dead already.

He called Claudio's number again, worry creasing his forehead when it went to voicemail.

"Motherfucker," he mumbled.

He rested his head back against the corrugated metal wall to wait.

Life was death, and death was part of life.

He glanced over at Dom's body.

Then why did death feel so good? Why did killing feel so right?

Something about killing a man like Alex felt extra good. He wished he could do it tonight. But he would wait.

The job first.

Murder second.

Financial freedom is third.

Silvio grinned to himself while waiting for Alex to arrive in the darkened corner of the warehouse. Despite the mistakes, everything was coming together better than he'd planned.

Much better.

Chapter 10

SARAH ROBERTS HAD STAYED off the main streets, using residential streets to meander back toward her apartment. Since her cell phone was left at the scene of a murder, the authorities would be looking for her. A police officer was killed. The manhunt would be intense. She needed to reach out to someone she trusted. Perhaps trust was too strong a word. Someone she could rely on and could work with, like Detective Ricigliano or Detective Marina Diner.

But how? She didn't have her phone, which stored all her numbers.

With no cash on her, she needed to get home to grab the money they had stashed in the apartment, then find a hiding spot to catch a few hours of sleep. She could buy a cell phone in the morning and start making calls.

She hadn't seen Disco's Hummer but hadn't expected to

as she'd left the area around the motel. Everything would look better in the morning. Darwin would be in Toronto tomorrow evening, and with his help, they'd find Aaron and Parkman.

She wiped at a few tears that spilled over her eyelids. Four months pregnant, and she was dealing with this without her sister.

"What's the plan, Vivian?" she asked under her breath. "You want to help us out over here? Not liking this shit one bit."

She stepped out onto Bloor Street and stood in the darkness between two streetlights, staring up at her apartment building. The sides of the twenty-story building were lit by random apartment lights throughout. The parking lot was mostly full as it was nearing midnight on a Saturday evening.

She couldn't see all the vehicles from where she stood, so there was no way to tell if police cars had arrived yet. The authorities would likely come by soon enough, and Sarah didn't want to be in the apartment when they got there. Figuring out this mess from inside a holding cell wouldn't work. Although, she had to risk access to her apartment, or she'd be stranded without cash.

She crossed the street and strode onto the well-kept grass outlining the parking area. Attentive to movement, she trudged through the parking lot and around the back of the building. Not a single cop car was visible.

Maybe they weren't here yet. A warrant to access her apartment would take more than an hour, but she thought they'd at least send someone to watch her building in case she showed up.

One hour wasn't much time for the authorities to get organized while still dealing with a fatal call. But since she wasn't getting any help from her sister, she had to risk entering her apartment.

When they left for dinner earlier, she couldn't have known the night would go to shit, so she hadn't even brought her house keys. Aaron had his keys on him, and that was all they needed.

That left only one option.

The superintendent would have to let her into her apartment.

Sarah stopped by a minivan and leaned against it, staying in the shadows. Besides the random car on Bloor Street, nothing moved in the immediate area. No one was out walking or watching the front doors of the building, as far as she could tell.

This was her chance—her *only* chance—to get in, get cash, and get gone because the authorities would be here soon. Of that, there was no doubt.

After one last look around, she stepped out of the relative safety of the shadows and strode purposefully toward the front lobby doors.

So far, so good. No cop cars were visible, and no one jumped out to arrest her.

She entered the main foyer and slapped the superintendent's buzzer. In the brightly lit foyer, she was completely exposed to anyone in the entire parking lot, like she was on stage with spotlights aimed at her.

She buzzed again and faced the interior of the lobby.

Mike finally answered. "It's late," his metallic voice

came through the speaker on the wall. "What do you want?"

"Let me in," Sarah said.

"Who is this?"

"Open the door, Mike."

"Just wait there. I'm coming out."

The speaker clicked off. Sarah waited without glancing over her shoulder. She was committed to this plan and had to see it through, even though it made her nervous.

She didn't have to wait long. Mike stepped around the corner and stared at her. Recognition changed his expression, and he quickened his pace until he smacked the door's handle, giving her access. But there was something else in his face. Something that looked like worry.

"I need into my apartment."

"No hello?" Mike asked, his voice shaky. "No, sorry for bothering you at this hour, Mike?"

"You're right. But I still need in my apartment, though."

Maybe she'd just woken him up, which was why he looked the way he looked.

He huffed out a breath and started toward the corridor that led to his apartment, avoiding her gaze.

"You don't have your own keys?" Mike asked without turning around.

Something was definitely different with him. She felt it right away and slowed her step. Was she walking into a trap?

Mike got to the corner and stopped. When he turned back, his face was a mask of worry.

"Sarah, you need to stop forgetting your keys."

This was the first time she'd ever asked Mike for access to her apartment. They'd dealt with him several times in the past, but it was always simple tasks. Passed him by in the hallways and offered the usual hellos and goodbyes, but that was it.

Someone was here.

But how? She hadn't seen any police cars.

Perhaps an unmarked cruiser she'd missed?

"Follow me, Sarah. We'll get the keys to your apartment. Just be ready." Mike nodded once, then turned back around and walked away.

Just be ready?

Someone was in her apartment already. The authorities had rushed over and got Mike to let them inside. They were waiting upstairs, and she could do nothing about it.

She followed him down the corridor. He was just entering his place when the thought hit her that she could be wrong.

The authorities weren't just in her apartment.

They were here, too.

She slowed at Mike's open apartment door, danger raising the hairs on her arms.

Then, it all became clear to her.

Why else would Mike come to the lobby to verify it was her with his own eyes? And why would he warn her to be ready back in the lobby when he could have easily spoken to her in private in his apartment?

Because someone was in Mike's place.

Sarah inhaled deeply, then stepped inside her superintendent's unit, staying close to the wall by the closet on the left.

A tall man in civilian clothes moved quickly, reaching for

her from the kitchen door. He wasn't taking any chances by talking or negotiating. She was going into custody, and he was going to do it forcefully because, after all, one of his gang had been killed earlier in the evening, and they suspected Sarah had something to do with that.

What he couldn't know was that Sarah didn't kill that cop.

He also didn't know Sarah wasn't going into custody today.

Sarah lowered her upper body and wrapped her arms around the man's knees. The man had lunged for her, and as he saw her drop, he adjusted himself to grab her about the waist.

Before he could get a solid grip on her, she locked his legs into her shoulder and lifted upward. He lost his balance with a grunt and fell forward, resting partially on the backs of her shoulders. Taken by surprise, he grappled for a hold as Sarah got several feet off the floor, then twisted in the tight space and released the man.

He dropped sideways, hitting the floor hard, and Sarah dropped beside him, shoving her weight into the elbow she had thrust outward. Her elbow struck the side of his head as it bounced off the floor. The man emitted a short moan, then his eyes rolled back, and he was out.

Blood oozed from a small wound where his head came in contact with the floor, but it was the elbow that had knocked him out.

"Holy shit," Mike said, watching from the alcove that led to his living room. "You put all your weight into that elbow. You knocked him out cold."

Sarah collected herself and got up off the floor, brushing at her pants, her hands shaking at the sudden violence.

"You could've warned me."

"I did warn you. Told you to be ready."

"Yeah, well, that could be misinterpreted."

Mike pointed at the man on his floor. "Evidently, it wasn't." Then he met her gaze. "But also, he suspected it was you from the intercom. Told me to bring you in here."

"Who is he? A cop?"

Mike nodded. "There's more."

"In the building?"

He nodded again.

"My apartment?" she asked.

"Sarah, you can't go up there."

"Shit. But I need cash."

Mike blinked once, then nodded. "I know who you and Aaron are. I know what you guys do. What I don't know is why four cops showed up tonight and ordered me to give them access to your apartment, then proceeded to invade my place while I was trying to watch my Netflix. It upset me. So, wait right here."

Mike stepped away, and Sarah lowered to her haunches. She tapped the man's pockets until she found his wallet and withdrew it. The man was a detective with the Toronto Police Services.

"Shit, shit, shit," she mumbled.

She didn't kill that cop by the motel, but she certainly knocked this one out. Although, people come to a lot faster than they do on TV. Mr. Detective would be awake within minutes or sooner. She needed to leave.

She stuffed the man's wallet in his pocket, then moved to the door and peeked into the hallway.

It was empty.

"Sarah."

She jumped and brought her hands up.

Mike stepped back, even though he was five feet away. "Sorry to startle you." Once he realized she wasn't going to hit him, he stepped over the unconscious detective on his floor and handed her a bundle of something.

"Take this," he whispered, as if the detective was simply sleeping and could be woken by loud voices. "Some tenants pay in cash, and with this being a Saturday, I haven't gone to the bank yet. Pay me back in a week or two whenever you and Aaron are safe and coming back around."

She opened her hand. It was a rolled-up wad of cash.

"There's got to be a couple grand here."

"Use what you need, then return the rest." Mike shrugged. "Or use it all. I don't care, Sarah. Just clean up the mess you made and know there are people out there rooting for you."

She slipped the money in her pocket, then jumped forward and hugged him.

"Thank you, Mike," she said into his ear, matching his whispering tone. "I'll be in touch soon."

She released him and checked the hallway again. Then she stepped out and moved toward the side door to avoid exiting at the front lobby.

When she got to the door, someone moaned or grunted loudly. She opened the door and entered the stairwell. As it closed, the distinctive voice of the cop coming to and screaming her name gave her chills.

She shouldered the side building door open and bolted out into the cool night air.

They were looking for her in connection to the dead police officer at the motel, and now they'd be looking for her because she'd knocked out one of their detectives.

From dinner out with Aaron to having every cop in the city hunting her, the night was not going well at all.

She ran for the nearest bushes and trees beyond, hoping to be lost from sight before anyone exited the building after her.

It was time to steal a car. She needed wheels. She needed to get clear of the area and fast. And instead of waiting until the morning to buy a burner phone, she needed to steal one of those as well.

Detective Ricigliano was about to get a phone call from Sarah as it appeared Sarah needed help.

After all, Ricigliano had thrown an apology party for Sarah about four weeks ago.

The detective would trust her story, wouldn't she? Sarah could only hope so as she ran along Bloor Street.

Otherwise, Sarah would be screwed and would be in jail by the end of the weekend.

Having her baby in jail and raising it behind bars was never something she could imagine, but it was looking more and more likely.

Chapter 11

Alex stopped walking when the man on the phone said the warehouse was just past Coxwell. He could jog there in thirty minutes. Since the meeting was an hour away, he turned back toward the dojo and broke into a run. He needed a few things to make this meeting more interesting.

Under four minutes later, he reentered the dojo, got what he needed, relocked the building, and then checked the time. Thirty-five minutes left until the hour was up.

Jogging down Queen Street wasn't going to work. He'd get there on time, but he couldn't have that. Being on time wouldn't offer him a chance to check out the building, see where the exit points were, where they'd be waiting for him —whoever they were.

He maintained a solid pace along the sidewalk, waiting for his opportunity. Calling a taxi would take too long. He didn't drive unless he had to, and even then, he only drove someone else's car as he didn't own one himself.

He watched a carpet cleaning truck pass him going the other way, but hardly any vehicles were going his way.

Ten minutes into the run toward Coxwell, what he was waiting for came along.

A large twenty-four-foot box truck lumbered along Queen Street, heading in the direction he was going.

He needed to go onto the road to gain access to the truck. What stopped him was car after car parked on the side of the road in an endless stream of metal and glass, nose to tail.

The truck was almost alongside him now. The timing was off. If he slowed down now, enough to skirt between two cars and then pick up the right amount of speed to hop on the back of the truck, it would leave him with low odds of catching it.

Without another thought on the matter, as he was out of time to debate it further, Alex leaped up onto the trunk of the nearest vehicle, hopped onto its roof, and then launched into the air just as the truck passed by.

Hands extended, feet ready to land, the truck edged by as he was airborne, the rear lining up with him as he dropped.

The timing was off by a mere second, but he could land his left foot on the small platform at the tailgate. Upon contact, his balance was off slightly due to the timing, making his right foot shoot outward. Because the truck was moving faster than he was, it threatened to dislodge him, but he could grab a steel handle and hold on, swinging his leg inward.

Once balance was regained, Alex pivoted around to place

his back against the rollup door, where he watched the road pass by, mentally noting how close they were to Coxwell. It was evident the driver hadn't noticed his new passenger through the mirrors because he didn't try to slow down or pull over.

Moments later, the truck did slow, but probably for a red light. Just when it was about to stop completely, the driver shifted gears, and the truck jerked forward, the engine revving in short spurts as multiple gears changed.

They went through the light at Coxwell. The guy on the phone had said it was a warehouse on the right, just past Coxwell. He'd said he would leave a light on over the front door.

Alex watched the right side. A retail store, a consignment shop, then a parking lot went by, and finally, a brick warehouse with For Sale signs plastered on the front of the building. The light over the front door was brightly lit.

He waited until the truck was half a block away, then pivoted around to see where he could jump off.

That's where his problems started.

The truck was picking up speed, the wind buffeting his short hair, making him close his eyes to slits so they wouldn't water in the cool evening air. He glanced back over his shoulder. The light over the warehouse's front door was rapidly moving farther and farther away.

On the side of the truck, there was nothing but concrete rushing by at bone-breaking speeds.

Maybe this wasn't a good idea after all.

Without many options left to him and the need to get off the truck as fast as possible, causing a sense of urgency within him, he smacked the side of the truck repeatedly until he caught the driver's attention in the mirror. The brake lights brightened beside him, and his left shoulder leaned into the truck as it slowed fast.

When it had almost stopped, Alex jumped off and ran into the shadows at the side of the road. The truck was no longer needed, and Alex moved along the sidewalk without looking back, even as the driver got out and shouted obscenities in his general direction.

By the time the light at the front of the warehouse came into view again, the truck driver had gotten back in and drove away, his interest in the unknown rider gone.

Alex moved closer to the warehouse and then stopped by a thick tree to scan the area for movement. Since the eye was naturally drawn to movement, he stared at one area for several seconds and then examined another area. Some sections along the side of the warehouse were bathed in darkness. A man dressed all in black could easily blend in, and Alex would have difficulty seeing him.

One more check on the time gave him just over ten minutes before the man's deadline of an hour was up.

Alex placed two small knives—red fury throwing knives —in his hands, the base of the knife attached to his wrist where a cloth strap held them in place. Even if he were knocked off balance and his hands opened to break his fall, the knives would be there when he got back up.

He stepped away from the tree, the knives in his grip, and sauntered up the street. He wasn't particularly concerned for his safety as he could defend himself, and the man had said something about having a job for him to do. Alex had to assume this job meant he wasn't walking into a trap.

At the corner of the warehouse, he could look down the length of the side of the building, but no one lurked in the shadows. He spun around and stared at the other side of the street. Still, no one was watching him. The street was nearly deserted, with no foot traffic and only an occasional vehicle passing by.

Instead of moving to the front door as the man on the phone asked him to, he slipped along the side where the total darkness concealed him. Tall grass and thick straw-like weeds restricted his movement and made considerable noise with each step, but he was able to stay up against the building where the shrubs were at their lowest.

When he came upon a window, he slowed, then stopped. A small amount of light emanated outward from the inside. The window was a large square with twelve smaller square panes inside the large frame. In three places, a pane had been broken out.

Alex checked his surroundings, saw no one watching him, then lowered to the ground and crawled under the window. After the count of three, he raised himself slowly to peek inside.

There was enough light that most of the interior was visible except for a few areas lost to shadows. A full-grown man could hide in those areas. He studied the back wall and discovered a garage door leading out into the warehouse's alleyway. Tire tracks were visible in the dust and grime on the warehouse floor.

Two other things stood out.

In the center of the warehouse, the couch from the

pictures he was sent was unoccupied. At one point within the past few hours, Parkman, Daniel, and Aaron sat unconscious on that same couch.

His emotions rose to the surface, and he had to choke them off, mentally force them down, and maintain an awareness of his surroundings. He was in full combat mode and would remain that way until their enemies were dealt with.

The second thing that stood out was the body on the floor beyond the couch. It was too dark to see which one of his friends it was, but he was pretty certain it was Parkman. Even in the limited light, he could see the blood that had pooled in a dark mass by the man's head. It couldn't just be someone lying there because of the awkward way the man's legs were twisted.

There was a dead man on the floor of the warehouse, likely from a gunshot wound to the head, and he had pictures showing his friends were in this very warehouse less than an hour ago.

Someone was sending him a message. One Alex couldn't ignore.

He lowered to the ground and was surrounded by darkness again.

They had taken his friends, taken Sarah. They had threatened their lives. Then whoever was doing this to them had killed one of his friends as a message. Luring him to this warehouse was so he'd find the body and do whatever the hell it was they wanted from him.

Whoever had orchestrated this level of attack on his group, his family, didn't matter anymore. It could be a street gang, the mafia, a group of rogue cops—none of it mattered anymore.

Because whoever did this had declared war on Sarah—a pregnant Sarah—and her closest people.

Which meant they declared war on everything Alex believed in and loved.

No one touched his family, and he walked away unscathed.

And yet, they made one major mistake, one deadly mistake.

They should have taken Alex first. They should have trapped him, killed him, or blown him up. But because they didn't, they would all die.

Every fucking last one of them.

Alex crawled away from the window, intent on finding a way inside the building from the back.

Whoever was still inside the warehouse waiting for him wouldn't be breathing within minutes.

For what they did to his family, he would go for arteries, eyes, crotches, and throats—then ask questions later.

Nothing was stopping him now from reaching his full potential as an accomplished martial artist. He drew this ire out of him. As John Rambo would say, they drew first blood.

They called this war. They started it.

Alex would end it—and them along with it.

Chapter 12

SARAH MADE IT A couple of blocks without being stopped. It was only a matter of time before the entire area swarmed with cops. The manhunt would be enormous, the fallout something she was afraid she couldn't live with. How could this come into her life as she was about to have a baby? They had simply gone for dinner. That was it. And now she was on the run from every cop in the country, and Aaron was gone, missing.

"You're missing, too, Vivian," she shouted, forgetting herself in her frustration and anger as she half jogged, half walked up Tomken Road toward Burnhamthorpe. "Pitch in a little. Tell me what we're up against."

Her sister was gone as if she'd never been there. In the past, this had caused her immense frustration and should piss her off this time, too. Generally speaking, her sister's absence was a blessing because her baby was coming, and she didn't want to keep doing what Vivian needed her to do with a little one at home.

The gas station at the corner came into view. Up ahead on Burnhamthorpe, a cruiser raced through the green light going at least a hundred kilometers an hour, lights flashing.

Backup was on the way. Within a half hour, every available cop would be in the area, essentially locking it down in their hunt for Sarah Roberts, alleged cop-killer.

How many scrapes had she been in, similar to this one? How many times did this shit have to happen before they realized she was on their side?

None of that was important right now, though. She had to leave the area as fast as possible without anyone knowing where she was going. She needed to regroup, try to reach her sister and get a grip on what was happening.

To stay less visible, she moved off the sidewalk and scurried across several front lawns until she reached the back of the gas station. Then she ran up to the building and walked the length of the side wall until she could see the pumps.

At this hour, no one was getting gas. A couple of cars were parked out front as their drivers had gone inside.

But none of their cars were left running.

If only she could've been that lucky.

She eased back into the shadows and debated her options. Step one was getting out of the area as fast as possible to avoid arrest. Contact Ricigliano was step two. She'd listen to her and know the truth when she spoke it. It would explain what happened without her being detained so she could figure out what was happening from the outside instead of sitting in some holding cell while Darwin and Disco tried to find Aaron.

Music blaring from car speakers caught her attention. She leaned around the corner of the building. One man—or a boy trying to be a man—had gotten into his late model Camaro, started it up, and was blasting the stereo. The driver ducked his head below the dash several times as if looking for something.

Another man exited the gas station convenience store and waddled toward his car, his arms full of two large Coke bottles and three bags of chips.

The Camaro driver was still looking for something as the other driver entered his car.

Sarah debated stealing one of their vehicles. She'd have to overpower the man, shove him from the car, and steal it, which was something she had no issue doing.

The second driver started his car, dropped it in gear, and backed out of his spot.

That left the Camaro.

On Burnhamthorpe, two more cruisers raced by, lights flashing. A serious response was descending upon the area.

Sarah needed to get out now.

The driver of the Camaro must've solved his problem because he put it in gear and was backing up.

Sarah moved out of hiding and strode directly toward him. As he started forward, she jumped in front of his car, making him hit the brakes.

Even though his music blared out the open window, she still heard him swear. The driver glanced down toward his lap and swore again.

Sarah smacked a hand on the hood of his car.

He jerked upward to stare at her.

"Are you fucking kidding me right now," the driver shouted through his window. "Spilled my fuckin' drink in my lap."

"We have to talk," she said without moving from the front of the vehicle. She couldn't afford him driving away.

"Talk?" He stared at her dumbfounded. "*What?*"

She withdrew the wad of cash Mike gave her, slipped a hundred-dollar bill out of it, and then shoved the rest of the money back into her pocket.

Waving the hundred back and forth, she said, "I believe this is yours."

His eyes softened at the sight of the cash. "Oh yeah, how so?"

Sarah had gotten his attention. He wouldn't bolt now.

She moved slowly up the car's passenger side and leaned in through his window.

"I need a ride. I'll give you one hundred cash for that ride up front."

"No shit?"

"No shit."

"Where are you going?"

"Away from here. Take me wherever you're going."

"You putting me on?"

She shook her head. "Here, I'll give you the hundred upfront. Stash it away before we leave."

She opened the door and slipped into the passenger seat.

"Hey," he said, leaning away from her. "I didn't agree yet."

She thrust the hundred at him with one hand and turned the volume down on the stereo with the other. "Take it and drive."

His eyes moved from the money to her, then back to the money.

"This isn't some sort of trick?"

Sarah looked back at him with sad eyes. "Abusive relationship issues. I need out. Nowhere to go, no car." She moved closer to him. "Please." Then she popped open the center console, dropped the hundred inside, and closed it. "Just drive. I'll hop out in ten minutes, twenty minutes, I don't care. Just get me out of here."

Another cruiser raced by. This time heading south on Tomken.

The young Camaro driver put the car in gear and exited the gas station. A minute later, they were heading up Burnhamthorpe toward Etobicoke.

"Where do you need to go?" he asked.

"Away from here." She faced him. "Where are you heading?"

"Home."

"Yeah, but where's home?"

"I can't take you there. My girlfriend would shit."

"I'm not asking you to take me there. Just tell me the general direction."

"Burnhamthorpe past Kipling. A little farther."

"That's perfect. Drop me anywhere past Kipling. I'll find my way from there."

They drove in silence for a few moments.

"You going to be okay?" he asked.

"I'm sure I'll make it. I always do."

"And you're willing to give me a hundred bucks for a ride a taxi might charge you twenty for?"

"Well." She turned to him. "The hundred is for two things."

A worried look crossed his face. He had been about to reach for what was left of his drink, but his hand stopped halfway.

"What's the second thing?"

"I need to make a local phone call on your cell. That's it. I'll be out of your hair in ten minutes."

"A phone call?"

She nodded.

"That's it?"

She nodded again, the seriousness in her eyes confirming her words.

He nodded and handed her the cell phone. "Go for it."

She dialed the Toronto Police Services line and waited until it was answered.

"I need to speak with Detective Ricigliano," Sarah said.

The driver glanced her way, then refocused on the road.

"I'm sorry, you'll have to call back in the morning, ma'am."

"That won't happen."

"Excuse me?"

"I'm calling now. Isn't there a way you could patch me through to her personal cell?"

"I'm sorry, ma'am," the woman said, her voice more brusque. "It's after midnight."

"Every cop in the Toronto area is looking for me," Sarah

whispered into the phone, attempting to keep that last bit from the driver so she didn't get kicked out of the Camaro early.

"What was that?" the woman asked.

"My name is Sarah Roberts."

The woman muttered something.

"And I need to speak with Ricigliano immediately."

"How do I know you're who you say you are?"

"The incident behind the Super 5 Inn might help. How about the incident at the apartment building on Bloor Street?"

The woman spoke softly and inaudibly, her voice muffled as if she had covered the phone with her hand.

Then she said, "If you'll hold a moment, we're trying to locate the detective now."

"I can hold for a few minutes, then that's it. Find her quickly."

The driver kept glancing over to Sarah. Finally, he asked, "Are you in trouble, Miss?"

Sarah shook her head, then lowered the phone from her mouth. "Nothing to worry about. I'll be done in a few moments, and you can drop me off."

He nodded and focused his attention on the road.

Sarah figured it was an entire minute before something clicked on the phone, and the woman was back.

"Patching you through now." Another series of clicks, and then a voice she recognized came on.

"Sarah?"

"Detective."

"Sounds like you've been busy."

That elevated her pissed-off meter.

"Really? You think this is all my doing?"

"I didn't say that."

"Then spell it out for me. I'd love to hear your thoughts."

"They have you at the Super 5 on Dundas. Sarah, we have a dead cop. Also, that cop at the apartment building called in. He said it was you. It's already been dispatched to officers in the area. You have to come in. We can talk, work it all out."

"That dead cop wasn't me." The Camaro braked hard. Sarah turned to the driver. "Keep fucking going. Do not stop." He had taken on a frantic look, his eyes wider. The Camaro coasted for a moment. Then he tapped the gas again. "We have a deal," she reminded him. He nodded twice. Two short jerks of his head.

"Ricigliano, you know me. The guy in that fake uniform behind the Super 5 wasn't a cop, and—"

"We know that now."

"He pulled the trigger. He killed your cop. They kidnapped Aaron from the restaurant and tried to take me, too. I fought back. When that fake cop approached me, he spoke into his cell phone, saying something about catching me and bringing me in. He called the person he was talking to *boss*."

"You know, Sarah, we went through some serious shit last month, and I went out on a limb—"

"And it paid off."

"It did. But this does not look good."

"What doesn't look good? That I ran from assholes who came after Aaron and me? How about you send officers over to Parkman's apartment? They grabbed him, too. And those guys were dressed as Toronto cops. You want more, Detective?" She was getting pissed now. "Look, I called you because I thought I could trust you. It would appear I made a mistake."

"Sarah, you didn't make a mistake. Come in, and we'll work it out."

"You want me to come in, and I'm telling you that isn't going to happen. The last thing I would trust right now is that blue uniform." Kipling was coming up soon. She needed to get off the phone. "Look, I have to go. I'll figure this shit out and give you the results when we've got the bad guys wrapped up for you."

"Sarah, wait."

"What?"

"I want to help. What can I do?"

"Find out what happened to Parkman. There was a waiter with a gray streak in his hair. He was involved in Aaron's abduction. Find the man with the gray streak, you find Aaron. Then, locate Daniel, Benjamin, and Alex at the dojo. Make sure they're safe. I texted them all but didn't hear back from Daniel and Benjamin, and then my phone was left at the scene by the Super 5."

"We know about your phone."

"Also, Darwin Kostas is flying in tomorrow afternoon. You remember Disco?"

"Of course I do. How could I forget him? But don't ask me to work with him again."

"Meet them at the airport. Disco is scheduled to pick up Darwin when he gets here. Darwin's a friend. Then come pick me up. We'll pool information and resources then.

Figure this shit out from there."

"Tomorrow afternoon?"

"Yes."

The Camaro slowed to a stop at the lights at Kipling. The driver put on his hazards and parked on the side of the road.

"What time is Darwin arriving? What airline?"

"Originating out of Rome. You'll have to use your detective skills for the rest. Just meet them, and then come get me."

"Where will you be?"

"I'll find you. I'll be in touch."

"Sarah, that's not good enough—"

"It'll have to do, Detective. Also, all the shit that's about to happen in the next twenty-four hours has nothing to do with me."

"Wait, what shit?"

"A storm, Detective. An entire shit storm with a lot of bodies."

Chapter 13

ALEX ENCOUNTERED NO ONE at the back of the warehouse. The place appeared deserted. The idea that he was being lured into a trap rattled him. Without prior knowledge of the building or who he was up against, he had to take every precaution while moving forward. What stopped his enemies from luring him into the building and blowing it sky-high?

Although he couldn't just walk away with the hour's timeframe exhausted. At this point, he needed inside.

Yet that body on the floor inside freaked him out, too. Who was it? Parkman or Aaron?

This was going to break Sarah's heart if it was Aaron. She'd never be the same. The father of her unborn child is dead.

Maybe she'd want to calm her sister down with the baby coming.

Alex glanced upward and followed the length of a drain pipe to the roof with his eyes. He slipped the knives back in their holders, then grabbed the pipe and shook it gently—no movement. The pipe held firm.

After one last look around, he grasped the pipe, placed his feet against the dirty brick, and, hand over hand, climbed slowly to the roof, checking each handhold as he went. The pipe offered a great climbing apparatus, not moving from the wall at all.

At the edge of the roof, he peered over slowly.

It was empty.

He climbed over the lip and onto the roof, then stood on the tar and gravel surface. Walking softly, he moved to the air conditioner unit. A few feet to the unit's right was what looked like a galvanized steel roof hatch. That would be perfect as long as the lock wasn't on the inside.

Alex lowered to check the hatch. No lock was visible on the outside. He could only hope and pray there wasn't one on the inside, either.

He slipped the knives back into his palms, then secured them properly in his wrist straps before placing his hands on the hatch.

Carefully, applying just enough pressure to raise the hatch with caution in case it made too much noise, he lifted upward, revealing the inside of the warehouse below.

Evidently, there was no lock on the inside.

He had a way in from the roof. It couldn't be more perfect if he'd planned it.

With the hatch open all the way and resting backward on the rooftop, he leaned over the square hole and stared down into the warehouse.

When he moved slightly inward, he could see the couch Parkman and Aaron had sat on in the picture. It was almost directly below the roof hatch. If he had to drop to the floor, the couch would make a better alternative.

He adjusted his gaze, scanning the interior as far as he could see without sticking his head down inside.

Someone coughed from within the warehouse.

Alex stopped moving.

At least that meant they wouldn't blow the building if their men were still inside. He'd heard one cough. That gave him nothing, though. No direction, no idea where they were hiding or how many there were.

"You think he's still coming?" a man asked.

"Shut up," another man said. "He could be here already, listening at the door."

"I hate waiting."

"Shut the fuck up, already. He'll be here."

Two male voices from either side of the warehouse.

They were waiting for him. For what? To attempt an ambush? Wouldn't they be surprised when he dropped in and ambushed them?

"I'm not waiting inside here anymore. Too claustrophobic."

Someone was walking now, heavy feet clumping along the warehouse floor.

"Get back to your hiding spot," the man from the other side of the warehouse said, his voice a hushed shout.

"No, fuck that guy. I'll do the job myself."

"What, you want to go to prison for this job?" The

second man's voice was closer now.

One of the men materialized below the square hatch, just slightly to the right. Alex stared down at him, almost twenty feet below.

The man stopped walking. Another moved up to stand beside him.

"Silvio, tell us the job. We'll do it."

Silvio? Alex didn't recognize the name. How could these people know about him and everyone else? What could they possibly be planning?

"It's not that simple," Silvio said. "It has to be Alex. He's got the skills—special skills."

"And if I shoot him when he shows up?"

"Yeah, then what?" the other guy asked Silvio, obviously supporting the notion that shooting Alex was a solid plan.

"Then I'll kill you both. We did not just kidnap all of Sarah's team to shoot Alex. The job gets done, then we kill him." Silvio pointed. "Now, get back to your hiding spots. He'll be here any second."

Alex wasn't going to wait. This seemed like the best time to crash their little get-together.

He placed his hands on the lip of the hatch, lowered his head into the hole first, then allowed the rest of his body to slip through, his feet taken with gravity. Still holding onto the hatch's rim, dangling, he swung back and forth quietly about fifteen feet over their heads. With a small adjustment, he could land on the two men standing side by side, talking to Silvio.

One of them mumbled something. Silvio asked him to repeat it.

Alex kicked with his legs, swinging forward, then backward.

"I was just saying ..."

Alex let go and dropped. The second he let go, he rolled his hands out and over the blades protruding from the wrist strap, gripping their handles tight.

Off by a couple of inches, his knees connected with the shoulders of the man on the left, crumpling him under Alex's body weight. As he angled away to break the rest of his fall with a hard roll on the warehouse floor, he left one blade embedded deep in the man's neck.

The roll was short and fast, bouncing him onto his feet and in his shuto stance, center of gravity low, hands at the ready, the second knife already prepped.

Silvio had stepped back but hadn't drawn a weapon. The third man had drawn a weapon, his hand raising to take aim at Alex.

So Alex threw the other knife with careful aim, hoping for somewhere in the man's face. The upper area would draw blood as foreheads often bled profusely. Extra blood would mess with the man's ability to see properly.

What he hadn't expected—he was in a rush when he threw the knife—was the knife going hilt deep in the man's right eye.

The urge to yell *bullseye!* overcame him, but he kept his mouth closed as the man with the knife sticking out of his eye dropped the gun in his hand and reached for the blade.

The man with the knife in his throat made choking, guttural protests as he dropped to the warehouse floor, his life blood oozing out through his fingers.

He needed both men on the floor, away from their guns, in order to talk to Silvio without distraction.

The man with the knife in his right eye had placed his hands on the hilt and was about to yank it out.

Alex lurched forward and kicked the man's feet out from under him in a slide that looked like he was trying to steal third in a baseball game. When the man dropped beside him with an audible grunt, Alex twisted his upper body and backhanded the blade deeper into the man's face hole.

Another short grunt escaped the man's mouth, something deeper, more subdued, as his body went into convulsions, vibrating on the warehouse floor as if he were being electrocuted.

Silvio still hadn't pulled a gun while he watched his two colleagues die in front of him.

He had pulled out a cell phone instead.

Alex rose slowly, allowing Silvio to savor the moment before his death to take it all in. After what they'd done to his friends, to Sarah, they would all be dead in short order.

This is what he'd been training in private for. One could never be lazy if you were Sarah's friend, colleague, and confidante.

The knife-in-the-neck man had gone still, eyes staring at the open roof hatch but seeing nothing. The knife-in-the-eye man had gone still now, too, the river of blood exiting his eye having slowed to a small stream and already stopping as his heart had.

Alex stepped over both of the dead men, feeling something akin to a sense of closure. He'd taken out men who had hurt Sarah and her team. Until he got everyone back safe, he would continue to hunt the people involved, hurting or killing them.

"Hey," Silvio said. "Take it easy, pal." He held up a hand to ward off Alex while stepping back. "We can work something out."

"Where's Sarah?"

Silvio lifted the phone to show it to him. "I didn't shoot you for two reasons."

"Where's Sarah?" Alex asked again, moving closer to Silvio.

The man stepped back again. "The first reason is I need you to do a job."

Alex stepped within two feet of the man and contemplated where he would hit him first. A throat punch, a fatal jab to the neck, or perhaps a broken bone to get the man talking.

"The second reason is," Silvio rambled on, "this phone is more powerful than a gun."

Alex stopped moving and glared at him while checking his peripheral vision for movement. As far as he could tell, they were alone in the warehouse now.

"How so?"

"With one phone call, everyone you hold dear, everyone you care about will die."

Alex grabbed him about the shoulders in a fit of rage, driving his knee into Silvio's stomach so hard he thought he connected with the man's spine. As Silvio bent forward, as victims of a violent attack on their midriff always do, Alex wrapped his arms around the man's throat and spun him around behind him, yanking backward.

Silvio's feet came off the ground momentarily, and then Alex dropped hard, sticking his right knee out. The man's back came down on the top of the knee and arched wide as Silvio shouted in pain, his arms splayed out, the phone leaving his grip.

He hit the floor hard and rolled several times, grunting and attempting to breathe. The stomach hit knocked the air out of him, and the spine to the knee contact caused intense pain.

Alex picked up the cell phone off the warehouse floor and glanced around his surroundings. There was just enough light to see in most corners, leaving only a few dark areas for inspection.

Silvio moaned and rolled onto his side, curling up, his breathing still ragged.

Alex glanced over at the body he'd spied through the side window of the warehouse. Aaron or Parkman?

After one more look at Silvio, Alex strode over to the body and was relieved to see it wasn't one of his friends even before he got a close-up. None of them had a gray streak in their hair as pronounced as this man.

Things were looking up already.

He pivoted back to Silvio and then tried to turn on the phone. It needed a password.

"Wait," Silvio muttered. "Stop," he breathed deeply, one hand on his back. "Stop hurting me, and I'll explain."

"Start talking."

Silvio nodded, tried to sit up, and then laid back down to stare at the roof.

"We have no intention of hurting Sarah or your friends."

"Then why kidnap them?" Alex moved closer until he was standing over the man.

"Because we wanted you to do a small job for us."

"Why not just ask?"

"You'd say no."

"Then you have my answer."

"Hence," he grimaced in pain, "the leverage."

"Leverage like that could get people killed." He gestured at the two men he'd killed and then pointed at the man with the gray streak in his hair. "You kill him?"

Silvio nodded. "Too stupid. A liability."

"You're all a liability." After a moment of staring down at Silvio, Alex asked, "Where is everyone? Let's go pick them up, and I'll think about letting you walk away from this with all your teeth."

"Not that easy."

"Why not?"

"I don't know where they are."

"You're lying."

"Insurance. We knew you'd be angry." He pointed over his shoulder at his dead men. "Although, not that angry. That sort of anger is reckless."

"How so?"

"One phone call ends Sarah's life. Parkman, Aaron, and Daniel, too."

"It also ends your life and the life of the man you call."

"So we all die, but you?" Silvio looked up at him. "How is that rational?"

Alex shrugged, seemingly indifferent. But he wasn't. Inside, he was searching for a way out of this, a way to save

Sarah and his family. "What you did isn't rational."

"You die, too, Alex," Silvio muttered. "How could you live with the knowledge that you killed your friends when you could've done a single job and saved them?"

He suppressed the fear of that sentence and asked, "What's the job?"

"Give me the phone."

"Fuck you. What's the job?"

"I have less than a minute to phone Randy. He has everyone. If I don't phone him, and he assumes something happened to all of us, he kills your group and heads for the border." Silvio sat up and grimaced, a hand on his stomach. "Now give me the fucking phone so I can save your friends."

Alex stared down at the cell in his hands, then leaned forward and gave it to Silvio.

"Don't fuck up," Alex said.

"How could I do that?"

"By talking in code. Or telling your guy to kill them. Your heart would stop within a minute of that sort of order."

Silvio nodded. "I understand, and I believe you."

He used his thumbprint to access the phone, then hit a button and placed it on speaker.

"Yeah," a man said.

In the background, Alex heard the rushing wind. A vehicle on a highway.

Silvio cleared his throat. "I'm safe and talking with Alex."

"Has he agreed to do the job?"

"We're getting there. I'll call back in fifteen minutes."

"I know what to do if you don't call back."

Silvio slapped the phone, ending the call. "So, you have fifteen minutes to agree to do the job or kill me. But if I don't call back, everyone you love will be dead."

Alex crossed his arms, afraid that if he didn't lock down his hands, he would strangle the man out of frustration.

"What's the job?" he asked.

Silvio shook the phone in the air again. "See how this cell phone is more powerful than a gun?"

"What's the fucking job?"

Silvio smiled up at him. "We want you to assassinate the Chief of Police for the Toronto Police Services tomorrow at a planned rally and speech he's doing at York University. His name is Thomas Clark. It shouldn't be too hard for a man of your talents. Once he's dead, your friends will be freed."

Chapter 14

Sarah Roberts had to pay another hundred before the Camaro driver would give her his phone and charger. Even though he probably suspected he was in the car with a cop killer, he pushed hard to keep his cell.

She strolled up Kipling, keeping to the shadows. There was a massive presence of police cruisers in the area as they were probably headed toward her apartment building to lock down the area. She was far enough away that they wouldn't get to her now.

Unless Ricigliano had pinged the phone, she'd just called her on.

Sarah quickly turned off the phone and slipped it into her pocket. There was no need to give them a beacon to her whereabouts.

Kipling was mostly deserted as she walked north. Her

stomach ached as she hadn't eaten her salad at dinner, but it also ached in longing. Where were Aaron, Parkman, and the rest of them? And when Disco couldn't find her and reported back to Darwin, they'd worry she was also taken.

Only when Darwin landed the next evening, and Ricigliano was there to meet him, would he learn she was okay.

Another cruiser approached, but this time, the driver had a spotlight on the outside of his cruiser, flashing it at the houses as he drove south on Kipling.

Sarah glanced over her shoulder and saw another cruiser coming north, watching the houses with a spotlight on her side of the road.

She had to get off the road. This told her that Ricigliano had pinged the Camaro driver's phone. Or the driver had gone home and called the police to absolve himself of any wrongdoing. He probably told them where he'd dropped her off and his cell number.

None of that mattered now as they were on to her, and they were here.

It was the same old story, the same old fucking song and dance, and Sarah was getting sick of it. Someone had gone after her man and her dearest friends, and while trying to stay alive, trying to save herself, she had to stay away from the police as well. They should be on her side here, but it never worked that way.

On a deeper level, she understood their reaction. One of theirs was killed tonight, and Sarah's cell phone was found at the scene, not to mention the cop who was killed had called in saying he'd spotted her. So, of course, every cop in the city, province, and country would want her apprehended. But she didn't kill that cop. Someone had brought this all down on her.

And yet again, as this rollercoaster of life went up and down, she had grown to accept it, to live with it, and not overthink it.

What stopped her was the baby. How could she bring a baby into this world, the life she inhabited? This had to be the end. There was no way she could go on while preparing to feed the baby and change diapers while running down back alleys to escape cops or murderers or whoever happened upon her at that time in her life.

Another cruiser turned onto Kipling.

The one heading north was ten houses away.

She broke into a run, staying on the grass and mostly shrouded in darkness to the right of the sidewalk.

An expanse of land opened up on her right. At first, it was too hard to see what it was—a field, a park, or just random undeveloped land—and then she got close enough that the streetlight shone on a walkway.

It was a golf course.

She hopped the small fence, dropped onto the manicured grass, and bolted into the darkness of the course. Far from searching spotlights, Sarah found a soft tuft of grass on a small rise by one of the side fences. She doubted the authorities would comb the entire golf course in the dark, so she laid back and stared at the clear sky above as the night chills gave her the shivers.

Adrenaline wearing off, she wrapped her arms around herself and curled into a ball wondering what had happened along the way. What had brought her to this moment in time? Why was she hiding out on a golf course overnight while Aaron, Parkman, and who knew who else were in trouble?

Vivian was done. She hadn't come around much in the last little while and had completely avoided Sarah since tonight's dinner with Aaron.

Just when she needed her the most, her sister abandoned her.

Maybe it was for the better. Sarah would get out of this on her own. Then they'd leave the city so they could have their baby and be left alone for a while.

She only hoped when they came to abduct Alex or Daniel that they'd put up a fight. She also hoped Ricigliano could identify the man in the fake cop uniform at the back of the Super 5 Inn and discover any known accomplices. Perhaps good old-fashioned detective work would solve this one because it seemed Sarah's celestial connection was gone.

"Vivian," she mumbled, surprised at the vibration in her voice. Maybe she was colder than she thought. "We're in trouble right now, and I'm four months pregnant."

Nothing.

"Sometimes I rant, sometimes I shout. But this time, I'm asking."

Still nothing.

"Give me something to work with, or don't come back. Family doesn't abandon loved ones in their time of need."

And like someone blowing smoke in her face, Sarah jerked back slightly as Vivian entered her consciousness.

Vivian rattled off several sentences quickly, telling her something unclear about a man named Thomas Clark. She added that Ricigliano would help, and the leader of the kidnapping ring would get away, but that Sarah had to let him go. Also, some cop would kill another cop, which was important but meant nothing to Sarah as it seemed wholly unconnected. Then Vivian told her to be at Keele and Finch by slightly after two in the afternoon the next day. As fast as she had arrived, Vivian disappeared as if she hadn't been there in the first place.

This sort of communication was so unlike Vivian, Sarah was reduced to snatching at the tidbits of information like they were puzzle pieces, attempting to assemble them all into something coherent.

Her sister's full communication was being blocked, probably due to something Vivian had said recently about greater things at work. But that didn't help them in the here and now.

And what was that about the bad guy getting away and letting it go? After everything that had happened tonight, she wasn't sure how she was expected to just let it go. And what cop was going to kill another cop?

"Wait, who the fuck is Thomas Clark?" she whispered.

The second she'd said the name, it felt familiar somehow.

Tempted to turn on the cell phone in her pocket to google the name, she grabbed it, then stopped.

They could ping it again once it was back on, even for a few moments, and then she'd be on the run all night.

As it stood, she was well hidden and in a comfortable spot, somewhat concealed from any sort of wind. Nestled in the soft grass, Sarah closed her eyes and reviewed everything her sister had said.

None of it made any sense.

None of it was a call to action. It told her to stand down.

Just more pieces of nothing.

When the sun rose in five to six hours, she would find a coffee shop, possibly some new clothes, and a motel that took cash. She needed to change, shower, and get ready for the day.

Nothing was clear in her sister's frantic presence, but something told her she would have a busy weekend yet, and it was only Saturday night.

As she attempted to sleep, her stomach twisted in worry, her anger brewing. Sarah thought of Aaron and where he might be.

And what about Parkman?

Were they still alive?

Vivian had said nothing about them. Why? To save her feelings?

Sarah adjusted her position and settled more comfortably on the ground. She glanced skyward again, her jaw clenching.

"Hey, you listening up there?" she whispered. "Whoever's blocking my sister had better know that what happens down here is their fault—all of it." She inhaled, trying to calm her insides. "If I lose one of my friends, there'll be hell to pay."

A tear slipped from her eye, sliding over her temple toward the ground.

Then, something moved inside her belly.

The baby?

Wasn't this just four months? Could it be too early?

She quickly counted the weeks and came up at sixteen, maybe seventeen.

One more soft movement brought her to tears and softened her resolve.

They were going to have a baby, and all the doctor's appointments had proclaimed the pregnancy was fine.

"Then what the fuck am I doing sleeping outside on a golf course on a Saturday night in early October while unknown criminals attack us and the police are hunting me for the murder of one of their own? Huh, Vivian? Tell me that."

There was no answer as Sarah was lost to tears for the world her unborn child would be entering soon.

She gently placed both hands on her stomach and asked out loud, "How could life be so cruel—so fucking cruel?"

Chapter 15

Parkman snapped awake. When he tried to lift his head, a wave of nausea washed over him.

The gentle vibrations under him weren't helping his stomach. He rolled to the side in case he was going to throw up. When he opened his eyes, Aaron was beside him, watching him.

For a brief moment, Aaron looked dead. His eyes were wide and unmoving.

Then he blinked, and Parkman breathed in deeply, relieved.

They were in a moving vehicle of some kind. A van, perhaps, or a larger truck. He glanced around and concluded they were in the back of a truck.

"There's three of us," Aaron said.

"Three?"

Aaron nodded. "Daniel, too."

"Any idea where we are?"

"No."

Parkman couldn't figure out why his hands weren't responding until he glanced down. His hands and feet were both secured with a thick amount of duct tape.

Who would kidnap them? And why? To get to Sarah?

"Where's Sarah?" he asked Aaron.

"Not with us."

"Is that sarcasm?"

Aaron stared at him momentarily, then said, "We were out having dinner. I think my wine was drugged. Sarah didn't drink."

"So they nabbed you but not her?"

"Yes."

"You feeling okay?"

"No."

"What's wrong?"

"Sick to my stomach."

"Me too."

They rode in silence for a few moments.

"You know," Aaron said. "This is bad, eh?"

Parkman stared at him a moment. "What do you think is going on?"

"No idea, but Sarah didn't see it coming."

"What do you mean?"

The truck they were in hit a pothole or something. The back bounced a couple of times, then resumed its normal vibrations. The bumps shook his shoulder, causing a slight pain. He was too cramped up and needed to stretch.

"She knew something was coming. She said she could feel it, but Vivian wasn't talking. I told her it was no big deal because if it were a big deal, her sister would step in and warn us. I tried to downplay it, even as I was being drugged."

"How could you know?"

Aaron's eyes had watered. "If Sarah had been drugged …"

"The baby is fine, Aaron. We'll deal with this and make sure Sarah is okay."

He nodded, the movement dislodging a tear. It dropped to the floor of the truck.

The truck slowed and turned onto another road. Parkman rolled onto his back to check out the interior. Their box-like cube had one access door at the rear, which was probably locked.

He twisted back to face Aaron. "We have to get this tape off."

"Can't. Already tried biting it. They've wrapped it so thick and covered the seal by placing it on the inside of the wrist. There's no way without a pair of scissors."

"You have keys in your pocket?"

He shook his head. "They cleaned out our pockets."

"There's got to be some way."

"There is. We wait until the door opens, and they cart us off somewhere. Then, we figure a way out of this. Besides, even if we got the tape off and found a way out that door, jumping at this speed would suck."

"True, but I want to be ready when they open that door."

"Me too," Daniel muttered behind him.

Without turning around, Parkman asked, "How are you

feeling?"

"Like shit."

"Any idea how to break these bonds?"

There was silence as the truck bounced over what sounded like a gravel road.

"None," Daniel said. "Absolutely none. Too tight."

"So we sit here and wait?" Parkman voiced the question for either man to answer.

"About sums it up," Daniel said. "I just want the truck to stop. This movement isn't helping my stomach."

As if on command, the truck slowed, angled into a turn, then stopped with a jerking motion.

The engine died.

One door opened and closed.

Without discussing it, all three of them knew they were dealing with one driver.

Parkman listened for any other noise, but nothing came to him. No one came to open the back door, which freaked him out. Had they been driven into the woods where the truck would be set ablaze? Were they waiting for other vehicles or more recruits to arrive? Was this a gang or actual cops like the two that showed up at his apartment and attacked him?

What could they possibly want?

The only positive takeaway from this was they were all alive.

"Where's Benjamin?" Daniel whispered. "He was with me at the dojo."

"It's just the three of us," Aaron said.

A cell phone rang somewhere up front. Someone

stomped hard on the ground outside the truck by the third ring as they ran by it. A door was yanked open, and then the ringing died.

"Yeah?" a man said.

There was a pause.

"What? Really? Joe's dead?"

Another pause.

"Motherfucker." There was a loud thump as if the man punched something. "What about Benjamin? He dead, too?"

Daniel gasped audibly behind Parkman, and Aaron's eyes widened in panic.

"Well, good. Find out for sure, though. Also, what about Claudio? Did he get to Sarah?"

Aaron jerked his hands in a frantic effort to yank himself from his restraints, but it got him nowhere. All he succeeded in doing was making noise.

"Claudio's dead, too? No fucking way. Did Sarah kill him?"

Aaron stopped moving and glared at Parkman. "I'll fucking kill them all."

"How?" Parkman whispered. "Sounds like they'll all be dead soon enough."

"I watched Silvio shoot Domenic in the warehouse … I know, what a fucking idiot." Another short pause, then, "Silvio's lost his shit. The man needs to be put down. Call the cops now. Remember to block your number and tell them you heard gunfire inside the empty warehouse."

Aaron began biting the tape on his wrists, but it was wound so thick and tight he wasn't getting anywhere with it.

"Look, man, I gotta go," the driver said. "I have to dump

these three at the farm, then get back to the city. When this is over on Monday, make sure you do as you promised. I just hope they pick up Silvio for murder. At least then he'll be inside—" he stopped talking, then laughed. "I know!" he burst out. "We'll deal with the rest of these assholes then."

Aaron stopped moving, and Parkman angled his body to listen better.

"Okay," the driver said. "This ends Monday, and I'll hit Europe after that. Go backpacking for a year with all the cash I'll have. Yup, you got it, man. I'll wait to hear from you that Silvio is in custody."

Something thumped up front, and then a door closed.

This time, Parkman heard footsteps as the man walked the length of the truck.

A lock clicked open, and after a metallic thunk, the back door pulled back.

"You boys awake?" the driver asked.

He leaned in close, then turned on a flashlight.

"Oh, great. I was hoping you were awake because when Alex decides not to do what he's told, I want you awake when I kill you all." The man zeroed in on Daniel. "I get to shoot you first for what you did to my face. But don't worry, you'll all be dead by Monday, even if Alex agrees. Then none of this will matter to you anymore."

The man laughed at a maniacal cackle, snapped several pictures of them with his cell phone, and then slammed the door closed.

Chapter 16

ALEX STARED AT THE man, dumbfounded. Murder the chief of police? To save the lives of his friends?

What an impossible position to be in.

He had never been presented with such a decision, one where there was no upside. Frustrated at the man in front of him—Silvio—he wanted to lash out, hurt the man, kill him. Then he would go find his friends and take out the man Silvio had just spoken to, and all would be right with the world.

But Silvio didn't know where Randy was, so Alex couldn't torture it out of him.

He was in a no-win situation. The only solution was to kill an innocent man, the police chief, or Sarah and Aaron, and everyone else was dead.

He'd always pick Sarah to live over anyone else if given

the choice.

And it appeared that choice was before him now.

"What guarantees do I have?" Alex asked as he walked in circles around the man, still debating if he would hurt him somehow.

"Guarantees?" Silvio guffawed. "None. Do the job, and your friends live. That's it. Don't do the job. I might die on this warehouse floor, but I assure you, all your friends will die as well." He shot up a hand as if he had just figured something out. "There it is. Your guarantee is that your friends will die if you *don't* do the job. The rest is a risk."

Alex stopped pacing in circles and stared at him. "You told those two something when I was listening on the roof."

"Oh yeah, what did I tell them?"

"You spoke about kidnapping Sarah's team. Your words were, 'the job gets done, then we kill him,' or something like that."

"Yeah, I was trying to appease them. They wanted to go after the chief on their own. My plea was to get them not to kill you tonight."

"They couldn't anyway," Alex muttered and went back to pacing.

"Evidently." Silvio glanced over at the bodies of the men he had been trying to appease less than ten minutes ago. "Nobody expected you to fall from the fucking sky."

"Roof."

"Sky, roof, what the fuck ever. Look, I have to call Randy back. We're down to a few minutes. You in or out?"

"If I were out, you wouldn't be breathing."

Silvio swallowed audibly. "Fair enough."

"Call him. Make sure he knows I'm in. Nothing happens to my people."

Silvio held up the phone, then paused. "How come I don't believe you?"

Alex stopped walking to stare at Silvio. "This is what you want, right? You went to great lengths to get my attention. Now you've got it. Don't fuck that up. Call this Randy guy."

Silvio lowered the phone to his lap. Alex decided he'd kill the guy on principle. What kind of a criminal taunted the power of a grizzly while standing beside it?

"I need to hear it in your voice."

Alex stared at him a moment. "What?"

"This job is important. I can't have you rethinking it in the morning and not showing up at the speech. It has to be done, and you're the best suited for the job."

"Because I'm expendable?"

Silvio nodded. "We don't care about you or Sarah or any of them, but knowing this job would require special skills, we find ourselves in this predicament. Your name came up, and the rest is history. But I'm not hearing conviction in your voice."

"Look, I'll do it. Call Randy."

The cell phone remained on his lap.

"The way I see it," Alex said, "is you don't call Randy, I'll kill you and go find my friends on my own. So, believe me, or not, your life hangs in the balance."

"But will you execute the police chief?"

"The odds of me getting arrested are high."

Silvio nodded. "High, as in likely. Year-long trial, prison, another ten years behind bars at least, probably fifteen." He raised a finger. "But Sarah, Aaron, Daniel, and the rest stay alive. You save everyone."

Alex glanced away to stare at the window he'd used to look inside the warehouse.

How could he agree to kill an innocent man?

However, the actual question he had was how he could *not* agree to kill an innocent man.

He'd sacrifice anything for Sarah, Aaron, his group, his family, his life.

He'd sacrifice his life for them.

Finding them before Randy executed his friends was nearly impossible. There was no way he could save Sarah without agreeing. There was a slight chance he could fix everything before he had to kill a man at the university tomorrow—a slight chance.

Alex spun back around and nodded. "Call Randy."

This time, Silvio lifted the phone. That movement likely saved his life. Alex was at the end of all the bargaining and negotiating. They were manipulating him, using him, controlling him, and they'd done a fine job of absconding with his people and keeping them at enough of a distance that even if he went on a psychotic rampage, he would recklessly and likely get Sarah killed.

That was something Alex could not live with. His freedom wasn't worth Sarah's life. He'd once told her he'd take hits for her, even die for her, and now that word was being tested.

He would not fail.

Although, he was still seconds away from throwing it all

in on a gamble and killing Silvio where he sat if this Randy didn't answer the fucking phone.

The phone rang on speaker.

"Yeah."

"He's in," Silvio said.

"Delightful. Tell him don't miss."

Alex leaned in closer to the phone. "Just make sure nothing happens to my friends."

"Fuck you, asshole. Do the job right, or I kill them all."

"Ahh, Randy, he's agreed. Don't taunt the guy. Everyone else is dead here. I saw Alex at work myself. He dropped in out of nowhere and took out Eric and Nestor in under half a minute."

"Then he's the right guy for this particular job," Randy said.

"Which is what I'd been saying since day one."

"Wait," Randy coughed. "Are you guys still at the warehouse?"

"Yeah, why?"

"Oh, just wondering. Thought you'd be done by now."

Alex stared at Silvio as he raised one eyebrow. Something was off. Something else was at work. Were these two on the same schedule? Why would it matter to Randy where they were? That question wasn't natural. It meant something to Randy, but what?

Had Randy done something? Was he setting up Silvio?

"Well, we're leaving now. I'll brief Alex on the kill site, and then we're gone."

"I'll keep Alex's friends safe. Once I hear the kill took place, I'll untie them and walk away."

Silvio clicked off. "There you have it." He got to his feet. "We have a deal."

"Fuck you."

"Now that's not very nice, speaking that way to a man you just entered into a business arrangement with."

Alex moved closer. "I didn't enter into a business arrangement. I was coerced and left with no other option but to comply."

"Okay, call it as you see it, but know that all business arrangements often have a currency and a value. You're getting the better deal here: one life for four or five lives."

"Four or five? You mean, you don't know how many of my friends you have?"

Silvio blinked and cocked his head to the side. "Okay, the truth?"

Alex nodded.

"Benjamin got away. We suspect he killed Joe and ran."

"Suspect?"

Silvio nodded. "Yeah, because Joe didn't come back with him."

The sound of sirens in the distance caught Alex's attention. Had someone called the cops randomly? Were they coming to this location?

Or did Randy call them on Silvio so he'd be found with all the bodies?

Alex jumped past Silvio, dropped to his knees, and yanked his red fury knife out of the man's eye. He wiped it on the man's shirt, then withdrew the blade from the other man's neck, wiping it off as well.

The knives back in their holders, he spun back to Silvio.

The sirens sounded about a block away.

"What time is the chief doing his speech tomorrow?"

"He's supposed to be there for two in the afternoon."

Alex launched toward the back door of the warehouse. "Consider him a dead man." At the back door, he glanced over his shoulder. "Those cops are coming here." He stared a moment longer as Silvio frowned. "Run!"

Alex kicked open the door and disappeared outside into the darkness of the back alley, where he disappeared over a fence. The headlights of a police cruiser lit up the fence seconds later.

Doors opened and closed. A dispatcher on the police radio inside the cruiser was easily heard from where Alex landed.

After he got to his feet and brushed himself off, he strode away from the area with a lot on his mind.

He didn't stop walking until the sun rose.

Chapter 17

THE TRUCK HAD DRIVEN on into the night after the man had warned them they'd all be dead by Monday. At some point, Parkman had fallen asleep again, which seemed to help with the nausea, but now he had to urinate and didn't want to soil his pants.

Having just woken back up, he wondered what startled him awake.

The truck wasn't moving now. Maybe that was it.

Why had the driver stopped? Was this the farm the driver had referred to? Were they going to be offloaded?

He listened intently but could only detect Daniel and Aaron's heavy breathing.

His hands were mostly numb, and his feet were of no use. The restraints needed to be removed soon, or he worried his extremities would face some sort of damage.

A door thudded closed somewhere, a hollow sound echoing throughout the area surrounding the truck.

Someone banged the side, startling Parkman, his head smacking the truck's floor. Aaron lifted up to glance around.

"What the hell?" he asked.

"We're here," Parkman whispered.

"Rise and shine," the man shouted from outside the truck.

"Where's here?"

"Your guess is as good as mine."

The door clicked, then swung open.

"Up and at 'em, boys. This is your final stop." The man jumped up into the back with a long pole. A rounded hook was at the end of the pole, like something that an entire carcass of beef would be suspended on.

Daniel stirred behind Parkman and tried to sit up on one elbow.

"You get a reprieve," the man said as he placed the hook between Aaron's legs and yanked it to the end, where the pound of duct tape secured his ankles. "Looks like Alex agreed to the job." The man smiled wickedly. "Can't kill you three yet, but I can certainly treat you any way I want because you'll all be dead by Monday anyway."

He yanked on the hook, dragging Aaron feet first toward the opening at the back of the truck.

"Hey, take it easy," Aaron protested, but he could do nothing. Nothing anyone could do bound the way they were.

The man yanked again, bringing Aaron to the mouth of the open door.

"Hey, don't pull him off," Parkman shouted.

The man glanced back at Parkman, a crazed look in his eyes. "Don't you go worrying about your friend here. Worry about yourself. You're all coming off the truck."

To Aaron's credit, he didn't protest. He simply waited for the inevitable.

After jumping down to the ground, the man's chest area even with the truck's floor, he took a tight grip on the handle of the pole, leaned into it, and yanked once more.

Aaron swooped toward the edge, then was lost to view as he dropped to the ground with a chest-rattling thud.

Parkman felt sick to his stomach watching that. The absolute glee on the man's face bothered him to his core. How could strangers behave toward others in such a disgusting way? This wasn't a vengeance thing. This wasn't retaliation for something. This was a hired thug doing his job, plain and simple—a job he enjoyed too much.

At that moment, even though he'd worked with Sarah for the past decade, he reached a deeper understanding of why she did what she did. It was because men like this would not exist without her. Because of Sarah and her band of friends, this man was the one who would be dead by the end of the weekend, and not them.

In the meantime, they had to take their hits without complaint.

Just like Aaron did when he hit the ground. Not a single peep or moan of protest. Aaron took the shot to the body that gravity delivered and shook it off.

Parkman only hoped he could do the same.

The man jumped back onto the truck, slipped the hook into Parkman's bound ankles, and dragged him toward the edge. Once the man hopped down, one final yank and Parkman was temporarily airborne.

The ground came fast—too fast. He didn't even get to hold his breath. It felt like being knocked into the air during a run for the end zone in football and dropping from five to six feet only to slam into the ground.

Ground, one. Parkman, zero.

The air shot from his lungs and his bladder threatened to explode through his jeans. Aaron panted beside him, eyes wild.

"You good?" Aaron asked. "Nothing broken?"

Parkman nodded a few short jerks of his head. "Yeah." He breathed in short gasps of air. "I think so. All good."

He rolled onto his stomach and hands, then continued rolling and stopped on his back, facing the roof of what looked like a barn. Several shafts of light peeked through wooden slats high up on the wall.

He rolled to avoid having Daniel land on him as he was being dragged to the edge of the truck's bed, but it was also to determine if anything had broken when he dropped to the ground.

Lucky for them, the man had tied their hands at the front.

Several seconds later, Daniel dropped with a thud two feet from him.

The man tossed the hook back inside the truck, then slammed the doors closed and turned to face them.

"Scream all you want, it won't matter. We're at least four kilometers from another house. Roll around this barn and get used to it. This is the last place on earth you'll see." He stepped away, then stopped and turned back. "Piss yourselves, shit yourselves, see if I care. When I return tomorrow morning, I'll be coming armed." He laughed that maniacal sputter again, grating on Parkman's nerves. "Think firing squad, up against the barn wall. Won't it be fun?"

"Can't wait," Aaron whispered.

The man shrugged. "I could kill you now if you want."

"Proof of life," Parkman whispered.

"What?"

"You need proof of life if Alex decides he needs a guarantee."

The man stared at him. "Well, aren't you Mr. Hot Shot Smarty Fucking Pants? So, let's pretend Aaron is dead, and Alex wants to hear his voice. I could play a recording."

"Won't work. Not with Alex."

The man glared at Parkman as he placed his hands on his hips. "How about all three of you shut the fuck up and stop talking to me. Confuse me, and you die anyway."

Parkman watched the man a moment, then turned his attention to Aaron. Their eyes met, and Aaron acknowledged him. Do not antagonize the jailer.

Daniel watched it all from the side, still gasping from the drop to the ground, his face lacking color.

"Fine, fuck it. I'm out of here." The man strode the length of the truck, Parkman watching his feet from under the large vehicle.

"I'll be back tomorrow." He mumbled something under his breath, then hopped up into the cab and slammed the door.

The truck started up and drove forward, easing out a large door on the other side of the barn, then it stopped just outside.

The driver appeared again, stared at them a moment, then slid a large door in place and snapped several locks together. The locks were big and loud enough to be heard on the other side of the barn.

A moment later, the truck's engine revved and then diminished as the driver exited the property.

"We have to get out of here," Aaron said.

Parkman twisted around toward him. "I agree. Otherwise, we're dead tomorrow."

"But also because Alex needs us."

"He does. Whatever they've manipulated him into doing, it has to be big and something he would never normally do —"

"Otherwise, why go to such criminal lengths to persuade him?"

"Exactly. It doesn't make sense."

Aaron averted his gaze to Daniel. "Where's Benjamin?"

"The driver and another guy attacked us. I fought with the driver until he shot me with some sort of tranquilizer. The last thing I heard was the front door of the dojo as Benjamin ran outside, and the other guy followed him."

Parkman stared at Aaron, unwilling to ask but having to anyway. "What happened with you and Sarah?"

"We were having dinner. I wasn't feeling good. A waiter helped me to the bathroom, but it wasn't a bathroom. Then I woke up with you guys."

"Sarah called me," Parkman added. "Tried to warn me. I didn't listen well."

"At least that tells me they didn't get her. What

happened? How did they get you?"

Parkman told them about the two cops at his door and the ensuing fight.

After a moment of silence between the three of them, Aaron scanned the building and then rolled toward the side wall of the barn.

"We need to get out of here for Alex," Aaron said as he rolled away from them. "And we need to help Sarah. She's probably losing her shit that she can't reach any of us."

"Okay, but how?" Parkman asked. "This building looks pretty secure."

"I have an idea, but first I gotta piss," Aaron said.

"Me too," Parkman echoed.

Aaron rolled until he got to the wooden wall of the barn. With his back aimed at them, he worked on the front of his pants, then moaned softly as he emptied his bladder.

"Parkman?"

"Yeah?"

"When I'm done, roll over here and piss in the same spot."

"What?"

"Just piss here."

"And why is that?" Parkman glanced at Daniel, whose color had returned to somewhat normal now. "Are we setting up a piss corner or something?"

"I have an idea."

"And what if this idea of yours means I roll into your piss?"

"Doesn't matter, just listen."

Parkman waited a moment, and when Aaron said

nothing, he frowned.

"Listen to what?" Daniel asked.

"Just listen," Aaron reiterated. "You can't hear it?"

Now, Parkman listened to the sounds outside the barn. Several birds whistled in nearby trees. He thought he could detect a breeze soothing the leaves of trees into a susurration of calm, but nothing else. Then he closed his eyes and drew inward, focusing on his ears.

Water.

A stream or a river of sorts was close by, barely audible.

"You hear it?" Aaron asked.

"Yes. Water."

"And what does water do to adhesion?"

"Weakens it."

"But isn't duct tape waterproof?" Daniel asked.

Parkman shook his head. "Water *resistant*, not waterproof. It can be used for a leak, but only temporarily. Water breaks down the adhesion." He faced Aaron, who had done up his pants, and rolled around to look at them. "But it takes time."

"So, we roll to the water source, dip our hands in, and wait. One hour, two? Who knows, and who cares? Once our hands are free, we untie each other and get the fuck out of here."

"Okay, but what does that have to do with pissing in the same spot?"

"I quickly scanned the barn while you and Daniel were dragged from the truck. It's fortified and well-built, but the walls are still wooden."

A plan formed in Parkman's mind. "Try to weaken the

wood by making it wet."

"Exactly."

"Then kick at that piece until it gives."

"Okay, boys, time to piss."

Parkman rolled toward Aaron as Aaron rolled out of the way.

"I'm next," Daniel said.

Once Parkman was set up, wetness soaked through his shirt at the waist.

"Fuck, I got piss on me now."

"Don't be a wuss," Aaron said, laughter in his voice. "You can jump in the river when we're free if you want. Just hurry up so Daniel can go. Then we kick our way out of here."

"How far is the river?" Daniel asked.

"That's the only part that'll suck."

"Why?"

"However far it is, we must roll all the way there."

"It can work if you raise your hands above your head."

"Smart, but what if it's just a thin path?" Parkman asked.

"Well then, we could be fucked."

Parkman finished and did up his pants, then rolled away.

"Daniel, you're up." He rolled a few more times until he was facing Aaron. "Doesn't matter how we do it, but we do it. We could even try to stand and hop all the way there."

"I agree. We do it. Regardless."

They nodded at each other.

"Who's kicking first?" Aaron asked.

Minutes later, the three men took turns kicking at the unforgiving wooden wall of the barn.

Wet wood or not, it wasn't going to be easy.

But they kept taking turns into the first hour, hope diminishing with each kick.

Chapter 18

AN ENGINE WAS CLOSE, the motor revving, slowing, then revving again. Light streamed through a window or something because it was too bright.

Sarah opened her eyes, then snapped awake, shielding her face with a hand. She was outside, lying in the grass.

It all returned to her in a flash, the morning sun warming her chilled skin.

A groundskeeper for the golf course was roving back and forth on the green of one of the holes, the flag stick on the ground at the fringe.

She scanned the area. Empty except for the one groundskeeper.

When she sat up, she rubbed her neck, the muscles stiff from an awkward four or five hours scrunched up on the hard surface.

The groundskeeper jumped off his machine, stuck the flagstick back in the hole, then got back on and rode toward the next green without looking in her direction.

She stretched, arms high, grunted, and tried to stand, all of her muscles feeling stiff.

From where she had nestled in for the remainder of the night, she could see Kipling Avenue. Not a single car drove by this early on a Sunday morning. It had to be slightly after six, perhaps going on seven.

What else had happened last night? She wished she could get an update on everyone. Where was Aaron, Parkman? How were Alex, Benjamin, and Daniel?

Sarah got to her feet, stretched again, brushed the grass off her clothes, and headed toward the street.

She needed a bathroom, a coffee, and some time to think. Darwin would be there within twelve hours. He was already in the air. Disco would be with them, too. Even Ricigliano could be counted on. Sarah just needed to stay off the street and hidden for the rest of the day, then find a way to get to the airport for five or six that night. Then, with Darwin's help —because Vivian was hardly around—they'd find a way to figure out what was going on.

But first, she would need to check in with Ricigliano. Vivian told her about a cop who would murder someone, which was not much to go on. But Vivian also told her the name Thomas Clark. Who the hell was that? Maybe before meeting Darwin, Ricigliano could look up that name. The one thing Vivian said about the leader of the kidnapping crew getting away and how Sarah had to let it go didn't sit well with her. That was something she'd have to decide at that moment.

At the street, she withdrew the cell phone, hit the power button, then trudged south on Kipling.

The phone dinged as it connected to the cell network. Two more dings, then a voicemail icon lit up.

Someone had texted the cell.

She opened the text option. It was Ricigliano. Sarah hadn't blocked the number, so, of course, the homicide detective would text her if she couldn't reach her, which was evidently something she had tried countless times throughout the night based on all the voicemails.

Sarah opened the text.

Is this the man with the gray streak in his hair that you mentioned on the phone last night?

Sarah frowned, then scrolled up to the picture of a dead man.

It was the waiter from last night. Someone shot the man in the head.

Sarah stopped and leaned against a light post, placing a hand on her stomach. What the hell was going on? Kidnap Aaron and Sarah—although he didn't get Sarah—and then deliver the goods only to get shot in the head? Who was behind all this? And where was Aaron?

Or was it Aaron who shot the guy?

There were more pictures below the first one.

Sarah lowered the phone and stared down the length of the road. If the next picture showed Aaron dead, she would scream. Then, she would resolve to make it her mission to end whoever was responsible for such a heinous act.

They were innocents out having dinner last night. How

could this shit keep happening to them? It wasn't like they were dealing with anything specific. They just wanted to be left alone to have their baby in peace, and now, less than twelve hours later, people were dead, every cop in the country was looking for her, and Aaron was missing—Parkman, too.

She raised the phone, steeling herself for what she was about to see.

The next picture was another dead man, but this time she didn't recognize him. However, that would have been a tall order because of the damage to the man's eye and face. The third photo Ricigliano sent her was yet another dead man. This time, his face was clear, minus a little blood, but his neck had a gaping hole.

Someone went on a killing spree last night, and they used guns and knives.

"What the fuck, man," Sarah muttered to herself as she started walking again.

The next one was a picture of a man she recognized: Benjamin.

He was lying in a hospital bed, a white bandage around his head and a cast on his left arm. He was smiling in the photo, which made her heart swell with happiness. They'd missed Benjamin. Somehow he'd gotten away from the assholes that had launched a late-night attack on them all.

She scrolled once more to another picture. A man who appeared to have been dropped from a building or something or perhaps hit by a car. His facial bone structure was dented inward, blood everywhere.

In the final text from the detective, Ricigliano explained

that the first three photos came from a warehouse on Queen Street, and the last one was a man who had tried to abduct Benjamin. They'd tussled and ran in front of a Brinks truck. This explained why the guy was dead, and Benjamin was in the hospital with what looked like a broken arm and a nasty bump on the head.

Ricigliano implored Sarah to call her as soon as she got the texts.

Sarah kept walking after slipping the phone back into her pocket. She wanted to tell the detective what her sister had told her, but not yet. Nothing would change that morning. She could call Ricigliano in an hour.

Twenty minutes later, as Sarah turned right onto Dundas, she spied a Tim Horton's coffee shop and headed directly toward it. Twenty feet from the door, the phone in her pocket buzzed.

Sarah slowed her pace and snatched it out.

Ricigliano.

She hit the answer button. "What?"

"Finally. I've been trying you all night."

"I'll call you back."

"What?" Ricigliano raised her voice.

"Yeah. Need a coffee."

Sarah clicked off, set the phone to silent, and entered the coffee shop. After using the restroom and washing her face, she got in line. She took a table in the far corner with a large coffee and breakfast sandwich in hand and withdrew the phone.

Ricigliano had called two times in the last ten minutes.

She dialed her back.

"What the fuck, Sarah?" Ricigliano snapped halfway through the first ring. "I've got bodies dropping all over the city because of you."

"Hey, hold up. I told you the storm was coming, the entire shit storm, and that none of the bodies were going to be my fault."

A couple sitting three tables away glanced over at the same time. Sarah offered them a warm smile until they turned away.

"Sarah, you're involved. There's no ifs, ands, or buts about it."

"Oh yeah," Sarah whispered into the phone. "I just woke up on a golf course. I'm four months pregnant, talking to you on a cell phone I bought for a hundred bucks from a stranger. I'm lucky I even have my freedom because Aaron was abducted last night, Parkman was taken by two men dressed as Toronto cops, and some other asshole in a cop uniform tried to nab me by the motel last night. Now I see Benjamin's in the hospital—"

"Sarah, I get it."

"No, let me finish. Benjamin is in the hospital, and you know he's there because someone tried to nab him, too. So, to conclude, an entire fucking team of assholes have descended on me and my family, my men, and you want to tell me it's all my fault. Rethink that, Ricigliano. Rethink, and fast, because I'm pissed and about to tear up the city to find my people and end whoever gets in my way."

When she glanced up, that couple was staring at her. This time, her smile wasn't so nice. They turned away and began to collect their things to leave.

"You finished?" Ricigliano asked.

"Fuck you." She took a bite of her sandwich. With her mouth full, she asked about Benjamin.

"He's fine. Bruised everywhere, cracked ribs, broken arm, smacked his head hard, and overjoyed at having not been shot."

"Of course, that guy is a bullet magnet. What else?"

"He said two guys jumped Daniel and him."

"And? Where's Daniel?"

"We don't know."

Sarah stopped chewing. "So, whoever they are, they have Parkman, Aaron, and Daniel. What about Alex?"

"That's where it gets tricky."

"How so?" She popped the lid on the coffee and took a sip.

"We got an anonymous tip that there were dead bodies in a warehouse—"

"The men from the pictures you texted me?"

"Yes, and that tipster said they saw a tall, thin man wearing some sort of black ninja gear entering the building. An eyewitness, a truck driver, came forward saying a man fitting that description hitched a ride on the back of his truck last night."

"You're thinking that was Alex?"

"Yes, we think so. Homicide was called to the scene, which is me. The efficiency of the kill is impressive. The one man had shoulder wounds, too. Like someone landed on his shoulders."

"How is that important?"

"The roof hatch to the warehouse was open. The two

bodies that were found stabbed were directly under the hatch."

"So you suspect their murderer dropped in on them wearing a ninja suit of some kind and executed them?"

"That would be a reasonable, plausible conclusion with what we have so far."

"And you have Alex pegged for that?"

"Let's just say we have to talk to him as a person of interest."

"Okay, so what's next?"

"I don't know, Sarah. You tell me. Where are the bodies coming from next? Another shit storm?"

"One second." Sarah bit into her breakfast sandwich and enjoyed the taste, savoring the freedom momentarily. Ricigliano could be pinging her cell phone again. Cruisers could be on their way as they chatted.

It was time to turn off the phone and get back on the road. Maybe she had to lose the phone altogether.

"Do you know a man named Thomas Clark?" Sarah asked.

"Why?"

"My sister gave me the name. Said he's involved somehow."

"Then your sister is wrong."

"How so?" She took another large bite, curious about what Ricigliano would say.

"Thomas Clark is the chief of police for Toronto. He's the boss of us all. Unless you're talking about a different Clark. I mean, I'm sure a few are in the city."

"The chief of police?" Sarah gripped her coffee, thinking

about her sister's words. "Vivian also said a cop will kill another cop."

"Oh, great. Seriously, Sarah? How is any of that helping? I need names, dates, and facts. Things I can back up and investigate. We call it evidence."

Sarah ignored Ricigliano's sarcasm. "The third thing she said was that the guy who is orchestrating everything will escape and that I'm supposed to let him go."

"Okay, call me back when you have something I can work with. None of this is helpful to me. I've got bodies piling up."

"How many are coming?"

Ricigliano remained silent for a long moment.

"You still there?" Sarah asked, watching out the window now.

"Yes, I'm still here."

"How many are coming?"

"How many what, Sarah?"

"Cops?"

"Coming where?"

"You really want to play with me? After what happened last month at the courthouse? You saw it through, and it helped your career. It didn't hinder it."

"For that, I'm grateful, but Sarah, you have to see this through my eyes. For starters, I've got a dead cop on my hands. Then I've got bodies dropping like flies. C'mon in, Sarah, talk face to face."

"Goodbye, Ricigliano. I'll deal with this shit on my own."

"Sarah, wait."

"For what? For them to get here?" She got up, stuffed the leftover sandwich in her pocket, and snatched the coffee off the table. "My ride's waiting anyway."

"You've got a ride?"

She pushed out through the door and stood beside the drive-thru lane.

"Ricigliano, you're either on my side, or you're not."

"You're wrong, Sarah. I'm on the side of justice, what's right and what's wrong. And we have to rely on detective skills, data, and evidence to solve crimes. We don't have sisters or people on the other side to guide us. I have a dead cop and you at the scene. Until this is over, you're suspect number one for that murder."

"Then we will talk again when this is over."

She killed the call but left the phone on, ensuring it was still silent. The vehicle she was waiting for was idling in the drive-thru. A dark blue pickup truck with a long-haired, blond female passenger. Sarah leaned nonchalantly against the building and waited.

Less than a minute later, the pickup eased forward and slowed as it passed her before turning in front of the Tim Horton's to head toward the parking lot's exit.

Sarah tossed the phone into the back of the pickup and strode the other way.

Minutes later, sirens wailed in the distance as they raced after the pickup.

She finished her sandwich, drank the rest of the coffee, and kept walking.

She'd be at Keele and Finch in about three and a half hours of straight walking. No taxis, no hired rides, and no

Uber. Something was happening around two in the afternoon that her sister wanted her to witness, and she planned to be there.

Once that was done, she had three more hours to kill before she needed to be at the airport to meet Darwin. Then, they would fix this and end it. She only hoped they'd be in time to ensure Aaron and everyone else remained on this side of the dirt.

With each step, she felt closer to solving everything. If only she could get the authorities' help instead of always fighting them.

Just once would be nice.

After all, Aaron, Parkman, and Daniel were gone somewhere—kidnapped—and Alex was now a suspect in a double homicide. They'd probably even try to pin the murder of the man with the gray streak in his hair on Alex, even though Alex didn't ever use a gun. There was an attempted abduction of Benjamin, and all the authorities wanted to do was go after Sarah.

"Where are you, Aaron?" she whispered to herself.

Unable to contain the tears and emotion welling up inside her at how crazy life could get in the span of twelve hours, Sarah wept while she walked, wiping the tears from her cheeks, realizing they would never be safe again. Not unless they moved up north somewhere and lived off the grid in a cabin, far, far away.

And that wasn't a life she wanted for her child.

But was this life any better?

Chapter 19

PARKMAN HAD ALREADY URINATED twice now, and they still hadn't broken through the wood.

"How much longer?" Daniel asked.

"Can't really tell," Aaron said as he kicked at the wall again.

Parkman watched him, then studied the wall around the area. "Tell me we checked that there's no support beam on the other side of that section."

Aaron stopped kicking. "This area had the weakest, oldest-looking wood. So I pissed here first."

Parkman took in the entire barn. It had to have been built many decades ago, but over the years, someone had rebuilt it, fortifying it. The floor was dusty, dirty concrete that led to the outer wooden walls. The door was brand new, similar to a strong steel garage door, and large enough for the truck to come and go.

He checked the corners and moved his gaze along the walls, watching for weak spots, but Aaron was right. The area he was in did appear to be the oldest. It even had a slight discolor to it, which denoted aging.

The duct tape was wrapped so tight around his wrists and over the tops of his fingers that he could barely use the tips of two fingers to pull down his zipper. If they had more movement in their fingers, they could've just pulled the tape off each other, but that wasn't happening. Each one of them had tried to bite it off, but the seam was wrapped over and under the inside of their hands. They wouldn't be able to bite their own, and the angle didn't work for another person's mouth because the final seam was in the center between the wrists. The ankles were the same, but in that case, the tape started at the base of the shoes and wrapped around and around to mid-calf muscle. It was like an entire roll was used on each man. It was so thick and tightly wound.

All options for removing the tape had been exhausted while one man kicked at the wall.

They'd been there for at least an hour, the barn warming up as the day progressed.

Aaron hooted from near the wall.

"You're not worried," Daniel said, "with that volume?"

"Remember the guy said we could shout that no one's around? Besides, you'll be happy with this."

Parkman placed his hands over his head and rolled toward Aaron. "How's it going? You break through?"

"Take a look."

Aaron laid flat, and Parkman sat up. A section of the wall

had cracked outward. Half a dozen, maybe a dozen more kicks, and they'd be out.

"Let me at it."

Aaron rolled away and laid out flat, staring at the roof.

Parkman applied his feet to the damaged area, lifted them, and kicked back onto it. The wood cracked and echoed throughout the barn. He kicked again, then again.

About ten minutes later, he'd managed to open a small enough hole for a man to squeeze through.

"We did it," he said, the triumph evident in his voice.

"As much as that's a great hole, how will we get out?" Aaron stared at him a moment. "We have to keep kicking. The way we roll, we'll never be able to inch out like a worm."

"We could try," Parkman said.

Worried about the lack of circulation to his reddened hands and feet, he couldn't feel any longer, and desperate not to be in the barn when they came back for them, he angled his head through the hole and checked the outside. It looked like any other woods in northern Ontario. Trees lined the side of the barn. Toward the front, a gravel road disappeared into the tree line.

Once his head was outside the barn, the sound of rushing water was much louder.

He breathed in the clean air and kicked his legs, trying to squirm through the hole. His shoulders barely edged past the wood, with it digging into his back slightly. Twisting and rotating from shoulder to shoulder, propelling with his legs as best he could, he was able to squeeze outside in under a minute.

"There, did it," he said. "Your turn." He rolled away to a grassy area and waited, panting with the effort.

Aaron's head poked through the hole. After a brief hesitation, he fought to get out as Parkman had, but this time, Aaron edged out on his back, which seemed smarter. Minutes later, all three of them were lying on their backs outside the barn.

"We have to move," Aaron said. "If they come back, we can't be caught out here."

"Agreed." Parkman didn't want to move. Every movement irritated his feet and hands. "What now? We roll on down the road?"

"Sure puts a new meaning on the term, Rolling Stones, eh boys." Daniel released a nervous laugh.

None of them would admit how scared they were. Bound, driven there by a madman bent on killing them, they could only imagine what was happening to Sarah and the others. How worried Sarah must be for Aaron, too. And neither of them had any idea what was going on or how they got into this mess.

"We have to start rolling toward the sound of the running water," Aaron said.

"I second that," Parkman said without much conviction in his voice. Rolling for several hundred meters or longer wasn't appealing at all. He'd do it, though, because the alternative was worse.

"Okay, guys, let's do this. Hands above your heads so you roll without scrunching them under you the whole time."

Daniel moved closer. "And if we find something sharp along the way ..."

Something sharp could cut the tape, but then what? Walk out of the woods? On feet that had lost enough circulation to be tingling.

Parkman glanced down at his hands. They'd gone a dark color as the oxygen had been fighting to get in. If they didn't get the restraints off soon, there would be lasting damage to their hands.

"Guys." Parkman raised his hands for them to see. "The blood flow is restricted, but I don't feel we've hit the point of no return yet."

"Meaning?" Aaron asked.

"These have to come off sooner rather than later. Like, within an hour is my choice."

"We'd be dead already if it wasn't for proof of life. Not sure that asshole cares about our hands in the long term."

"Agreed. But we care, so we roll."

"Let's get rolling then."

"And let's keep a steady pace to get to that water as our lives depend on it."

Daniel nodded and started rolling around the barn toward the tree line.

"Let's hit it then," Aaron said and rolled away, his hands thrust over his head as if he were about to dive into a pool.

Parkman took a deep breath, raised his hands over his head, and followed Aaron and Daniel as they rolled into the woods toward the water.

Chapter 20

Alex checked the time again: 13:02.

The police chief would be on stage on the university grounds in one hour. They had already begun assembling the makeshift stage on the edge of the lawn in front of the glass building called Kaneff Tower.

In the middle of the night, Alex had snuck back inside the dojo through the rear door and retrieved more weapons. In their storage locker, they had a collection of knives, swords, throwing stars, and many other martial artist weapons that some advanced classes used.

Alex worked like an automaton without a plan other than following through on his word to get Sarah and the others released.

Not convinced he'd actually be able to do it, but seeing no other way out, the path led him to the grounds of York

University in preparation for the kill. He'd changed back into civilian clothes to avoid standing out in the crowd.

There were several options he was mulling over in his head. One was to get as close to the intended target as possible, then go for it, dropping anyone who got in his way. Once he was on the chief of police, several knife jabs to the carotid would do the trick.

But *could* he do it? An innocent man? Wasn't there a better way?

He considered explaining everything to the authorities. Tell them what had happened to Sarah and the others to convince them of the severity of the situation, and then have the police chief allow Alex to *pretend* to kill him on that stage. Once Sarah was released, they could investigate from there.

But that idea died in its infancy. There was no way the chief of police would go along with the hysterics of a murder in order to have Sarah released from kidnappers. Sarah Roberts was no friend of the cops, and they made that clear often enough.

And even if he was able to convince them of the urgency of the situation, he highly doubted they'd allow him to carry on his business due to the bodies he left behind in that warehouse last night—two of which he killed with his own hands.

Since last night, when he felt like he was literally stuck between a rock and a hard place, he had thought he'd come to some conclusion that would allow him to avoid the actual murder of Thomas Clark, Toronto's police chief. Still, he was one hour away from the deadline, and no magical solution existed yet.

So, here he was, armed with several knives, dressed like an average student at the university, watching as workers assembled the stage, the sound system, and a drinks table where it appeared volunteers had placed large containers of juice and pop.

Why here? Why so public?

Even news vans were arriving to capture the event.

There had to be a reason why Silvio needed it done this way. Was it simply to have Alex taken out of the picture? Because surely other officers would attend the talk, and he was sure they'd be armed. If they didn't kill him on the bright green grass of the university lawn, then he'd be taken in and charged with attempted murder or first-degree murder in the event he proved successful.

So why such a big show?

Alex moved to the side and sat on a bench that lined one of the walkways.

He had forty-five minutes to figure it all out and felt that he was getting somewhere with it. Because if all Silvio wanted was for the chief to be killed, the easier solution was breaking into the man's house at two in the morning and slicing his throat.

No, Silvio wanted a show, a presentation. Whoever had hired Silvio needed a public display that he could get to anyone, and only Alex had the special talent to circumvent a dozen men in uniform to get to the target.

The twist in Alex's stomach wasn't due to nervousness, as much as letting Sarah down. If all it meant was someone had to die to save her and the others, then in theory, that worked like if Hitler had been killed in 1939.

But it didn't work in this case.

And if Alex failed to act, would Sarah be murdered? Aaron? Parkman?

He blinked once, then blinked again.

The solution hit him like a slap in the face.

He blinked again and wondered why he hadn't thought of it before. He could keep his word to Silvio without killing the chief, and he only hoped Sarah and everyone else made it through their ordeal.

Because in the end, when he went home to meet his maker, he couldn't have his soul marked in such a way.

Alex was no murderer—in the cold-blooded sense.

As much as anyone was a murderer to protect themselves in a kill-or-be-killed scenario, Alex could not outright kill a man who wasn't threatening him or someone he loved.

Sarah would understand that.

He told her he'd kill for her, but it was never meant in this sense.

The idea, the solution he'd come up with, accounted for that.

But he would have to sacrifice himself for it to work.

He checked the time: 13:18.

He would do what he came here to do in just over a half hour, although with a little less conviction.

Alex's journey here was coming to a close.

His final wish was for Sarah to be proud of him for his decision.

Although, he wouldn't live long enough to know, which saddened him further.

It had been a good run.

Alex smiled at the memories he'd created with the boys who had become family.

And then he lowered his head and wept, alone, on the bench while he waited for the kill.

Chapter 21

Daniel hollered first, then Aaron. Parkman had been slower, but this rolling in the dirt had produced so many bruises and cuts he was wondering if a man could kill himself by just rolling for several hours.

He slowed to catch his breath and stared at his fingers. In the afternoon sun, they were a dark red, almost purple. The duct tape had to come off soon, but it was close to half an inch thick and wound so tight onto itself it would take days of biting to get anywhere with it.

How fast would the water work, though? Dipping their hands in a river or stream sounded like the best idea at the moment.

"Parkman," Aaron called from up ahead.

"Coming," he shouted.

At least they weren't still in the barn waiting to be

slaughtered like the farm animals it once housed.

He positioned himself, then rolled, only slowing to ease over a large rock protruding from the ground. The water was much louder now, but he couldn't see it yet.

Aaron and Daniel had stopped up ahead. They were watching him from the bottom of a small rise. Parkman rolled down the rise and slowed a few feet from them, the rushing water even closer.

"Found the river," Daniel said.

"Great. Where is it?"

Aaron jerked his head to indicate it was behind him.

Parkman leaned inward, then twisted around to look past the other two men.

He could hear the water but couldn't see it yet.

Then, it all became clear when he sat up.

Daniel and Aaron had stopped because they couldn't roll farther. They were lying at the edge of a small cliff.

Parkman wormed closer and glanced over the edge.

Water rushed by in a fast current about twenty feet below them.

"Shit," he yelled. "We can't reach that."

He looked left and right, but this entire side of the river, as far as the eye could see—about fifty meters each way before the river bent to the right—was a cliff. In some spots, the cliff edge was higher.

"Now what?"

"Look for sharp rocks," Daniel said.

"There aren't any. This is a forest filled with grass and trees. The path we took was more dust and shrubs than anything else. There wasn't even hard wood we could rub the tape against."

Aaron stared at the river. "Even if we found a rock, who would hold it? All of our fingers are discolored and jammed together because of this fucking tape."

"Biting at them would take a few days, and I think that would be faster than a rock."

"These restraints were never meant to come off, were they?" Daniel asked in a dejected tone.

Aaron tore his gaze from the rushing current below. "Hence, they weren't too worried about circulation problems, thinking we'd never need our hands anyway."

"Solutions?" Parkman asked. "We need one, or they win." He waited a heartbeat, then added, "We've broken out of the barn and come this far. Tell me that wasn't for nothing."

Aaron faced him. "We're dead anyway, right?"

"Not if we can get these off and walk out of here."

"Right, but if we can't?"

"Yeah, dead."

"Okay, then. I've got a solution."

"What's that?"

"Same one as before."

Parkman glanced over the cliff's edge again. "It's too far to dip our arms in. The water is rushing by too quickly, too. We'd be swept under with the current." He glanced back at Aaron. "Unless you have another idea on how to lower you twenty feet, then I don't see how the water plan works."

"Dead anyway means …" He angled closer to the edge.

"Aaron, what are you doing?"

"… I've got nothing to lose here."

"Wait, let me."

Aaron stared at Parkman for a brief moment. "I'll be back to untie you both. If I don't come back, find another way out of here and tell Sarah I always loved her."

"Aaron, wait!"

But it was too late.

Aaron had rolled over the edge.

Parkman glanced down in a panic as Aaron hit the dirt shore and bounced into the water, his mouth open.

The hit on the dirt must have knocked the wind out of him. When he hit the water, he kicked and frantically waved his hands, but the water embraced him and swept him away at an incredible speed.

"Aaron!" Parkman yelled.

His friend's head dropped below the surface and didn't come up right away.

Daniel mumbled something continuously under his breath.

Parkman watched the area he thought Aaron would surface due to the strength of the current, his gaze following the water as it traveled away from them.

Over fifty meters away, he thought he saw Aaron bob up once, but then he was lost again.

Parkman stared at the rushing river water for over ten minutes, knowing Aaron was gone by then. Even if he was still alive, he'd been out of sight as the river meandered to the right.

He rolled over, stared at the sky, and heard what Daniel said.

Daniel was whispering a prayer for Aaron's safety over

and over. He had never struck Parkman as the religious type.

But if someone was going to pray, now was the time.

Whispering Aaron's name, Parkman joined in the prayer.

The two of them stayed like that for a long time, begging for Aaron to survive the river, even though Parkman was sure no one could, even if their hands and feet weren't secured in such a way.

There was still a chance.

Thin as it was.

Chapter 22

THE CROWDS HAD ASSEMBLED for the chief's speech, taking spots all over the lawn. The news vans had circulated with cameras, cameramen, and women checking their microphones and testing their equipment.

He counted six vans, over a dozen crew, and almost twenty uniformed police officers, not including the crowds that had taken up residence on the grass. There had to be two hundred people milling about, waiting for the police chief.

So far, Alex had gathered that the speech was about campus security, overall crime statistics, and the humanization of the Toronto Police Service's officers.

Meanwhile, Alex's actions would throw a monkey wrench into all that.

More officers exited the Kaneff building doors in preparation for the chief's arrival.

It was 14:12 now, and the speech was set for 14:00.

How much longer would the chief make everyone wait?

Alex got to his feet and nonchalantly wandered to the side near the news vans, waiting for the chief to arrive. Once he was on stage and the cameras were rolling, Alex would expedite his plan and make sure the cameras caught it all.

At the side of the building, he leaned on the wall and lowered his head, breathing evenly, thinking about Sarah and his friends.

The only regret was he wouldn't get to say goodbye to them all.

The pain wrenched at his heart, and he prayed this wasn't all for naught.

He wouldn't fail. He would do as he planned.

It had better work. Silvio had better keep his word because if he killed Sarah and her friends, Darwin would find him. Bruno would come. Disco, too.

In the end, Silvio needed to release everyone and run.

And in the meantime, Alex had a job to do.

He was more than ready.

If only the fucking chief of police would show up, then he could attack him.

Why couldn't people be on time for their own funeral?

***

Deputy Chief of Police Roger Sterling sat the phone down and gawked at the chief.

"Sir, wait," he gasped.

Thomas Clark was adjusting his lapel in the full-body

mirror. "What is it now, Sterling?"

"We just got a tip."

"A tip?" Clark stopped what he was doing and turned his attention to his deputy police chief. "What kind of tip?"

"A homicide detective called about the murders in the warehouse."

"What's that got to do with my speech? I'm on in"—he glanced at his watch—"five minutes."

"The person of interest for those murders is a man who goes by the name Alex."

"No last name?"

"It wasn't supplied."

Clark looked away and continued to adjust his attire in the mirror. "We can discuss this after the speech." He brushed himself down once, then pivoted to stare at Sterling. "Ready?"

Sterling shook his head. "I'm afraid you can't go out there."

Clark frowned. "And why not?"

"Homicide believes this Alex is here, hiding somewhere in the crowd."

Clark raised his eyebrows. "Why would that be?"

"They have intel that leads them to suspect he's here to execute you."

Clark guffawed. "Right, in front of all these people, those cameras?"

Sterling nodded slowly. "That's what their intel says."

They stared at each other a moment longer.

"Shit," Clark said, slapping his hands once. "How ironic, considering the speech I've prepared."

"We have to get ahead of this."

"Thoughts?" Clark asked.

"Call in uniformed officers. We need a quick five-minute meeting."

Within a few minutes, over twenty uniformed officers stood at attention in a classroom the university offered them to use.

Sterling moved to the front.

"Ladies and gentlemen. A credible threat to the chief of police has come to our attention. Outside, in that growing crowd, a man named Alex may be lurking around, waiting for the chief to step on the podium."

He paused to let that sink in.

"According to homicide detectives who are on their way here now, this Alex is a person of interest in the murders that happened in a warehouse on Queen Street last night. Homicide believes he's here to attempt to kill the chief of police."

A low murmur rumbled throughout the classroom.

"We have not been able to obtain a photo in this short time, so we will have to spread out on the lawn and watch for anyone acting suspiciously."

"Are we canceling the speech?" an officer asked.

"No. I've spoken with the chief, and he's still going out there, but he's wearing a slash vest now."

"A slash vest? Why not Kevlar?"

"Alex isn't known to use guns. He's a martial artist known for knife play."

"Bit of a risk," another officer said. "We should cancel."

"The chief feels strongly about this speech. Showing

strength for the students will be a demonstration in and of itself."

"By being bait?"

"Please, the decision has been made. We've got officers out there now scouting the grounds. Alex hasn't been found as of yet, but we're looking. There's a chance he isn't even here. But if he is, the chief must step outside to draw this man out of hiding."

Many officers were nodding, while others sported concerned looks.

"Okay, disperse and find this man before he does any harm. The chief will be running late, but he will exit the building soon in the event Alex is not located."

Everyone filed out of the classroom, with Sterling leaving after it was empty.

He sidled up beside the chief again.

"They have their marching orders. A couple of dozen officers are out there looking for Alex."

"Good, then we're ready."

"Let's give them a few more minutes to be sure."

"Then you go out and tell the crowd that I'm coming and apologize for my tardiness."

Sterling nodded and stepped away. At the doors, three officers escorted him outside. He scanned the crowd of more than two hundred people and realized finding Alex among them would be too challenging.

He tapped the microphone at the podium and received heavy feedback for his efforts.

"Ladies and gentlemen, I'm Deputy Chief of Police Roger Sterling, Specialized Operations Command. The chief of police has had a few setbacks. We apologize for his tardiness. He will be with you shortly."

The crowd cheered softly and then clapped like Sterling had performed a song or something similar.

He backed off stage and headed toward the Kaneff building. Officers opened the door and let him back inside, where Clark was waiting.

"We set?" Clark asked.

"Give them five minutes. If they don't find this Alex character in that time, then we're good to go."

"I'll be ready." He spoke the words, but his face said otherwise. The worried look and the sweat beading on his forehead told another story altogether.

The chief of police, Thomas Clark, had been through so much over the past few years that Sterling wasn't surprised the man had a death wish.

At least then, he wouldn't have to face the damage he'd done.

Something only Sterling knew.

Something Sterling wasn't prepared to take to the grave.

The timing was important with everything.

All in good time.

***

Alex watched as the doors opened and several uniformed officers escorted a man to the podium. This was it, the chief of police.

He slipped behind a news van and started toward the front of the press line, giving him ample access to the stage.

"Ladies and Gentlemen," the chief started.

Then, the man explained that the chief had been delayed and would be out shortly.

Alex slowed his pace.

This wasn't the chief.

He stopped behind a CP24 News van, glanced inside the front cab, and watched the stage through the van's windows.

The man, surrounded by uniformed officers, was already heading back inside the Kaneff building.

The chief would be out soon. Five minutes or less.

Dangling from the rearview mirror of the van was a press pass. After a look both ways, Alex tried the door.

It was unlocked.

He opened it, grabbed the pass, removed it from the mirror, and quietly closed the van's door.

Someone was walking his way from the front area. He acted like he was supposed to be there, glancing down once at the name on the press pass.

The man slowed as he approached.

Alex stuck out his hand. "CP24 News, the name's Mike Smith. Gonna be a great speech."

The man frowned, knitting his eyebrows together as he stared at Alex.

"I'm with Global News. Haven't met you before."

"New on the job."

Alex stretched out the lanyard and slipped the pass over his head as he lumbered by the man. "Let's go for beers sometime."

The other guy continued walking away.

The press pass wasn't for this event. It was for some

political speech two years ago when the prime minister had come to Toronto. Perhaps the news van driver was patriotic, keeping the pass as a souvenir.

Who would know it wasn't a proper pass for this event at first glance, though? It had the big media badge sign on the front.

Wouldn't it be too late, anyway, if someone were to call it out?

The Kaneff doors opened. A tall man in an official-looking uniform stepped out of the building, surrounded by six officers wearing Kevlar and two men in suits.

What the hell? Did they know he'd be here? Or did the chief of police always travel with such an entourage?

Alex took a moment to scan the crowd. Over twenty police officers roamed throughout the people sitting on the grass, stepping over lunch baskets, purses, and bicycles. Other officers had made a solid perimeter along the walkway.

They had to expect something was going to happen today. Had Silvio set him up, or did he actually want the chief of police killed?

Did it really matter? Sure, people's lives hung in the balance, but what was up and what was down? Nothing made sense.

For example, when Randy asked if they were still in the warehouse last night, it was an odd question because why would he expect them to leave? Then, the cops came to find the bodies.

Did Randy call them? If so, why would he do that when he was working with Silvio?

Nothing made any sense, and the more he thought

everything over, the more fucked up it seemed. Although, no amount of thinking got him out of the hole he was in. He had seen pictures of his friends being held captive. He'd gone to the warehouse, saw the couch, took out several of their members, and still had no choice.

The sweat forming on his neck had to be from the direct sun on his back. He wouldn't buy into the fact that he was nervous.

Attacking the chief of police in the presence of so many armed police officers was a form of suicide. He knew that, and Silvio knew that.

So, was the end result the chief's death or Alex's death?

Or both?

The chief stepped up onto the podium, hunched down to speak into the microphone, then smiled at the assembled crowd.

"I apologize for the delay. It seems there might have been a security breach."

Alex listened to the chief drone on momentarily, stunned at what he heard.

A security breach?

They already knew about him.

Then, there was nothing left for him to do.

With no intention of actually getting close enough to kill the chief, he left his knives in their slots as he stepped out from around the news van and started toward the side of the podium.

He caught the eye of several law enforcement professionals as he approached, the media badge giving him a pass. They glanced down, saw the company name, and nodded as he walked by them. He caught two men staring at his waistline in search of a weapon, but they wouldn't see one.

The chief droned on about safety and security as Alex approached the steps at the side of the podium where two officers stood guarding the access.

One officer leaned toward Alex. "No media on the stage."

Alex smiled and shot a hand up into his ST 09 and 10 nerve in the neck, slightly to the right of the man's Adam's apple. While the man placed his hands on him, he jabbed at the other man's nerves in his neck with his free hand.

Hitting this nerve with just the right amount of force—not too much. Otherwise, there could be lasting damage to the trachea, but not just a soft jab, either—it tricks the nerve into shutting down the body by lowering the blood pressure. A full-grown man can be knocked out in as fast as six seconds with this blow, and Alex could smack both men with efficiency, stepping around the first man as he was already falling.

The reaction was swift as the two officers dropped to the ground at the base of the stairs. Someone shouted, a woman screamed, and men surged to the podium's edge. Alex detected footsteps charging up behind him.

It was now or never. He only hoped, if they shot him, that the final bullet would be painless, like a shot to the spine or brain stem.

As the men ran to form a line at the podium's edge, he expected them to rush the chief off the other side.

So, instead of attempting to run through the line of men,

he dropped to the ground and rolled, coming up on his feet slightly behind the makeshift stage, where he encountered a couple of men who were easily dropped to their knees with short jabs.

He twisted out of one man's grip, then dove over another as he bent down and lunged at Alex, similar to a linebacker going for the tackle.

Imagining he carried the football, Alex dodged as many men as he could in his attempt to get close to the chief, surprised none of them had a Taser or had tried to shoot him yet.

Maybe they hadn't shot at him because he hadn't produced a gun.

But he'd assaulted officers and knocked them out. Surely, they'd up the ante at any moment.

The chief jogged by about ten feet to his right, completely surrounded by an entourage of men in uniform.

There was no way he would get close enough now.

Pandemonium ensued as people ran in all directions, and yet another dozen men ran toward him.

Alex dropped his center of gravity and bolted under a couple of men grabbing for him, lifting them off their feet as he broke free of a group. An open section of grass was laid out in front of him.

He took the chance to run at the chief and got within a few feet of the group surrounding him when he pulled out a knife.

"Chief Thomas Clark," he shouted.

The chief glanced over and stared at Alex, his eyes going to the knife in Alex's hand.

"I held the power of life and death—"

Someone knocked into him from behind so hard that the knife was lost from his grip.

More men landed on him until bodies obscured the sunshine. Men shouted and wrestled for his arm, his legs.

He let it all happen.

Silvio got his show, but he didn't get his kill. In the end, Alex couldn't kill an innocent—not even for Sarah.

She'd understand and forgive him for not saving her.

Handcuffs were slapped on his wrists, and he was hauled to his feet. The rest of the weapons were carefully removed from his person, and he was guided to a police car roughly.

They shoved him in the back of the cruiser with no regard for his personal safety, which he understood because, after all, he'd just tried to attack, harm, or kill their police chief. There would be no doubt in their minds that he was going after the chief.

Although, he had no intention of killing the chief. Would they believe that? And how he was still alive was a mystery. In cases like the one the officers just faced, didn't they shoot to kill when one of their own was in mortal danger?

He righted himself in the back of the cruiser as it pulled away from the curb, the driver cursing at him from the front seat.

Alex blocked the verbal abuse and stared out the window as shocked students and teachers watched the cruiser leave with its captive.

There was one consolation.

At least he had the skill set to defend himself in prison.

Chapter 23

PARKMAN HAD EXAMINED EVERY option, talked it out with Daniel, spent at least a half hour gnawing at the tape and getting nowhere, then laid back down and stared at the sky.

It was no use. They weren't getting through the tape with their teeth alone. It was just too thick. Daniel was exhausted and getting more and more worried about the color of his hands.

Parkman thought the same, but his thoughts were drawn more to Aaron. A river as deep as the one below them, with that much current, would challenge anyone to swim with their hands and feet free of restraint. The way Aaron was bound would make swimming an impossibility.

If they made it out of this in one piece but Aaron didn't, what would he tell Sarah? That Aaron just rolled into the river in an attempt to get the tape wet? The danger and risk level was too high when freedom equated to death. Even though death was another sort of freedom, it wasn't Aaron's intention in this case.

Someone shouted in the distance, making Parkman return to the here and now.

"You hear that?" he asked.

"Yeah," Daniel whispered. "Sounds like the assholes are back."

"Maybe we should follow Aaron. We could roll into the water."

"Not me. Can't swim that well. I'd drown."

"That's the point."

Daniel looked over at him. "Suicide?"

"Not exactly. Going over gives us a chance. Staying here and getting retaken guarantees we die."

"A bullet is faster than swallowing water. And until they shoot us, I'll have time to figure a way out."

"I'm going the river route." Parkman twisted his body around and rolled to the edge.

"Parkman," Daniel pleaded. "Wait. There's got to be a better way."

He glanced back over his shoulder. "They're closer," he said. "Tell me this better way."

Daniel waited a moment. "I said there's got to be a better way. I didn't say I knew what it was."

"I don't want to roll over this edge and leave you alone." Parkman turned back to Daniel.

"Then don't. We'll face what's coming together."

"Come with me, is what I meant."

"Parkman, I have more hope in staying. That water is

certain death."

"Is that what you think happened to Aaron?"

Daniel glanced away, but Parkman saw his lower lip quivering before he did.

The voices of men were much closer. Parkman heard three, maybe four different men. They were so close now. The stomping sounds of moving through the brush were loud enough to hear each step.

Daniel turned back to face Parkman. "I fear the worst for Aaron and think we will die if we go in that water. I'm sorry, but I'm staying."

This was their point of no return. By Parkman's guess, Aaron was gone close to an hour now, and the men coming through the woods would be upon them in less than a minute.

They had to go into the water now or seal their fate with their captors.

With Daniel refusing to go, Parkman wouldn't go either.

He rolled away from the edge and maneuvered himself to be closer to his colleague, his friend.

"We got this," he said. "Whatever happens."

"Whatever happens. Together."

A man in a red and black lumberjacket broke through the woods, a long rifle in one hand.

"Hey guys," he yelled over his shoulder. "Found them."

He stomped toward them as other men came out of the woods. All of them were armed.

Parkman tightened his jaw and waited for a bullet. What a great place to execute them. They had rolled their way to the edge of the river. The men could shoot them in the dirt, then roll them into the river, where they'd wash ashore a mile or two south of here. It would take the investigators forever to find this spot if they ever did.

Parkman counted three men, then four as they burst through the woods.

"How the hell did you boys get out here?" one of them asked, shaking his head.

Another man was shaking his head, too.

"Parkman? Daniel?"

A familiar voice.

He jerked his head to the right and saw Aaron walk out of the woods. His eyes widened when he saw the man, his hands and feet free, hair still wet and askew.

"Happy you guys waited for me," he said. "That river was too dangerous."

Parkman was speechless, as apparently was Daniel.

Aaron continued. "If it weren't for Jim here, I'd still be floating down the Grand River. He saw me bobbing up ahead and waded in to drag me out." Aaron raised his hands. "Then he cut the tape off and listened while I breathlessly told him about you two."

"Oh my shit …" Parkman breathed. "You did it."

"And here we are. Jim brought his brothers along in case we encountered trouble. Oh, and he's agreed to lend us a pickup truck to get back to the city and report this to the police."

"Motherfucker," Daniel muttered.

"Let's cut that tape, boys," Jim said, dropping to his knees. He produced a knife and began slicing at the tape on Parkman's hands.

"Thanks, Daniel," Parkman said.

"What did he do?" Aaron asked.

"Saved our lives. He convinced me to stay and not float away."

Chapter 24

Tʜᴇ ᴄᴏᴘ ɪɴ ᴛʜᴇ front seat had calmed down enough to speak with dispatch on his radio several times. He still made furtive glances at Alex in the back seat, but his streak of cursing seemed to have subsided for the moment.

Alex avoided his gaze by staring out the side of the cruiser while they headed south on Keele Street. They slowed for a light at what Alex suspected was Finch Avenue. After edging forward a few moments, Alex glanced through the windshield. A long line of cars were being guided into one lane due to construction, which was slowing how many cars got through the green light. They would get to Finch when they got there. As it stood, Alex had more time on his hands than ever before, so it didn't matter to him.

Thoughts of Sarah and Aaron and where they might be filtered through his mind. How were Parkman, Daniel, and

Benjamin faring? What kind of conditions were they all being subjected to? He could've done something more useful to save them, but instead, he had attempted to kill the police chief, and where had that gotten him?

When they sat him down in the interview room, he would tell them about Silvio and why Alex was there today. He would explain that Sarah and his friends were being held captive somewhere, and they'd ask him why he didn't bring it to their attention instead of doing what Silvio asked him to do.

Would they expend resources to find Sarah, to locate Parkman and the rest of them? Would they actually search for them or wait for their bodies to turn up somewhere?

Alex watched random people on the sidewalk and envied their freedom. To be able to walk where they wanted and go where their heart desired.

One woman caught his attention. She wasn't walking anywhere, just standing on the side of the road watching the cars go by on Finch. Even with her back turned to him, it warmed his heart to watch her because she looked just like Sarah from behind, with her long blonde hair and athletic build.

The cruiser edged forward, and the dispatcher called officers to a domestic in the Finch and Dufferin area.

They were ten feet closer to the woman. If Alex didn't know Sarah was being held captive somewhere, he would've sworn this woman was her.

Although, Silvio only *told* him he had Sarah. Alex hadn't seen her in the photos.

He sat up straighter, begging the woman to turn around.

The cruiser edged closer.

The woman turned around.

It was Sarah Roberts.

Their eyes locked, then hers widened. His followed.

She wasn't being held captive. A breath caught in his throat. Everything he'd just done was for nothing. What the hell was going on? Did Silvio even have Aaron, Parkman, and Daniel?

Sarah started across the grass toward the cruiser.

What the hell was she doing? There was nothing she could do for him now.

When she got to the passenger window, the driver saw her and waved her off.

Sarah knocked on the window.

"We're busy," the driver said. "You need police help? Call them."

Sarah knocked again, this time much harder.

It warmed Alex's heart to see her. This was the Sarah he knew and loved, the one he'd sacrifice himself for.

The cop lowered the window a few inches. "We're in the middle of traffic, lady. What do you want?"

"I just wanted to tell you that Darwin will be here in four hours, and we're going to the Disco. It'll all be okay soon."

Sarah didn't look back at Alex once, but he understood what she was saying. Every word out of her mouth was for him.

"Who the hell is Darwin?" the cop asked. "And what Disco?"

"Don't worry, sir, we'll get them. Although, we could use your help, if possible."

"You need my help?" the cop asked. "Just call 911 if it's an emergency. They can send someone right over. I'm transferring a prisoner here." He proceeded to close the window.

"We all love you and will get you out of this," she said the moment before the window closed entirely.

The cop clucked his tongue and hit the gas, pulling away from Sarah, leaving her at the curb, and wiping her eyes.

Alex lowered his head. What had he done? How could he be so stupid?

Sarah needed him. His purpose had been restored.

He had four hours until Darwin landed at the airport. That gave him four hours to escape police custody.

That was plenty of time.

Once they booked him and got him to the interview room, holding cell, or wherever they would place him first, he'd have a better idea of how to get out.

The issue wasn't whether he would be able to break free. That part he was clear on.

The issue was how he'd do it.

How could Sarah know he'd be there at that time?

It had to be Vivian.

Her sister was back. Her sister was telling her what to do.

He relaxed in his seat, knowing everything would work out now that Vivian was in Sarah's head.

Or would it?

Alex closed his eyes and meditated on slipping out of the handcuffs, then exiting the police building unscathed.

So many options and so many ideas.

None of them appeared easy, and they often entailed

violence.

Although, he was not one to shy away from violence.
He'd do anything for Sarah.

Chapter 25

AARON SAT BY THE passenger door, Daniel in the middle, and Parkman drove.

"Where do we start?" Aaron asked.

Parkman maintained a steady speed, shaking his head.

"We can check my place first," Aaron continued. "To see if Sarah's there. Or maybe she's been home and gone. I'll grab my spare cell phone and make some calls."

They stopped at a red light several blocks from the turn to Aaron's apartment. On the street to Aaron's right, a *Toronto Sun* newspaper box displayed the front cover for today's news.

He recognized Sarah's and Alex's faces from the passenger seat, which caused an instant reaction in his nervous system. A shakiness overtook his limbs, his hands. He wanted a copy of the paper, but fear stole his voice.

Parkman accelerated when the light turned green, then took a right onto Bloor Street.

Aaron's heart raced. He gulped down a few breaths and tried to speak up, but then nothing came. Those pictures, the news, had muted him.

Instead, he pointed.

"What?" Parkman asked.

"Pull in," he gulped, "here."

Aaron pointed at the strip mall on Runningbrook Drive.

"You need something?" Daniel asked.

Aaron nodded.

Parkman turned at the lights and pulled in. Aaron dropped out before the pickup stopped and strode for the convenience store, his legs feeling rubbery.

Behind him, he caught the muffled sounds of Daniel and Parkman asking each other what was going on.

Did the paper report their deaths? Was that why their faces made the front cover?

Many Torontonians knew Sarah's name. Some thought she was great, others didn't. Sarah never concerned herself with what other people thought of her, though.

But the front page? Sarah's face? Alex's face? To sell more papers?

Whatever it was, it wasn't good. The media aired dirty laundry, so if Sarah's face was on the front page, it was because she was either dead or the authorities were looking for her.

Inside the store, the clerk nodded at him. Aaron and Sarah were regulars, as this mall was the closest to their apartment building.

He grabbed a *Sun* without looking at the cover, flipped a dollar coin on the counter, and strode for the exit.

Once outside, he leaned against the brick wall and glanced down at the front page.

Manhunt was the first word he saw above Sarah's and Alex's head. A cop was dead. The authorities were looking to speak with Sarah in connection with the officer's death. A colleague of Sarah's, Alex—last name unknown at the time of printing—was a person of interest in the murder of three men found in a warehouse on Queen Street last night. The article considered both armed and dangerous and advised against approaching them. Several phone numbers were listed, along with Crime Stoppers, a tips line, and a direct line to Homicide.

"What's going on?" Parkman asked as he stepped up to Aaron.

Daniel was close behind.

Aaron glanced off toward the road and handed the paper to Parkman, then moved a couple of feet away to compose himself.

Parkman gasped behind him. "What the hell ..." he muttered.

Aaron pivoted back around, wiping his face with a hand, his resolve hardening. "Someone took us out of the picture last night, then set them up somehow."

"No shit." Daniel nodded.

"There's no way Sarah would've killed a cop unprovoked. And Alex? Three dead bodies? No way, not unless he was attacked or something."

"Let's go." Aaron started for the pickup. "We need a

phone. We have to call that homicide number and speak to Ricigliano. She was there for us last month. Shit, she even threw a cop party for us. If anybody knows what's going on, she will."

They piled back into the truck and were parked at Aaron's building a few minutes later. In the front foyer, Aaron buzzed Mike, the superintendent.

"How can I help you?"

"Mike, it's Aaron Stevens. I don't have my keys."

"Hold up. I'll be right there."

They waited in silence. Seconds later, Mike came around the corner and approached the door, a worried look on his face.

He opened it and let them in.

"The cops just left," he said.

"Just left?" Aaron asked.

"Come to my apartment for privacy. We should talk."

Mike led them down the hall and into his place. Once the door was closed, he nodded at Parkman and Daniel, then stared at Aaron.

"You guys want a drink, some water or something?"

Aaron shook his head. "Tell us what happened."

"You wanna take a seat in the living room?" Mike gestured behind him.

Aaron shook his head again. "No, we need to make some calls. We're in a hurry. Just tell us what's going on with the cops."

"Sarah almost got me arrested last night."

"What?" Aaron gaped at him. "How?"

"Last night, after whatever Sarah was up to, a handful of

cops showed up here. A few of them went up to your place to wait—"

"You let them in?"

Mike shrugged. "They said the warrant was coming and that a cop had been murdered. They were pretty angry."

"What else?"

"They had one cop in here asking me a bunch of questions about you two."

Aaron crossed his arms. "What did you tell them?"

"As little as possible, except for a batch of nice things, like how wonderful you guys are."

"You said this all happened last night. Why were they still here this afternoon?"

"Because Sarah showed up last night and came here to get me to let her in your apartment."

Aaron turned back to Parkman and Daniel. "She made it out of that restaurant, guys. That could be good news." He turned back to Mike. "What else?"

"When she came in, that cop I told you about was in my apartment. Well, he tried to grab Sarah, and she knocked him out cold."

"That's my girl."

"Then I gave her about two grand in cash."

"You did what?"

"Now, c'mon, Aaron, we both know she wouldn't kill that cop like they're saying, so I gave her some cash to get around until all this goes away."

"That put you at risk."

"No one knows. The cop was out cold." He shrugged again. "Besides, by the time I could wake him up, Sarah was gone. They tried to lock down the area, but they missed her. Then they stayed with me all night, and this morning, they were waiting for Sarah to try to return. And this one cop drilled me for hours, thinking I gave her some code to signal the cop was here. Like I was warning her of something."

"You did good, Mike. And we appreciate it."

"You think she's okay?" Mike asked.

"That's what we're going to find out."

Parkman stepped forward. "And you're sure the cops all left?"

Mike nodded. "The last one just left an hour ago."

Parkman faced Aaron. "I'm not sure they would completely leave. There's got to be one cruiser outside watching for Sarah, just in case."

"We didn't see one when we came in."

"That's the point. He'll be hidden well in an unmarked cruiser. Also, he's looking for Sarah, so they may not have noticed us or cared."

Aaron turned back to Mike. "Come up with us and let me in. I'll take my spare key with me so we don't trouble you again."

"Oh, it's no trouble." Mike nodded at the door. "You need money, too?"

"No, thanks, Mike." He patted the man's shoulder. "I've got some stashed in the apartment."

They rode the elevator in silence. At Aaron's door, Mike slipped his key in and opened it.

"Thanks, Mike, for everything. When this is over, we'll get your money back to you."

"No worries," Mike said as he shuffled down the

hallway.

They stepped inside, and Aaron closed the door.

"Boy," a woman said. "Am I glad to see you three." Detective Ricigliano stepped out of the kitchen area with another woman trailing her. "We've got a lot to talk about. Aaron, Parkman, Daniel, meet my new partner, Ingrid CK."

Chapter 26

ALEX SAT AT A metal table in an interview room, his right hand cuffed to the table. They'd left him there for at least an hour, which was an hour he couldn't waste. Sarah needed him, and he had to get to the airport by six. Yet, that task seemed completely insurmountable in the middle of a police station cuffed to a table.

The cuff was tight, but the hinge between the cuffs was breakable. All he had to do was lean forward, twist his body, then push off the wall. With his body weight and the proper amount of torque, the hinge would snap. During a session at the dojo on breaking holds and countermeasures over a year ago, one of his students presented handcuffs. They'd all learned several ways to remove them.

Once he was free, then what? Walk out into a room with dozens of armed police officers?

He would have to wait until the time was right. He'd meet them somewhere later if he missed meeting Darwin and Sarah at the airport for six.

This wasn't over. Whoever was behind this had outmaneuvered him and lied to him. He would deal with the charges brought against him when their enemies were found and stopped.

The door clicked, unlocked, then opened.

Without looking up, Alex detected one man entering the room. The man closed the door and stepped around to face Alex.

"They taking care of you here?" he asked.

He recognized the man from earlier. The same rugged features, the same chiseled jaw. He had taken the stage to announce the chief's delay. The deputy chief of police had removed his hat and held it between his biceps and chest.

"How do you think that went?" the man asked. "Wasn't your best performance."

Alex frowned. Performance? What an odd word to use.

"I'm Deputy Chief Roger Sterling, Specialized Operations Command." Sterling took a seat opposite Alex. "I've had the cameras turned off and all recording devices shut down." He stared at Alex, his eyes boring into him. "You've been a busy man."

Alex stared back without saying a word.

"I didn't agree with this outrageous plot of setting traps, but Silvio pushed, saying it was the right way to go."

That got Alex's attention, making his heart race. How high did this go? Were the authorities involved in the attempt on the police chief's murder?

"Well, you did good," Sterling continued. "Although I would've liked to see more effort in the attempted murder department, what you did will work. The knives you carried on your person and those bodies you left behind in the warehouse last night." He shook his head. "You did exactly as you were supposed to, so far."

Alex's eyebrow twitched before he could stop the frown. "So far?"

"That's right. You were employed to send a message."

"A message?" Alex asked.

The deputy chief leaned back in his chair and crossed his arms. "You were never supposed to kill the police chief. That was part one."

All he could offer the man was a blank stare. This was beyond his realm of understanding.

"The attempt was all that was needed," Sterling said.

"You knew I was coming?"

Sterling nodded. "Randy's people coerced you with the traps they set for your friends, and you played it right. Randy said he and Silvio organized everything. Now, as I understand it, you killed most of Silvio's men, which makes the attempt on Chief Clark even better, more credible." Sterling laughed. "I bet Silvio is happy. The money will be divided among the remaining few. You've made him even richer by your deeds, and you're still in the same spot, which is right where he wanted you, or rather, where I wanted you."

Alex leaned forward, then eased back. It was almost time to snap the cuff and do some damage to this man. He understood he'd been played when he saw Sarah back at that intersection, but he had no idea how bad it was.

"We needed the chief to know he wasn't above the law. That man …" Sterling glanced down at his lap, shaking his head. "That man runs his office like a high school principal, but this principal is dating the students."

"So you arrange for his murder?"

Sterling lifted his head and raised one eyebrow, appraising Alex. "No, you would've never been able to murder the chief of police—"

"In your opinion. I *chose* to let him live."

"Okay, fair enough, believe what you want. That press badge was smart, gotta hand it to you, but we knew you were coming, and we knew what to expect."

"Why me?"

"Does it matter? How about asking yourself that question when this is done because your task isn't over?"

"Sure it is. Fuck you." Alex rattled the handcuff for emphasis.

"Then your friends will die, and we all call it a day. Like I care." His right shoulder lifted as if indifferent to the idea. "I'll find someone else tomorrow, set new traps for another professional."

"You don't even have my friends. You're lying."

Sterling uncrossed his arms and produced a cell phone from the pocket of his pants. After accessing it and typing several times on the screen, he turned it for Alex to see.

Parkman, Aaron, and Daniel didn't look so good in the photos. Their wrists were bound, and it appeared their ankles were as well. Someone had placed a flashlight on them in the back of a truck and snapped their photos.

"We had set a trap for Sarah, but we missed her. Why she

didn't drink the wine was beyond us. She ended up killing our guy and getting away, but that doesn't matter now because she also killed a cop. Sarah will be picked up and arrested before the day's end. She's out of the picture and has nothing to do with this anymore."

Alex jerked the cuff again. *Traps* was the operative word. They'd all been trapped.

"And we missed Benjamin, but he's in the hospital." Sterling shrugged. "Who knows if he'll make it out of there alive."

Heat rose to Alex's face. Darwin was coming. Disco, too. With Sarah, they would be unstoppable. Even if he couldn't join them, the man sitting across from him would soon learn the reality of fucking with Sarah and her people.

Sterling flipped the picture until he showed Alex his friends from another angle, then pocketed the phone.

"So, if these three men mean anything to you, you'll continue to do as you're told."

"What do you want me to do?"

"The original task of killing the chief was to have you arrested, to bring you to me. Now you're here. Tonight, you'll be interviewed by detectives for most of the night. Tomorrow morning, you'll be brought before a judge in an arraignment process. At which point, you'll be remanded into custody as you are too dangerous to be released until trial. Are you following me?"

Alex nodded.

"Good. Once you're in the remand center, you're to find a man named Kevin Logan."

"Why?"

"He's the target. Kill Logan and your friends will be released." Sterling slapped his hands together. "It's that simple. That's part two, and that's the end."

"So I was never meant to kill the chief? This Logan was the job from the beginning?"

Sterling nodded, the edge of his lips rising in a half smile. "If we asked you to get arrested to get to Logan, it wouldn't have worked too well. By doing it this way, we also sent a strong message to the chief that he isn't above the law. If we want to take him out, he's touchable."

Alex stared at the man sitting across from him. "You smug son of a bitch."

He nodded. "That I am. Tell the investigators whatever you want tonight. They'll never believe you. It'll add to the remain-in-custody order."

"Why the chief? Why such a high-profile target in front of so many people? Why not an attempted murder charge on a John Doe? I'd still be sitting here before you."

"There are reasons that we needn't discuss here. The actual relevance means little to the actual job."

"Fuck you. I'm not doing it. Logan lives."

"Aww, are your feelings hurt because we didn't tell you the whole plan from the start?"

"Nothing to do with my feelings. I don't work for you."

Sterling laughed. "Sure you do." He placed his elbows on the table and leaned closer. "As long as I have the life of your three friends in my palm, you will do as you're told. And once Sarah's brought in, who knows what'll happen to the bitch while in custody? There are a lot of my men who'll want a crack at that ass."

The urge to kill the man overwhelmed Alex. He focused on the pain in his wrist when he held the cuff at the end of the chain hinge.

"How do I know this is the whole job? What's to stop you from naming another kill, then hurting my friends anyway?"

"Nothing, really, but I give you my word. Kevin Logan is the target, was the target, and will be the only target. You are all free to walk away when Logan is dead." He offered Alex that smug smile again. "Well, perhaps not you, as they'll have you on another murder charge then. Think of it as a sacrifice. You have to take one for the team."

Alex fidgeted with his fingers, wanting to wrap them around Sterling's throat. He stared down at his hands. "I overheard Silvio's men talking before I surprised them in that warehouse."

"Oh yeah? Did they say something interesting?"

"They argued with Silvio about the job. Said they should just do it instead of all the trouble of getting me involved."

"And?"

"When one guy said, 'I'll do the job myself,' Silvio responded with something like, 'What, you want to go to prison for this job?'"

Sterling nodded. "Then you were close to hearing the whole thing right there. This job needed someone in custody at the remand center to get to Kevin Logan, someone with your special skill set." Sterling pushed on the table, rising to his feet. "You've got your marching orders. Talk all the shit you want to whomever you want, I don't care. But at the end of the day, when you arrive at that remand center, Kevin

Logan must die, and it has to be tomorrow, which is a Monday. Logan's coming to court on Tuesday. You won't get another chance." Sterling moved to the door.

"And if I don't?" Alex asked.

Sterling nodded. "They'll never find the bodies of your friends. Silvio will die, too. I'll take care of anyone who knows the entire plan and start again. Logan will still die. Whether it's you or someone else, Logan has to die."

"Why is he so important? And why don't you handle it yourself?"

"C'mon Alex, you're smarter than that. I am handling it myself. I'm just not getting my hands dirty."

"Why Logan? What did he do?"

Sterling eyed him a moment, then cleared his throat. "Let's just say Logan has dangerous material that, if leaked, could hurt important people. A dead Logan hurts no one." He knocked on the door twice, opened it an inch, then pulled it shut. "We're all in this together, bound at the hip until it's done. And until it's done, we won't meet again. I'll hear about Logan's death and tell Randy to release your friends. You've got roughly twenty-four hours to complete the job." Sterling pushed the door open to leave.

"You're wrong," Alex whispered.

Sterling stopped, glanced down the hallway, then leaned back inside. "About what?"

"You said we won't meet again."

"We won't."

Alex turned bodily in his seat to face him. "Yes, we will. And when we do, you won't walk away from that meeting like you are now."

Sterling stared at him a moment longer, something akin to fear in his eyes, then closed the door rapidly.

Alex turned back in his seat, already forming a new plan.

Chapter 27

"This is madness," Aaron said. He jumped from his chair and strode to the window to peer over Mississauga. Ricigliano and her partner, Ingrid, just spent most of the hour reviewing everything they knew. "How long before your people grab the carpet truck?"

"Who knows, Aaron," Ricigliano said. "I've called it in. If they can find it, they will take it."

He checked the time. "One hour before Darwin lands." He turned back to everyone assembled in the room. "Are we all going to meet him?"

"Ingrid and I will try to get in to talk with Alex."

"I'm going to stop at the hospital to see Benjamin," Daniel said, "to let him know we're all good."

Ricigliano got up from her chair. "Call me once you meet with Darwin and Disco and bring them up to speed. By then, we'll be done with Alex and can figure out what to do next."

"In the meantime," Ingrid said, "don't talk to local cops or try to explain your abduction. The more hands in this water, the muddier it'll get."

"Ingrid's right," Ricigliano said. "We keep it to ourselves until tonight. Once we have everything, we'll act from a position of strength."

"Tell me once more about the bodies you found last night in that warehouse. They're known to the police?" Parkman asked.

Ingrid nodded. "We have a long list of petty crimes for all three of them. Never really spent much time on the inside. Always had a good lawyer, a solid defense."

"Known associates?"

"Always running in the same circles, but more of a gun for hire. Think small-time local mercenaries. Nothing the mafia would depend on, but if you wanted your cheating spouse to be beaten up, these guys were your best bet."

"What I'm getting at is, are you aware of others they're known to hang with, guys you can round up and sweat for information?"

Ingrid glanced at Ricigliano, who nodded and stepped forward. "We're looking into that."

"Well, we have to look harder, faster, because we need to find Sarah."

"We tried. She ditched her phone in the back of a truck. We pulled over the wrong guy."

"Okay, then that's that." Aaron started for the door but stopped when Ricigliano's phone rang.

Everyone stared at her as she grabbed her phone and

stared at the screen.

"It says private caller."

Aaron gestured with his hands to answer it.

Ricigliano tapped a few buttons. "Detective Ricigliano here."

She'd placed it on speaker. All five of them in Aaron's living room moved closer to form a circle around her.

"Detective," a familiar voice said. "Alex is in police custody."

Aaron would know Sarah's voice anywhere.

"We know. I'm heading in to talk to him now."

"Sarah," Aaron said, leaning closer. "Where are you?"

"Aaron?" Her voice cracked. "Is that you?"

"Yes, honey, it's me. Parkman and Daniel are here, too. We're organizing our next moves with Ricigliano and her partner, Ingrid."

"Oh my," she broke off. They all heard a muffled gasp as if she was trying to collect herself. "I thought …"

"We did, too," he said. "But we broke free. It's okay now, Sarah. Whoever is doing this got Alex involved somehow. Ricigliano and Ingrid are heading in to talk to him. We're going to the airport to meet Darwin. Where are you?"

"Outside a Tim Horton's on Airport Road."

"The one a little ways from Carlingview?" Parkman asked. "That same one we sat at while waiting to stop the matador beside Wendy, or a plane would crash?"

"The exact same one. Where I asked you about your name, Parkman."

Aaron frowned at him. "Your name?"

"Yeah," Sarah said. "We only know him by Parkman.

Oh, and those toothpicks of his."

"Which reminds me," Parkman said, heading toward the kitchen. "I've missed my toothpicks. Being abducted will do that to you."

"Okay, back on track, Sarah," Ricigliano said. "It looks like your boys will come meet you and get Darwin. Then we all need to meet somewhere and compare notes."

"So you're not pinging this phone, trying to arrest me anymore?"

"Sarah." Ricigliano glanced at the faces watching her. "I needed to be the one who picked you up so you wouldn't get hurt. We've got a dead cop out there, and we all know how other cops respond to that. And since talking with Aaron and figuring this shit out, I can see you guys were all set up and kidnapped. I'm on your side, always have been."

There was a pause as everyone waited for Sarah to respond. "I know where we'll meet," was all she said.

"Tell us."

"At the Wealth Exchange Building, downtown."

Ricigliano frowned. "That thirty-story glass tower on the corner of Yonge and Adelaide?"

"That's the one."

"Why there?"

"I'm not entirely sure, but my sister told me to set up a trap of our own."

They all exchanged a glance.

"Sarah," Aaron said as Parkman reentered the room, a toothpick in his mouth. "A trap? What kind of trap?"

"I'll know more once we're with Darwin. Come get me."

"Are you saying this ends tonight?" he asked.

"No idea. Vivian just told me where to be and how to set up the trap."

"What are we trapping?" Ricigliano asked.

"No idea."

"Your sister doesn't offer much, does she? Sounds frustrating."

"That's an understatement."

"Until then," Ricigliano said loud enough for everyone to hear. "We've got four hours. You guys meet up, and my partner and I will talk to Alex. See you all at the Exchange building for nine."

"That works for me," Sarah said. "Guys, come get me. I'll wait for you here. Damn, I'm happy you're all safe."

"On our way, Sarah. Don't move."

The line died.

"Well, that makes me feel better," Parkman said.

"What? The toothpick?"

Parkman scowled. "No, that we're going to pick up Sarah and then Darwin. Benjamin is safe in the hospital, and Alex is in custody. No one has died yet."

"Yet?" Aaron echoed. "This isn't over."

"Yet," Ricigliano repeated as she headed for the apartment doors. "Let's go. We've got four hours to figure this shit out."

"Hey," Aaron said, catching up to the detective. "That thing you said, what Sarah told you about a cop committing murder, did she elaborate on it?"

Ricigliano stopped in the hallway outside Aaron's apartment door and studied his face for a moment. "No, she didn't. Why?"

"I just need to know you'll be able to handle that if it happens in front of you."

"Aaron." Ricigliano's expression hardened. "Murder, or attempted murder, is still a crime where I come from. A private citizen or a decorated police officer—it doesn't matter one bit to me. Either one is going down."

"That's all I needed to hear."

Aaron watched Ricigliano and her partner head for the elevators without another word between them.

Something told him it would end tonight, whatever *it* was.

Based on the Sarah Roberts he knew there would be more bodies at the end of this long and dangerous road.

A powerful person with a lot of money and influence had to be behind all that had happened to them over the past twenty-four hours, and that didn't always mean he was a bad guy.

Sometimes, it was one of the good guys who had turned bad that made life miserable for so many others.

Sometimes, it was a cop who committed murder.

Chapter 28

Deputy Chief Roger Sterling poured himself a shot of whiskey to calm his nerves. It would all be over by this time tomorrow, and life could get back to normal. Until then, they had to keep their heads and wait for Alex to do as he was told.

He would gather them all for a meeting at his office and lay down the rules. The entire operation had gotten off track from the beginning. So many of Silvio's men had died, but that was their own incompetence. Fewer men meant fewer mouths that could tell a tale.

With his glass in hand, Sterling moved to the window and stared out over his fine city. One day, he'd be the chief of police instead of the deputy chief, and he'd definitely do things differently. The only chief he'd respected in the years past was Julian Fantino. That man got in front of the cameras, drove to the crime scenes, and managed to get his face in all the papers. For the people of Toronto, he gave them a chance to get to know him.

Chief of Police Thomas Clark wasn't like that at all. He kept it behind closed doors and avoided the cameras and the people.

The reason he did this was because of his affairs.

His time in office will be short-lived, and Sterling would see to it.

"What a disgrace," he mumbled to himself, then took a sip of his beverage.

After another few moments of contemplation, he lifted his phone and dialed the chief's direct line.

"Clark here."

"Hello, Clark. How are you feeling after this afternoon's brouhaha?"

"Brouhaha? Is that what we're calling it?"

Sterling sneered. "Call it what you like, Chief. A fiasco, kerfuffle, a fracas, or even chaos, but it still boils down to an attempted murder of the chief of police."

"That it does." Clark cleared his throat into the phone, then asked, "What can I do for you, Sterling?"

"It's a Sunday, and you've been through a lot today. I wanted to invite you to my office for a drink later this evening."

"Your office here?"

"No, in the investment tower. You know, I still hold an office on the top floor as part owner."

"I don't know, tonight's probably not good."

"Why's that?"

"I was planning on taking the wife to dinner. You know, have a quiet evening at home."

He just made that up on the spot. Sterling was sure of it.

"I'll make it interesting." Sterling sipped more whiskey, waiting for Clark to respond.

"How so?"

"Randy will join us."

Clark didn't respond immediately, as if he was trying to ascertain Randy's connection with his deputy chief.

"Do you mean the Randy I know?"

"The same one."

Another pause, then, "Well, Sterling, after today, I think it's better if I stay home. Having your life threatened in such a manner puts one off of social gatherings for a while."

"Come anyway, Chief Clark." Sterling deepened his voice to emanate a more serious tone. "We will be discussing a man named Logan."

Sterling could swear he caught a gasp of breath on the other line.

"Logan?" the chief whispered. "Kevin Logan?"

"I understand you might know him. Come to my office at eight this evening. We'll discuss it before Randy arrives at nine."

Sterling hung up the phone before he heard another whiny refusal. Then he dialed Randy's number and let it ring. Moments before he thought it would go to voicemail, Randy answered, sounding out of breath.

"What?" he shouted into the phone.

"Randy, it's Roger Sterling. What's going on?"

"Oh shit," he gasped out the words. "You don't want to

know."

"I most certainly do. Tell me what's happening."

"I drove back to the barn by the Grand River, which was empty."

"Empty?" Sterling shouted. He set his drink down to avoid spilling it. "How could that be?"

"They broke through the wall."

"But how?"

"Who fucking knows? I tracked them to the river."

"The river?" Sterling leaned against his desk. This was all falling apart at a rapid pace. None of Silvio's men knew what they were doing from the start.

"Looks to me like they rolled into the river. They're probably dead somewhere. Their bodies will turn up one day. Nothing to worry about."

"You'd better hope they're dead." His words seethed with anger.

"Hey, back off me. This wasn't my fault."

"Why are you running? Trying to find them?"

"No, when I was heading back to the truck, four or five cruisers pulled into the barn area and surrounded my vehicle."

"You stupid fuck. Nothing to worry about, eh?"

"What?" Randy shouted back at him.

"They aren't dead."

"How would you know?"

"One of them had to make it out alive to tell the cops where they were being held."

"Oh, damn." Randy paused. "Hadn't thought of that."

"Come back to Toronto."

"Why?"

"The chief and I are meeting at my Adelaide and Yonge Street office at nine. You need to be there."

"Well, I don't have wheels anymore."

"Find some. Just be here. And call Silvio. Tell him to be here too, or he won't get paid."

"He won't like that. He's lost several of his team members."

"Yeah." Sterling scoffed. "Like that'll be a hardship for him. The money was going to be divided among you all. Those dead team members just means the portions are higher per person."

"Oh, right. I guess there's that to consider. Is everything still a go?"

"Yes, everything is still a go. As long as Alex doesn't find out you've lost those three men."

"He won't hear it from me."

Sterling squeezed his free hand into a fist, clenching his teeth. "Look, let me worry about Alex. He's already been told about Kevin Logan. Everything is in place. Just like the original orders that you and Silvio received, it's almost done."

"Boy, we're sure glad you were in our corner for this."

"Just be at my office in the Wealth Exchange Tower at nine."

"Okay, I'll rent a car or steal one, but I'll be there."

"Silvio has to be there, too. Tell him."

"Will do—"

Sterling hung up and reared back his hand to throw the phone, then thought better of it. He needed his phone. What he didn't need was the anger.

He dropped in his chair, panting the anger out in controlled breaths.

The incompetence was off the charts. Not a single member of Sarah's group was in their possession anymore. After all the traps Silvio had planned, even delaying the first traps until Saturday night, knowing full well this operation had to be handled by Monday, was a foolhardy mistake. So many things could've gone wrong—too many—and they did go wrong.

And now they had no one. Silvio was roaming the streets of Toronto somewhere, thinking he had done his part and would be rewarded on Tuesday, while Randy was on foot, running through the woods near the Grand River, over an hour's drive away, the final two members of Silvio's bumbling gang of idiots.

Randy was the mistake. From the beginning, this was a dumb plan, hence the reason Sterling got so involved in it, so wrapped up. Someone had to salvage a sinking ship, even if he was the only one who could see it was sinking.

He set his phone down and stared at it.

The meeting tonight would put everyone on the same page. They would understand the stakes, who would live, and who would die.

It was the only way to success.

It was the only way for Sterling to find success.

Even though he didn't initiate this huge mess, he was the one who would see it through to the end.

If his hand was forced, he wasn't above murder.

At least he knew how to cover it up.

"Fucking jackasses," he muttered and got up from his chair.

He had things to plan for tonight's meeting.

Just in case …

Chapter 29

THEY HAD GIVEN HIM an egg salad sandwich and a bottle of water. Alex ate, savoring the taste, wondering when he'd be released back into the world. Could they hold him for several years? What would prison be like?

He already lived a disciplined life in his tiny apartment, at the dojo all day, then back to his apartment. With no family in the area and only the dojo to fall back on, Aaron and the rest of them had become his family.

Who could not respect Sarah for all she had done for the unjust, the ones who needed someone to stand up for them?

She still ran into every skirmish headlong without specialized training like he had. That sort of bravery moved him emotionally over the years. He'd do anything for her— anything righteous, noble.

If she knew he was being ordered to murder Kevin

Logan at the risk of having Aaron—Sarah's future husband and the father of her unborn child—killed, Alex believed she'd still tell him not to do it.

So, right up until Monday, when he got to the remand center Sterling spoke of, he would let Sterling believe he would follow through with the murder.

That would give Aaron, Parkman, and Daniel a chance to escape their current situation and survive this insane ordeal. Because after tomorrow, everyone was on their own. He couldn't save them all.

Sterling had mentioned traps.

That was exactly how Alex felt—trapped in his current situation, cuffed to a table, waiting for the investigators to come and ask a million questions. Trapped while he waited for the arraignment tomorrow morning. Trapped as he would be in the remand center and, finally, prison.

Sterling was right. Who would believe his story? The red fury throwing knives they removed from him when they arrested him would match the killing tool that executed the two men at the warehouse. During an autopsy, anyone worth his salt would figure that out. Before long, Alex would be charged with two counts of murder and one count of attempted murder of Toronto's chief of police.

Head hung low, his future looking worse by the second. He tried not to think about it, which was almost impossible considering where he currently sat. Overthinking caused a form of depression, and the last thing he wanted was to be lost down that rabbit hole again. Aaron had brought him out of it all those years ago.

And for that, he owed Aaron a debt that a lifetime of

service couldn't repay.

But murdering an innocent wasn't paying Aaron's debt.

Like a vicious circle, he was back to thinking about it—

Someone knocked on the door, then it popped open, and two people slipped inside, the door closing gently.

Alex detected them but didn't look their way. What was the use? He wasn't going to talk anyway. Nothing he said would be believed.

"Alex?" a woman said. "You okay?"

He recognized that voice. *Detective Ricigliano?*

A quick pivot of his head, and he peered up at her in her business attire, looking professional as always, with a slight bulge where her weapon was stashed under her light jacket. A blonde-haired woman stood beside her.

"Alex, this is my new partner, Ingrid CK."

He nodded at them, then stared back at the table. This was a pity call, a sorry-this-happened-to-you call. We'll do everything we can to help—the usual platitudes.

Chairs scraped the floor as they both sat.

"Have you lawyered up?" Ricigliano asked.

He shook his head out of respect for her and how she helped Sarah last month. Resolved to not talk to investigators, he'd at least show Ricigliano respect and, by extension, her partner, Ingrid.

"Can I get you anything?"

He shook his head.

"You don't want to talk?"

More head shaking.

"Then we'll talk."

This time, he glanced at her, leaned back, and nodded.

Ricigliano and Ingrid spoke to him for over fifteen minutes, telling him about Darwin coming and how Aaron, Parkman, and Daniel had escaped and were on their way to meet Sarah and Darwin. Benjamin was in the hospital and expected to fully recover after a tussle with a Brinks truck. Ricigliano went on to tell him that Sarah was about to execute some plan to set a trap for whoever was behind everything and that the detective would do everything she could to clear Alex's name.

"But for me to help you, Alex, you've got to tell us everything."

The relief was overwhelming. Everyone was free and safe and soon to be with Darwin. He could forget the entire plan to go after Kevin Logan. None of his people, his loved ones, were in jeopardy.

He slumped in his chair, the pressure on his shoulders oozing off him in waves. Letting out a huge breath he'd been holding, he glanced heavenward, lips parting, and thanked whoever looked down upon them that everyone was safe. Then he sat still to let the relief sink in as Ricigliano and Ingrid stared at him.

"Alex?"

He blinked, his gaze lowering to Ingrid's face, then Ricigliano.

"I never intended to kill anyone."

"We know that." Ricigliano didn't sound convinced.

"No." He leaned forward, the single handcuff on his right wrist clanging with the movement. "The attempted murder charge. The one that implies intent is wrong. I did what I did for show."

Ingrid frowned. "For show?" She glanced at her partner, then back at Alex. "Why would anyone put on a show of killing the chief of police?"

Alex faced her. "Because I was told to kill Thomas Clark, your chief, or the people behind the abductions of my friends would kill Aaron, Parkman, Daniel, and Sarah. If I'd known they weren't still being held captive, I wouldn't have even been in the area. They showed me pictures of Aaron and Parkman tied up."

Ricigliano leaned forward. "Tell us everything. What did they say, exactly? Where did you meet?"

Alex shook his head. "This room is live. Others will hear. It's too dangerous."

"But Alex, two things are wrong with what you just said. Whoever listens in on this room will be investigating these crimes. That will benefit you. And how could your friends be killed if they aren't captive anymore?"

"You'll have to think about it. Unfortunately, I can't spell it out for you because this room is wired."

Ricigliano and Ingrid shared a look.

Ricigliano opened her mouth. "Sarah said something about a cop—"

"Wait," Ingrid broke in. "Not here, not now."

Ricigliano's eyes widened, and then she got up from the table and exited the room, the door slamming behind her.

Ingrid sat quietly, drumming her fingers on the table. Alex sat with his own thoughts, wishing he was on the outside, helping Sarah and Darwin.

The door opened several minutes later, and Ricigliano retook her seat.

"Recording's off."

"Completely?" Alex asked. "Everything?"

She nodded.

"Still not safe."

"How so?"

"Ingrid." Alex turned her way. "Any chance you could go out and keep an eye on this room? Ensure no one is listening in or watching us, trying to read our lips?"

"Seriously?"

The silence in the room held weight.

After a moment, she rose from her chair and exited the room.

"You must have something important to tell us."

"I do," Alex whispered without moving his lips. After a few moments, when he suspected Ingrid was in place, he leaned closer to Ricigliano and told her everything. Starting with Sarah's text asking if he was okay, to a planned meeting at the dojo with Daniel and Benjamin, the warehouse—mentioning the men died as Alex was defending himself, which was partly true—all the way to Kevin Logan and what the deputy police chief, Roger Sterling, asked of him.

"Roger Sterling?" Ricigliano whispered. "No fucking way."

Spent, Alex leaned back in his chair until the hinge on the cuff stopped him.

"It goes that high?" she asked.

"Find the link to Kevin Logan," Alex whispered. "You'll find your answers."

"Because having Logan killed is a coverup."

Alex nodded. "What is it about Logan that has the deputy

chief afraid? Has he got something on him? Whatever it is, Logan is in court on Tuesday, and Sterling can't afford that. He wants Logan taken out tomorrow. That's why I'm in here."

"Something doesn't add up."

"Ask me."

"Why try to kill the chief of police? What if you were successful? Then what? I mean, how could they know they could stop you, whoever they are?"

Alex shrugged. "That part I'm not clear on, either. Sterling claimed to know I was coming and told me I wouldn't've gotten close enough to do the job, but he was wrong. If I wanted the chief dead, I would've killed him."

"See, and I believe that. I know you guys. Sterling doesn't."

After a few moments of silence, Ricigliano stared at him, shaking her head slightly. "You've been set up from the get-go. You were attacked and had to kill those men in the warehouse—"

"But not the other guy. I don't shoot people. Silvio did that."

She nodded. "And after the warehouse, you were given an ultimatum and couldn't do it. Your attempted murder charge is bogus because you didn't *attempt*"—she used air quotes on that word—"to kill anyone."

"Innocent if you were a jury of one."

"Which makes all the sense in the world for Sarah and her group." Ricigliano pointed at the door. "But all those people out there think you'll do twenty years, easy."

"And Sterling will guarantee that because I won't kill

Logan—"

The door smashed open as if it was kicked. It snapped to the extent of its hinges, then rebounded into the two men barging in.

"What's the meaning of this?" the tallest man shouted. "Who the fuck are you?"

Ricigliano's face hardened as she got to her feet slowly. "Exit this room. We will take our beef outside."

"No fucking way." The man stepped forward in a challenging manner.

If Alex was ever going to break the cuff, now was the time.

"This is our case," the man yelled in Ricigliano's face. "He went after the chief of police." He pointed at Alex without looking at him.

Alex bent the hinge back, leaned his body over it, and then twisted himself, using the wall to push off from.

The hinge snapped just like it had in his attempts at the dojo last year. The minimal pain in the wrist fired him up.

The man hovering over Ricigliano caught Alex's movement and started turning his way when Alex launched upward, his arms wrapping around the large man's neck. Seemingly weightless like a monkey, Alex let his lower body swing past the man's back as he locked his right arm onto the carotid and clamped down. Alex's body weight added to the pressure and caused the man to spin toward the wall, his large body acting as a shield in the event weapons were drawn.

"Alex!" Ricigliano shouted. "Don't."

But they were already falling, Alex behind the man, his

body in front, as weapons were drawn.

Alex ignored them as he tightened his grip. The large cop grappled with Alex's forearm, but nothing would make him take that arm away. He was too angry, too pissed off with all that had happened. The unfairness of it all infuriated him.

Men shouted, and guns were drawn. Others pushed into the tiny interrogation room.

Ricigliano pulled her weapon, but she aimed it at the other cops filling the door.

"Everyone calm down," she shouted. "Calm the fuck down." She refocused on Alex. "Let him go."

Alex waited, the struggle in the man decreasing, the oxygen to his brain limited.

"Alex, please."

"He threatened you," Alex said to stall her. He needed five, maybe ten more seconds. "No one threatens a woman like that. Only a wimpy bully would be such an asshole."

Ricigliano pushed one of the men as they moved closer. "Get back. Give us some room." She slipped her weapon back in its holster. "Okay, Alex. C'mon, this isn't the way."

The man was out, his hands having dropped from Alex's forearm.

He waited another three seconds, then released him.

The cop slumped to the floor beside him, and three men jumped on Alex.

He considered fighting them, taking a weapon, and escaping, but then he'd dig a hole he could never climb out of. A leg here, an arm there, all the pressure points he imagined jamming. Even when they grabbed his wrists, he considered two different ways to snap out of it and break a few bones.

Ricigliano shouted for them to be gentle, to go easy on him.

Alex felt the punches rain down. His anger spent for the moment, he allowed the abuse.

At least it wasn't Ricigliano getting hurt.

Or Sarah.

Chapter 30

After meeting at the coffee shop, then heading over to arrivals at the airport, Darwin exited right on time.

Sarah kept her hair up under a hat to avoid detection by members of the Toronto Police Service and even stayed outside the terminal when Aaron and Parkman went in to meet Darwin.

Outside, when Darwin saw her, he set his bags down and wrapped his arms around her.

"Congratulations," he whispered in her ear. "This is the first time I've seen a pregnant Sarah." He leaned back to stare at her. "No real bulge yet, though."

"Soon," she said, placing a hand on her stomach. "Soon."

Darwin addressed Aaron, then shoved out his hand. They shook. "Congrats, man."

"Thanks. We're just hoping this shit will all go away so

we can, you know, raise a family in peace."

"I hear you." Darwin glanced around at Parkman and Daniel, nodding. "Great to see everyone is here and healthy. Where's Alex and Benjamin?"

"More later," Sarah said. "Let's get you settled."

They led Darwin toward the borrowed pickup truck they were still driving.

"That's not going to fit all of us," Darwin said.

"Where's Disco?" Sarah asked. "We thought he was meeting you here."

"He is, but not *at* the airport. Too public for his face. He's waiting at the hotel."

"Which one?"

"The Carlingview Inn."

Parkman stepped forward. "I know the one. Daniel and I will take a taxi. Darwin, just go with Sarah and Aaron, and we'll meet at the hotel and get everyone up to speed at the same time."

"Any chance I could catch a nap and have a shower?" Darwin asked. "Long flight and seven hours' time difference between Italy and Toronto."

"Nope, sorry," Sarah said, leading him toward the pickup again as Parkman and Daniel veered off toward the taxi stand. "We have one hour to talk, grab a bite, then go set a trap for someone."

Darwin stopped walking. "A trap? For someone?"

Sarah nodded and gestured toward the pickup.

Darwin stayed rooted to the spot. "You don't know who you're trying to trap?"

"We know they're involved in everything that's

happening, but we don't know who they are."

"Great." Darwin started walking again. "Nothing's changed a bit, has it?"

The three of them piled inside the pickup and exited the parking lot with Aaron driving. Ten minutes later, they pulled into the hotel's parking and saw Disco's Hummer at the back of the lot.

"I'm willing to wait, Sarah," Darwin said, a smile creasing his lips. "But the curiosity is killing me. When you called and asked me to come to Toronto, someone had jumped Parkman, Aaron was gone, and the cops were chasing you. You mentioned something about a gut feeling and Vivian being quiet. I show up at the airport just now, and you're all together. How did that happen? Are you guys working miracles?"

"Not sure about miracles."

"I'm so curious as to what happened."

"The whole story is coming, told once, in front of everyone, Disco included."

Darwin nodded. "That's what I thought."

They exited the pickup with Aaron pulling one of Darwin's bags and headed toward the lobby. Parkman and Daniel were just exiting a taxi when they got there.

The lobby stood out as clean and well-decorated. Several couches were arranged throughout the open space, with a cavernous sixteen-foot ceiling echoing their footfalls.

The clerk glanced up and edged toward the counter to address them, but the man sitting alone on one of the couches in the lobby caught their collective attention.

"Disco?" the man asked, rising to his feet.

Sarah and Darwin nodded at the same time.

"He's waiting upstairs."

With Darwin's two bags, they needed two elevators to rise to the fifth floor. On the way up, Sarah checked the time. They had one hour at the most. Then, they had to get downtown.

The trap had to be set as Vivian suggested, or whoever they were trying to trap would get away.

At seven, she would call Ricigliano to ensure she was coming, too, provided she hadn't heard from her by then.

Could everything come together tonight and end this current nightmare? Would Alex just be released from custody, and they could all return to their lives after this?

She highly doubted that was the case.

Even though Vivian hadn't told her specifically it would end tonight, Sarah was sure this mess would be with them for quite some time.

As of tomorrow, she and Aaron would have some hard decisions about when and where they would have their baby.

And where they would want to raise him or her.

Because nowhere seemed safe anymore.

Chapter 31

Deputy Chief of Police Roger Sterling checked his piece. The weapon was ready if he needed it. No harm would come to Thomas Clark, though. Sterling was readying his weapon for self-defense because Silvio wouldn't like what he had to say—or rather, Silvio wouldn't like Sterling's questions.

They would get to the bottom of it all tonight, and then they could all go their separate ways, with everyone on the same page.

Sterling opened the rooftop patio and stepped out into the fading light of the October sky. He inhaled deeply, content with how he'd handled everything thus far. He'd committed no crimes himself. Coordinating with Randy by phone and speaking with Alex in the interview room could be construed as an accessory. Still, no one would suspect the special operations commander as consorting with criminals.

He moved to the railing of the thirtieth-floor patio and glanced down at Yonge Street. After watching the cars edge up and down the street, a few horns sounding, he strode to the other side and stared down at the alley behind his building.

When he gave Alex his marching orders, which was something Randy was supposed to do, but he was too busy fucking everything up, Sterling could be construed as being *involved* in criminal activity, but how would that ever come up? Alex's word against a decorated deputy chief's word? It was highly unlikely that anything would ever come of it unless the person behind the operation got more involved and outed him. But even then, he was in too high a position ever to be mistaken for a common thug.

Considering every angle, thinking of all the possibilities, Roger Sterling could not come up with a single moment where he made a misstep.

Yet something nagged at him. Like capture was right around the corner.

He leaned on the railing and wondered if that was guilt talking. Wasn't fear the basis of all guilt? The fear of getting caught? Fear of being exposed for who you truly are?

However, Sterling had always been fearless in his career and personal life. His divorce had cost him dearly, but fearless to the core, he fought through that, and now his ex-wife was married to some security guard.

To see this through, he had to remain fearless for several more days and not let doubt overtake him. But doubt that he'd dropped the ball somewhere, that a dozen cops were about to barge through his door at any time and arrest him for accessory to murder, pulled at his thoughts.

He needed a drink but waited until everyone left the meeting. Once the Chief of Police, Thomas Clark, was up to date, they could proceed cautiously.

Alex was dealt with. Kevin Logan was as good as dead. That was in motion, and nothing could stop that from happening now.

When he'd discovered Randy had fucked up and lost his three captives, he'd called the station and assigned two trustworthy detectives to Alex's case, with explicit instructions that no one spoke to Alex without his approval.

Sterling checked his watch. They'd be talking to Alex now.

The buzzer rang inside the office.

Chief of Police, Thomas Clark, had arrived.

Sterling trudged back inside, saw Clark in the lobby on the little camera by the door, and clicked the button to give him access.

"Come on up," Sterling said.

He stared at the camera for several heartbeats, but no one else entered with Clark. The door closed behind him without interruption.

Sterling clicked on the camera to his right.

Clark was at the elevator, patiently waiting for it to arrive. A moment later, the man got on the lift when the doors opened and began his ascent.

The chief was military with his punctuality. Not just on time but fifteen minutes early every time.

Sterling adjusted his shirt, checked himself in the mirror to ensure his piece couldn't be easily seen under his suit jacket, and then went to the door.

When he opened it, the elevator was just arriving.

Clark stepped off, his face a mask of concern.

"Clark, so good to see you." Sterling offered his hand to shake.

Clark clutched it, shook quickly, then dropped his hand. "This better be good, Sterling." Then he strode past him and entered Sterling's office. "Got anything to drink?"

Sterling hesitated a moment to collect himself. The chief was in a serious bind, and all he wanted was a drink.

Clark rummaged around in the office kitchen in the first room to the right of the door.

"Found one," Clark said.

Sterling entered his office, closed the door, and locked it behind him.

"Join me on the patio, will you?" Sterling said as he passed the open kitchen door.

Clark followed him, a glass with amber-colored liquid in his hand. He swirled it around, ice cubes clinking against the edges.

"What's this about, Sterling?" They stepped out onto the patio. "Wait, don't tell me. You've found out who hired that kid Alex, and you wanted to tell me in private so I'm not shocked in front of others. Is that it?" Clark sipped his drink, the ice cubes irritating Sterling.

"No, that's not why you're here."

Clark frowned, then moved to sit on one of the patio couches. He kicked a leg up to rest on the other leg and leaned back, totally relaxed.

"Then why am I here?" He drank more, this time gulping

back a mouthful.

This impromptu meeting was obviously bothering the chief.

"Look, Alex tried to kill you today."

"Right." He nodded. "I was there. And I have to thank you."

Now, it was Sterling's turn to frown as he sat opposite the chief. "Thank me? Why's that?"

"You saved the day. You rallied the officers and kept me safe. That man is quite something. It took several officers to bring him down. Without you in my corner, I'm not so sure we could've stopped him." Clark raised his glass in a toast, then drank from it.

"Well, sir, I was just doing my job."

"That you did. Now, why am I here and not at home with my wife?"

"Because of your connection to Kevin Logan."

The look in the chief's eyes told Sterling the man knew exactly what he was talking about.

"Connection?" Chief Clark said, his Adam's apple bobbing as he swallowed. He drank more, the glass almost empty. "What connection?"

"Look, Chief, let's be frank, shall we?"

The chief nodded. "By all means. Say what's on your mind."

"I have been made aware of your relationship with Randy."

The chief stopped moving, the ice in the glass gone quiet. He stared at Sterling, and then, after several moments, the chief blinked, and the spell was broken. He leaned back farther, if that was possible, like he was sinking into the couch, placed an arm up on the back of the sofa, and drank more of his beverage. The two fingers he'd poured were almost gone.

"Relationship?"

"Don't insult me, sir." Sterling had gone out of his way to protect the chief, and he wouldn't have him drinking his whiskey on his terrace, disrespecting him.

"Okay, so …" the chief trailed off, inhaled, set his glass down, and leaned forward, elbows on his thighs. "What does my relationship with Randy have to do with the attempt on my life today?"

"That's what I was hoping to find out tonight."

"And how are we going to achieve that task?"

"By speaking with the man who was hired to do the job in the first place."

"What job?" Clark got to his feet and moved to the railing. The sun's waning light cast a soft, orange glow on the chief's face. "Wait, speaking with the man who was hired for the job in the first place leads me to Alex." He spun around to face Sterling. "You're bringing Alex here?"

Sterling rose from the couch and moved beside the chief. "No, I am not bringing Alex here. That man is in custody, and I've got two of my best investigators interviewing him as we speak. Johnson and his partner."

The chief shook his head. "No, they're not."

Sterling's eyebrows knitted together. "Excuse me?"

"Some homicide detectives got to Alex first, and when your boys showed up, there was a fight."

Sterling stepped back and glanced around. What the hell

was happening? Silvio's men bungled everything at their end, and now his own detectives were fucking things up.

"You seem concerned," Clark said.

"I am concerned, Chief because I gave explicit orders that no one was to speak with that prisoner except my two detectives. That boy is up on some serious charges, and I wanted two of my personal best men to handle this case so nothing was missed or screwed up. And now I hear—wait, what homicide detectives?"

"Ricigliano and Ingrid."

His right hand clenched into a fist, his left cupping it. He should've figured it out. That bitch was known to work with Sarah Roberts in the past. They even collected a bunch of cops and threw a party for Sarah and her friends at the dojo on Queen Street last month. Considering what had happened of late, when the media ran with it, the department would be embarrassed. Could things potentially get worse?

"What was she in speaking with Alex about? Have you heard the recordings?"

Clark shook his head. "Ricigliano had all the cameras and audio silenced. Ingrid stood guard outside to make sure no one listened in."

"You said there was a fight. What happened?"

Chief Clark stared at him momentarily, then moved back to the couch, picked up his glass, and downed the rest. Then he dropped back onto the sofa.

"You brought me up here to ask about activity at the station?"

"No, there's more to discuss." Sterling checked his watch. Silvio and Randy would be there in just over a half hour, provided Randy found a ride from up north. "Just tell me about this fight first."

"From what I understand, your men discovered Ingrid first. Then they barged into the interview room and shouted at Ricigliano, demanding to know what she was doing in there."

"So far so good. She had no right to be speaking with Alex."

"Well." The chief shrugged. "That's a matter of opinion. She's point on the murders in that warehouse on Queen Street, and she's homicide, so there's that."

"Fine, what happened next?"

"Alex jumped Johnson."

"Johnson?" Sterling asked, his mouth dropping open. "Johnson's got to be two-hundred-fifty pounds of muscle."

Clark was nodding. "The same Johnson. I heard Alex knocked him out in less than thirty seconds. Guns were drawn, but luckily, no one fired a shot in such a confined space."

"What the hell?" Sterling couldn't believe what he was hearing. "Wait, wasn't Alex secured? Handcuffed to the table?"

Clark was still nodding. "He snapped the handcuff."

"The handcuff?" Sterling's voice rose several notches. "How the hell does someone do that?"

"Well, not the handcuff itself. I understand it was the hinge."

Sterling stepped away and gripped the railing, looking out over the sprawling city of Toronto. A helicopter circled the CN Tower, and the city was a bustle of Sunday night activity.

He collected himself and turned back to Clark.

But the chief was gone.

"Chief Clark?" he called.

"In here," the man's voice came from inside the office. "Getting another shot of that whiskey."

"Grab me one, too."

A minute later, the chief stepped back onto the patio with two glasses, offering one to Sterling. He took it and drank, letting the whiskey burn the back of his throat.

"So," Clark said. "You were talking about finding the people involved in the attempt on my life. Are you saying Alex wasn't acting alone?"

Sterling shook his head. "Someone is pulling the strings."

"Tell me what you know."

"Ever heard of a man named Silvio?" They retook their seats. Deputy Chief Sterling was in his element. Just two men discussing crime on a rooftop patio while sipping whiskey.

"Silvio?" The chief seemed to mull it over. "Just one name?"

Sterling shrugged. "We don't know his other names. It may even be fake."

"Okay, how is this Silvio involved?"

"He was hired to take out Kevin Logan."

Clark spit out his whiskey and leaned forward, wiping at his mouth. "What?"

"Silvio was hired—"

"I heard you the first time," Clark snapped. "Why would anyone want Logan dead?"

"Because Logan has court on Tuesday."

"And? What's that got to do with anything?"

"Word is, Logan has damaging information on you."

Now Clark looked completely stunned. The man leaned forward and set his glass on the table. Sterling even detected a subtle shake in his hand. If Chief Clark knew any of this beforehand, he was putting on the performance of his life. Histrionics aside, that was one of the reasons he wanted a private meeting with the chief. To feel him out, drop a few informational bombs on the man to see how he'd react. So far, the chief was innocently deceived and completely out of the loop, which was bittersweet. Sterling wanted the chief's job, but he didn't want it due to the chief being removed from office because of the crime of murder. There were other ways to obtain a new job.

"What kind of information?" the chief asked.

"The damaging kind."

"You said that." Clark glanced up at the purplish clouds easing by. Sterling kept his eyes glued to the chief's face. "So, more people know about Randy and me?"

"I believe that to be the case."

Clark closed his eyes, then opened them and met Sterling's gaze. "When should I expect the world to know I'm gay and that I've been cheating on my wife for years with Randy? I mean, that's what this is about, isn't it? You wanted to tell me first, to my face?"

"Chief Clark, I've known your secret for quite some time. Perhaps a few others in the department know. But who cares? No one has ever brought it to my attention. You and Randy kept it to yourselves quite well."

"Randy was a good cop coming up through the ranks, and now he's a solid undercover cop."

Sterling nodded. "I know."

"When he went deep undercover, we had a meeting, and it all sort of, you know, came together."

"When was that?"

"About three years ago."

"And since Randy was undercover for so long, running with street gangs and trying to infiltrate local mercenaries, he was accessible to you without anyone knowing."

The chief nodded. "I would like to avoid my wife hearing it from someone else." The man's eyes had glazed over. "I need to be the one to tell her."

"That may not be necessary."

"Why not?"

"Only Logan wants this to come out, and someone hired that man I mentioned moments ago, Silvio, to deal with Logan."

"Sounds like they hired Alex to kill me, too." Clark covered his face with his hands.

"Silvio is connected to a small group of criminals that had recently employed Randy."

The chief removed his hands from his face and stared at Sterling. "What are you saying? That Randy has been hired to kill me now?"

Sterling shook his head. "No, absolutely not. Listen, Randy got called in on the job, and when he showed up, he heard the name Logan, knew who Logan was, and called me."

"Why would he call you?"

"Because he didn't want to upset you, and Randy knew I'd do the right thing by you. We're all in this together."

"I'm so confused. In what together?"

"Kevin Logan is set to blackmail you, and Silvio was hired to take out Logan. Silvio's brilliant plan was to get Alex to be jailed at the remand center to do the deed, but to convince Alex, he had Alex's friends abducted, which are Sarah Roberts and her people."

"That's what's been happening all over town for the past twenty-four hours?" the chief asked. "Holy fuck." He placed a hand on his forehead and stared skyward.

Sterling nodded, then sipped from his drink. Clark was so grief-stricken that he'd forgotten about his beverage.

"The problem is, Alex's friends—Sarah Roberts and her team of martial artists—are a hard group to control."

"Hence the carnage that has beset the city. Those murders in the warehouse."

"Exactly." Sterling checked the time, then stared at his chief. "But I have Silvio coming here in fifteen minutes. We'll get to the bottom of this."

Clark jumped to his feet. "Are you insane?"

Sterling smiled and slowly got to his feet. "You have other options?"

"You're bringing a criminal here? To discuss his activities with the chief of police and the deputy chief? A man we know to be responsible for murder? This is madness."

"Chief Clark, you've dealt with men like him in the past. Consider Silvio a criminal informant, a CI with the best sort of information. Randy will be here soon as well. Your deep undercover boyfriend will arrive with Silvio to help us discover the truth."

Clark glanced at his drink, then huffed a heavy breath and turned toward the railing again. At the railing, he stretched his back in a nervous gesture, faced Sterling, strode back to the couch, plopped down, and emptied his glass once again.

"What is this truth you speak of?"

"I want to learn who hired Silvio so we can arrest the bastard. Whoever that is will be arrested for the murder of the police officer behind the motel in Mississauga last night, as well as the murder of Domenic in that warehouse. Sure, Alex can stay in prison for years for his role in all this, but Silvio will go a long way in offering us the true criminal mastermind behind it all, and Randy will testify about his role in the kidnappings. He witnessed Silvio murder Domenic. I'm sure Silvio would love to give up the person who hired him for a plea deal. What are your thoughts?"

"I feel sick to my stomach that all this was happening behind my back. No wonder Alex tried to kill me today." Clark seemed like he was trying to collect himself. "Have you got anyone in mind?"

"In mind?"

Clark stared into his eyes. "Who hired Silvio?"

"Yes," Sterling nodded. "But I'll keep that to myself until the man arrives. Wouldn't want to open Pandora's Box with suspicions."

Clark nodded, then grabbed his empty glass and strode back inside.

Sterling let him go this time.

From the beginning, he didn't want to tell the man that he suspected Randy, the chief's lover, in the plot.

Because it was Randy who was cheating on the chief.

It was Randy who leaked the affair to Logan in the first place.

And now it was Logan who was doing all the threatening because he was hurt. The man was about to spend serious time in prison, and with the chief of police as a part-time lover for years before Randy came into his life, Logan is angry and wants some sort of vengeance.

So, of course, Randy, a deep undercover cop with a stellar reputation, would need this information muzzled at all costs.

Which was another reason Randy was invited to the meeting tonight. Sterling needed to look in his eyes and watch the tells of a liar.

It had to be Randy behind it all. No one else fits the profile.

Sterling checked his watch again.

They would be arriving at any time.

The shit was about to get real.

He followed the chief inside.

Chapter 32

SARAH GOT OUT OF the Hummer and stared up at the building.

They had briefed Disco and Darwin at the hotel, then after hearing from Ricigliano and Ingrid, they all met downtown and were just now parking half a block from the Wealth Exchange Building on Adelaide and Yonge Street.

"Everyone knows the drill," Sarah said. "We're all going in blind. Vivian has not told me a thing other than to be in the lobby of this building tonight. I have no idea why, but everyone should be on the lookout."

They strode up the sidewalk, meandering around others as the streets were still bustling on a Sunday evening.

"What are we looking for again?" Disco asked.

"Anything suspicious, a familiar face, anything."

Aaron slowed at the streetlight on Adelaide and glanced upward. "Tall building," he whispered.

Sarah followed his gaze. "Hey, is that someone standing on the roof?"

Ricigliano stepped up beside her. "Looks like a rooftop balcony of some sort." She glanced back down as the light changed, and they started to cross the street. "If you're ever up on the CN Tower and looking down at all the smaller buildings, you'll see how many have patios, rooftop pools, and gardens, too. The rich know how to live."

"Doesn't the Royal York Hotel have a rooftop garden they use for their restaurant's kitchen?" Sarah asked.

Ingrid nodded. "I've heard they do."

Once they were across the street, they all entered the Starbucks, got a coffee, then met by the access to the building's lobby.

"Once more," Sarah started, "we're acting a little like security guards and just watching the entrances and exits. I think we're the trap for whoever is in this building."

Everyone nodded. Darwin yawned.

"You going to be okay?" she asked him.

He nodded, his eyes bloodshot. "After this, though, I'm heading to bed."

"Of course." Sarah faced Disco. "You armed?"

"Yes." He shot a glance at the detectives, but neither one acknowledged his comment.

"Okay, then we're set. Everyone's lapel mics work?"

Disco had provided five microphones, similar to the kind the Secret Service uses, where the device was in their ear, and the mic was on their lapel. There were seven of them, leaving Aaron and Ingrid without Disco's device, but that worked because Aaron was staying close to Sarah, and Ingrid was sticking with her partner.

"The building closes at nine," Sarah said. "After that, the doors automatically lock on a timer." She checked her watch. "This is it. We have five minutes. All set?"

Everyone nodded.

"Then let's do this. As planned, from the map on everyone's cell phone, we each take an exit point and watch it."

They filed into the lobby of the Wealth Exchange Tower through the Starbucks access.

"How long are we here for?" Parkman asked.

"One hour, maybe two. Could be less."

Several of them nodded, then they dispersed. Ricigliano was to take the main lobby with Ingrid sitting off to the side in case security came to clear the building. The plan was they'd show their badges and stay on site.

Sarah and Aaron would take the rear exit by the alley, which was in earshot of the two homicide detectives. Parkman was taking the underground garage access at the street, with Darwin at the west exit and Disco at the east.

As far as they could tell, they had everything covered.

At the back exit, Sarah slid to the floor, her back against the wall, staring out the glass door to the back alleyway.

"Any idea why we're here?" Aaron asked from a few feet to her left. "You know, something you haven't told everyone else?"

Sarah waited a heartbeat, then met his gaze. "You know me too well."

He offered her a warm smile. "Tell me."

"Death."

"What do you mean, death?"

"People die within the next hour or so."

"Who?"

"I have no idea. That's all Vivian said."

Aaron leaned against the wall. "Death," he whispered to himself.

"Yeah," she whispered back. "Sucks."

"And you don't think we should tell the others?"

Sarah shook her head. "They won't die."

"Then who dies?"

Sarah looked away, staring outside again.

"Not sure, but I know it's not one of us."

"Why aren't you sure, though? Sounds risky to me. Sarah, we've got five other people here sticking their necks out for you. Benjamin's in the hospital, and Alex is in custody. Tell me something more than, I'm not sure."

"I'm unsure because Vivian told me to keep it to myself." She didn't want to look at him. Otherwise, he'd see the anger in her eyes. "Don't put this on me," she whispered. "I didn't do this. It was done *to* us."

"What?" Aaron asked, his voice rising.

"Aaron." She faced him now. "There are people here who wouldn't believe me." She pointed at the homicide detectives near the front of the building. "So, for now, until we see this through, we keep it to ourselves. Vivian has not expressed danger to them, and we're all professionals. Everyone here knows the risk."

"Ricigliano would believe you. Tell her."

"You know what, that makes sense. But this one stays with me. For now."

Aaron nodded after several moments. "I'll back that."

"Good." She stared outside at the fading light of day and waited for whatever was coming.

According to Vivian, they wouldn't have to wait long and couldn't stop it anyway.

Better to let things be as they were.

And keep the information close to her chest.

Chapter 33

Silvio entered the foyer and slowed at the sight of two well-dressed women. What was this? A shakedown?

Both women appraised him, checking him from head to toe and back. Their eyes met, and at that moment, Silvio knew they were cops or detectives or something. They worked for Sterling. They were guarding the lobby. That had to be it.

He nodded.

They nodded back.

He moved toward the elevator, listening for their footfalls, but neither woman moved from where they stood by the front glass doors.

When he pushed the button to summon the elevator, he glanced back.

The women were staring outside, not interested in him at

all. The one on the left checked her watch and shook her head.

He exhaled slowly. They were waiting for someone. A ride, maybe, someone who was late. The women had nothing to do with him.

The elevator door opened in front of him, and someone whispered something to his right at the same moment. Silvio stepped forward onto the elevator, glancing over his shoulder. At the end of the corridor, a man leaned against the wall with his back to Silvio. Someone sat at the man's feet, but he couldn't see that person.

The doors began to close.

He almost opened them to get a better look at the couple by the back exit but thought better of it. As the elevator rose to the thirtieth floor, he considered the man he'd just seen and how close he resembled Aaron's broad shoulders and height.

But that was impossible. Why would Aaron Stevens be idly standing at the back exit of the building where they would meet about Logan?

Something wasn't right. His stomach twisted at the thought, so he checked his weapon to comfort himself. Fully loaded and ready to go.

Silvio slipped it back into his pants and stared at the door as the elevator slowed. A moment later, he stepped off and glanced both ways.

No one was waiting for him.

That was a good sign.

The buzzer for the thirtieth-floor suite was lit up on the right. He pressed it and waited.

The door opened, and a man he thought he recognized from the TV smiled.

"Silvio, please come in."

The man stepped aside and gestured for him to enter.

Silvio hesitated.

"You're among friends here," the man said.

The weight of his weapon reassured him, so he moved inside the suite cautiously.

"A drink, perhaps?" the man asked.

Silvio nodded.

"Help yourself. We're out on the patio." The man gestured at a drinks table, then pointed at the expansive deck. "Randy will be here soon. Join us."

Then the man stepped away and moved out onto the patio, where Silvio heard whispered chatter as two men spoke to one another.

What the hell was happening? Randy said he was contacted by the man who was helping him on the inside. Some friend he had on the force. Nothing to worry about, but they all had to be here tonight to get paid.

When Silvio pressed, Randy had said this was the guy who delivered the Logan message to Alex for them. Silvio had worked with Randy in the past and trusted him. When the concept of Alex getting arrested came up, it was Randy's idea—well, Randy's inside guy's idea, but Randy agreed with it—to have Alex attempt to execute the chief of police. That way, the chief would know he wasn't above their reach, that they could get to him if they wanted. Randy said it would send a message and have Alex arrested and kept in custody simultaneously—a dual purpose.

Silvio agreed, thinking it was brilliant, and so here they were. Alex was in custody, Logan was to be taken out tomorrow, and the man who was Randy's inside guy was inviting them for a drink on a Sunday night to iron out a few final details.

Show up or leave town broke, was how Randy had put it. He swore they were among friends. Nothing to worry about.

Silvio didn't get this involved, only to leave town with nothing in his pockets. The money promised for the job was large, and the woman who arranged the entire gig gave him fifty grand up front. He still had that, which was something he'd kept to himself. Even Randy didn't know about the fifty grand.

Silvio poured himself a whiskey, thinking he could use a drink to calm his nerves. This close to the end of the job made him nervous. So much had gone wrong, but they were still in place to end this.

Worst case, he'd kill these guys and escape with his fifty grand, set up in Vancouver or somewhere, and Logan would still be dead. No one was getting to Alex again. That man was lost to the system now.

Silvio moved toward the patio, sipping once on the way.

At the door, he stared over at the two men watching him, then stopped.

The Chief of Police, Thomas Clark, stared back.

"What the fuck is this?" Silvio asked.

The urge to drop his drink, pull his weapon and shoot the fucker in the face overwhelmed him. Instead, he tightened his grip on the drink.

Both men smiled at him.

"Come, sit down." The man who had let him in pointed at the sofa opposite the chief. "We'll talk and figure out what went wrong while we wait for Randy."

Silvio checked over his shoulder. The inner office area was empty.

"No one is there," the man said. "We are alone."

Silvio stepped out onto the terrace like the professional he was, then moved to the railing and stared out at Toronto. He could play their game. Whatever they were up to, he'd play along.

"We wanted to ask you a few questions."

Silvio turned toward them, staring at the man he didn't recognize. "Who are you?"

"I'm Deputy Chief Roger Sterling."

"You're our inside guy?"

"You could say that."

The chief glanced at Sterling, his eyes not hiding their animosity.

"So, you saved his life?" Silvio pointed at the chief.

The chief got to his feet and stared at Silvio. "Are you the man who sent Alex to kill me?"

The tension thickened between them. Were they recording this? Trying to extract a confession, maybe?

"Who's Alex?" Silvio asked. He had to keep from incriminating himself.

"Okay, cards on the table," Sterling said. "Let's get this preamble out of the way so we can talk freely."

Silvio shrugged nonchalantly. "Works for me."

"I'll start." Sterling got up and stood between Silvio and the chief, who remained standing by the sofa. "You were hired to take care of Kevin Logan. You assembled your team, which included Randy, a friend of mine. Worried about the job, Randy came up with the idea for how Alex would get arrested in order to be on the inside—"

"What?" the chief shouted. "Alex's attack on my life today was Randy's idea?"

"Chief Clark," Sterling said. "Calm down and sit down. Hear us out. Your life was never in danger. I was aware Alex has been coming since last night."

Clark reared back as if punched. "You fucking *knew*?"

"This ends unless you calm down, sir. We are here to find out who hired Silvio. Then we go our merry ways and bring that person to justice."

"Hired Silvio?" The chief sounded like he was in a daze, then his eyes refocused, and he stared at Sterling. "You were on your phone …"

"What?"

"Today, at York University, you were on your phone before I was to go out on stage."

Sterling just stared at him.

"I saw you hold the phone to your ear. You said you had just gotten a tip from a homicide detective. They'd called and warned you that I shouldn't go on and do my speech. I asked you why, and you said because there was credible evidence that Alex was out there to execute me."

Sterling nodded.

"There was no one on that phone, was there?"

Silvio leaned into the railing, sipping his whiskey. It was fun to watch two assholes fight about lying to each other. A much different world than he was used to, where men fought over money or women because everyone lied to one another.

Sterling glanced at Silvio. Silvio raised his glass slightly and nodded in a go-ahead-and-tell-him gesture.

"No, there was no one on that phone call."

"This has been all you from the start, hasn't it?" the chief shouted.

Sterling moved closer to the chief. Silvio wondered if he was about to grab the guy. Was it about to get violent?

"This has not been me from the start," Sterling shouted at the chief. "Just shut up and fucking listen. All I've been doing is protecting you from the start. That was me covering your ass."

"How does that make a lick of sense?"

"If you would sit back down and shut up, it will all make sense in minutes."

They stared at each other for what Silvio thought was a full minute before the chief dropped to the sofa.

Sterling adjusted his shirt and pulled up his pants. Probably some sort of gesture to calm himself.

"So, when Randy informed me of the job to take out Logan and what Alex would do at your speech earlier today, I was aware of the attempt on your life. All this time, it was Silvio," Sterling pointed at him, "who came up with the idea to use Alex and how to get him to do the job."

"Okay," the chief said. "Knowing all this information now, what am I expected to do with it? Let it go? Walk away? How can I walk away from this?"

"How you walk away from this is to find out who hired Silvio's team in the first place. Whether Logan's dead or alive doesn't matter anymore. What really fucking matters is who stands behind the money? Who hired Silvio?" Sterling pivoted away from the chief and addressed Silvio, his arms crossed. "Tell us who hired you."

Silvio shrugged again. "Your guess is as good as mine."

"How did they do it? A meeting? A phone call?"

"Fuck you guys. I don't have to tell you shit."

Silvio started toward the door, setting his whiskey glass on the table as he passed it.

"Walk out that door, and you'll be arrested before you hit the ground floor."

Silvio stopped, thinking about those female cops at the front doors in the lobby, that man he thought was Aaron, and that person sitting by the back exit. They let him come up to the thirtieth floor but wouldn't let him leave.

"Was this a trap from the beginning?" Silvio asked without turning around.

"No, this is not a trap." Sterling moved around in front of him. "The person who hired you is a threat to the chief. I'm on the inside, helping to control that threat. You're on the outside. We pool information, discover who hired you, and remove that threat."

Silvio stepped away from Sterling. He didn't like being so close to the man. For all he knew, Sterling hired him, and tonight, he was killing the contract because he just lied to the chief.

"Earlier, you mentioned we should put our cards on the table," Silvio said as he approached the railing again. It was almost full dark now, the sun gone below the horizon. Small lights lit the terrace, offering it an ambiance Silvio didn't feel. He glanced down into the back alleyway behind the building.

"I did." Sterling retook his position by the chief, who had remained quiet after being stunned by the knowledge Sterling knew about the attempt on his life.

"Okay, then, why are you lying to the chief?"

Sterling narrowed his eyes and glared at Silvio. "Lying?"

"Yeah, you told the chief it was Randy's idea to send Alex after him at the university."

"It was."

Silvio shook his head. "I was standing beside Randy when he called his inside man, which I'm now learning is you. Once we got the job and decided to do it, we talked about getting someone inside the remand center. Randy called his friend on the inside, which is you, because I recognized your voice, and he put you on speaker. I heard you tell us to have Alex attempt to kill the chief at the university speech."

Sterling's jaw trembled, and his hands twitched at his sides.

The chief stared at Sterling with something akin to hatred.

"I heard you laugh when you said it would show the chief he wasn't above the law and that he could be taken out if someone wanted him dead bad enough." One more shrug from Silvio, then he clapped his hands a couple of times. "I guess you did that to make yourself look good by saving the police chief. It all makes sense now."

"You motherfucker," the chief whispered. "I'll have you in jail for this."

Sterling jerked to the right. "Shut the fuck up," he

snapped at the chief. "We will see who is going to jail when this is over. I've been saving your ass since day one, and I'm still doing it. So just shut up and stay seated." Sterling withdrew a weapon. "Or I will make you shut up."

Silvio pushed back into the railing as he fumbled for his gun.

"Don't," Sterling shouted at him now, moving closer.

The deputy chief of police stood five feet from him, the weapon leveled at his face.

"Who hired you?" Sterling asked.

Silvio stared at the gun as it vibrated in Sterling's hand. "I have no idea. Was it you?"

"How did they make contact?"

"A phone call."

"Man or woman?"

"It was a woman. But her voice was disguised."

"Disguised how?"

Sterling held the weapon with both hands now. If Silvio had taken his time answering, Sterling would have to lower the weapon. He couldn't hold it much longer before his arms would tire.

"Metallic sounding. Like she used a device to disguise her voice."

"Do you think you would recognize it again if she called?"

Silvio nodded. "If she used the device, sure. Without it, how could I know who called?"

"Could it be Sarah Roberts who hired you?"

Silvio couldn't suppress the short laugh that escaped his lips. "Why would Sarah organize all this? You're delusional."

"How did she get you the money?"

"Haven't been paid yet." He tried to hold Sterling's gaze but couldn't.

"You're lying." Sterling changed hands, the gun still aimed at Silvio.

"Sterling," the chief said. "Put the gun down. We don't have to do it this way."

Roger Sterling glanced over his shoulder at the chief, and Silvio took his opportunity.

He gripped his weapon, pulled on it, and brought it up to aim at Sterling when it went off.

Something thudded into his shoulder.

He stared down at his gun, wondering how he had fired it when it wasn't even out of his pants yet.

Blood dripped onto his hand.

"What the hell, man," he muttered, wavering on his feet.

He glanced at his shoulder and saw a hole in his shirt. It wasn't his gun that had fired. It was Sterling's weapon.

When he looked up, Sterling scowled at him, a deep redness on his cheeks.

"You shot me," Silvio whispered, an uncomfortable tugging coming to his right chest area.

He dropped his weapon and took a step to the side.

"You drew on me," Sterling said. "Self-defense all the way. A righteous kill."

He fired again. Then again. Silvio felt each bullet, but no pain yet.

Something grabbed him as he fell to his knees.

Then he was falling faster. Much faster.

Did Sterling throw him over the railing? How could he

shoot him and then—

His thoughts were cut off with a violent thump, then nothing.

Chapter 34

Sarah tilted her head sideways. "Did you hear that?"

"Hear what?" Aaron asked.

"Gunfire."

They listened in silence.

"I'll be right back." Aaron moved into the main lobby. "Everything good up here?" he asked.

Ricigliano answered in the affirmative.

"You two hear any guns firing?"

A muffled no, then they said something else Sarah couldn't pick up.

"Yeah," Aaron said. "Exactly, probably just a car backfiring outside."

He started back toward her.

She kept her head tilted to the side.

Then, in rapid succession, a weapon fired several more

times. She was sure of it. She'd heard enough guns in her life to know that distinctive sound.

She jumped to her feet and opened the back exit to see what was outside when Aaron grabbed her shoulder, stopping her.

"Sarah, let me go first."

The baby in her womb offered her a sense of compliance, so she eased back and allowed Aaron to go out first.

"Guys," she spoke into her lapel mic. "We have gunfire outside the back of the building. We're stepping outside now to investigate it—"

A heavy thud erupted from five feet to Aaron's right.

They both jumped and looked over at the same time.

A man's twisted and bloodied body had smashed onto the concrete, his eyes popped out of his head, and his skull snapped and broke with a cracked crease at the forehead. His shirt had been opened, and Sarah saw his skin split upon impact. Legs and arms splayed at unnatural angles offered up a macabre scene, a grotesque image of a human body destroyed.

"Sarah, don't look." Aaron hugged her and tried to turn her away. She pushed him aside.

"Do we recognize him?" she asked.

Darwin burst through the door behind Sarah. "I'll check for ID."

Sarah turned around as Disco came through the door next.

"You guys okay?" he asked.

Sarah nodded. "Just a surprise." She faced Darwin, who was on his knees beside the body. "Check for bullet holes."

Without protest, Darwin straightened the man's shirt, then nodded.

"He's been shot at least twice. Hard to tell with the skin split like this."

"Someone's upstairs," Sarah whispered. "Someone shot him and threw him off the roof."

A man stepped into the alley from twenty feet away. He stopped and stared at the assembled group huddled around the jumper, then turned and bolted back around the corner.

"Motherfucker," Aaron shouted. "That's the guy who kidnapped us and drove us to that fucking barn. I can tell by the swelling around his nose." He started running. "C'mon guys."

Aaron, Disco, and Darwin took off running after the man who had stopped to stare at them for all of three seconds.

"What the hell is going on, Vivian?" Sarah asked.

Ricigliano and Ingrid moved outside to stand with Sarah. Parkman was behind them.

"Someone's upstairs somewhere," Sarah said.

Ricigliano and her partner stared at the body, then looked at Sarah.

"They shot this man several times, then tossed his body," Sarah added.

"Where did those guys go?"

Sarah glanced down the length of the alleyway, her heart racing at how everything was unfolding so fast. "Aaron saw the man who kidnapped him, Parkman, and Daniel."

"He did?" Parkman looked that way, a toothpick flicking in his mouth.

"Leave it," Sarah said. "I need you with me, Parkman."

"Why?" He turned to her. "You okay?"

"I'm fine. But whoever shot this man is coming down to the lobby any second."

"Vivian, tell you that?"

She frowned. "No, but a body attracts attention. This area will be teeming with cops in minutes. Whoever did this will want to be far from this building as soon as possible."

"I'll head back to the parking garage."

Sarah shook her head. "They parked off-site."

"You know this for a fact?"

"It's what I would do."

Inside, through the door Ingrid held open now, the elevator dinged.

They all stared at each other.

"Here we go," Sarah whispered.

Ricigliano pulled her weapon and jumped inside first, followed by Ingrid, who also had her weapon in her hand. Parkman followed, with Sarah taking up the rear.

A man stepped off the elevator.

"Stop right there," Ricigliano ordered.

The man stopped and turned slowly to glare at Ricigliano and Ingrid. He took in their guns, then his gaze wandered over their shoulders to Parkman and stopped on Sarah.

"You," he whispered. "How is it you're all here?"

"How about we ask the questions, sir?"

Sir? Who the hell was this guy?

"I outrank you both by a hundred degrees. I order you to lower your weapons."

Ingrid lowered hers, but Ricigliano aimed hers at the man's chest.

"Where were you, sir?" Ricigliano asked.

"That's none of your business." He spat the last word. "I won't tell you again. Lower your weapon, Detective."

Ricigliano paused a moment, then lowered it slowly. Something told Sarah this wasn't good—not good at all.

"Why are you all here?" the man asked. "And why haven't you arrested that fugitive, Sarah Roberts?" He pointed over Ricigliano's shoulder at Sarah.

Ricigliano moved closer to the man, her gun still in her hand.

"Sir, I need you to tell us where you were."

"I will tell you no such thing," the man stated.

Parkman moved in front of Sarah, shielding her from the action. He must've felt something in the air, too.

"Deputy Chief of Police, Roger Sterling," Ingrid said. "A man fell to his death back there." She pointed past Sarah and Parkman. "He had been shot. Are you armed?"

So that's who the man was: Roger Sterling. No wonder the detectives listened to him when he ordered them to lower their weapons. He was also the man who gave Alex the kill order.

"Of course, I'm armed," Sterling said through clenched teeth. He was obviously seething mad.

"Then we will need your weapon," Ricigliano said. "The building is closed, sir. A man was shot, then he fell to his death. Moments later, you come off the elevator. You are now part of the murder investigation whether you like it or not."

"Plus," Sarah spoke up. "Conveniently, the man who kidnapped Aaron and Parkman just showed up in the alley behind the building. They'll grab him and be back at any moment."

The look on Sterling's face was a twisted expression of anger and disgust. The man looked caught between his pride and his ego. He was used to having people listen to him because of who he was, yet these two detectives were telling him what to do. They wanted his weapon, and Sarah Roberts was calling him out in a suspicious way as if he was connected to the kidnappings—which they all knew he was because of what Alex had said.

Ricigliano raised her weapon again and widened her stance.

"Sir, I spoke with Alex today. He told me about your little meeting. About the hit planned on Kevin Logan in the remand center. There's a body out back and a kidnapper being chased around the corner. We will need your weapon. Ingrid, prepare to handcuff the deputy chief of police."

"This is disgusting," the deputy chief snapped. "I will not comply with the orders of a lowly detective like yourself."

Ingrid yanked out cuffs with a snap of her wrist, her gun still in her other hand.

"Sir?" Ingrid said, stepping forward. "Your weapon?"

Sterling stared at them all momentarily, understanding dawning in his eyes that the detectives wouldn't let him leave without relinquishing his weapon.

"Okay," he whispered under his breath. "Take it easy. Due process and shit. You can have my weapon."

The deputy chief slipped a hand inside his jacket.

"Easy," Ricigliano said.

He withdrew it and swung toward Detective Ricigliano.

A weapon fired.

Then another.

Parkman jumped back and wrapped himself around Sarah, bringing her to the floor in a twisting movement of his upper body that had her land on him to cushion the fall. Sarah heard the air shoot from his lungs with the impact, but he was already wrapping himself bodily over her as another weapon discharged behind them.

And yet another weapon fired.

Then, a deafening silence followed.

One more shot echoed throughout the lobby before it all ended.

Chapter 35

Sarah sat at the head of the table in the green room of their favorite steakhouse while everyone around the table ate and chatted about the past few weeks.

Something about what Vivian had said still bothered her, though.

She glanced around the table, fortunate that everyone was safe and healthy. Well, Benjamin still wore a cast on his arm, but overall, he made it out okay.

"When are they taking off the cast?" she asked him.

He finished chewing what was in his mouth. The others stopped talking to hear his answer.

"Doctors said another few weeks. I complained that it'd been six weeks already, and the doctor told me to be grateful it wasn't longer. Depending on how bad the break is, some people have the cast on for twelve weeks."

Aaron slapped his good arm. "Hey, at least you didn't get shot this time."

Benjamin nodded, then shoved a chunk of meat in his mouth. "There's that," he mumbled.

Sarah glanced at the faces around the table. Darwin had stayed longer in Toronto, which pleased her, and everyone was bonding with Disco. They had both shown up ready to fight for them but didn't have to do much after all.

Parkman was still Parkman, a toothpick in his mouth, smiling at her when their eyes met.

Daniel had fared well and stayed with Benjamin for an extra couple of days until Benjamin was discharged from the hospital.

Then, they had all gone through a series of interviews with the authorities. From the moment the traps were set, all the way to the shooting in the lobby of the Wealth Exchange Building, Sarah had gone over her story two dozen times.

It was later confirmed that she wouldn't be charged in the murder of the police officer behind the Super 5 Inn, nor would the restaurant be pressing charges for not paying their bill that fateful night.

For the first few weeks before the news caught wind of the Kevin Logan affair, as it was being called in the media, they all knew some of what to expect because they'd had a chance to meet with Alex while he was still in custody. He'd explained everything that had happened, not just to Sarah and the others, but to every investigating officer who would listen.

In the end, with Ricigliano's statement and her partner Ingrid CK's statement, all the charges were dropped, and

Alex was a free man.

Sarah moved her gaze farther to the left and watched Alex eating. This mess had taken an emotional toll on him. He'd withdrawn into himself again and spoke less. Truly, he was acting like the Alex she had known for years, but it saddened her to see the regression.

His release had come from the top. Chief of Police Thomas Clark, the man Alex was charged with attempting to kill, believed Alex was set up and forced to do things beyond his control. In the end, Chief Clark claimed Alex had no intention of killing him—which was the truth—and made sure all charges were expunged.

Alex may be a free man, but the chief wasn't.

Kevin Logan came out with his damaging story of a torrid love affair with the chief, which lasted several years behind the back of his current wife. This sort of thing was not a legal matter but a personal one.

The chief's wife was reportedly leaving him, and the chief had resigned, leaving his position eight months early. The media called for his resignation immediately following the death of the Deputy Chief of Police, Roger Sterling.

That gunfight in the lobby of the Wealth Exchange Building left Ingrid in the hospital with a bullet to her arm and Sterling dead.

If it weren't for Ingrid's expert shot, the deputy chief would've killed them all. He shot Ingrid, fired at Ricigliano, then aimed at Parkman and Sarah on the floor.

Ricigliano returned fire several times but missed him completely.

It was Ingrid's shot that stopped the man.

Cool under fire, a bullet already in her arm, she aimed from a few feet away and shot him in the forearm, dislodging his weapon before he could fire on Parkman and Sarah.

She fired once more.

The second bullet entered his right eye and exited the back of his skull.

Deputy Chief of Police, Roger Sterling, was dead when he hit the floor.

The investigation that followed showed it was his gun that killed Silvio Rossi, who lay dead on the concrete in the back alley. They also found Silvio's prints in the thirtieth-floor office, a company of which Sterling was part owner.

The investigation concluded that Sterling was trying to stop Logan and had been working with Silvio to do that.

They even brought in a deep-cover operative named Randy Wilson, who had worked with Silvio's team in the past, to fill in the blanks. Randy was the man Aaron and the others had chased. Showing up late for the meeting, Sterling had summoned them all to his office on the thirtieth floor.

Showing up late and getting away from Aaron probably saved that undercover detective's life. If they'd caught up to him, Aaron might have done damage the man wouldn't have walked away from.

Yet, something still didn't sit well with Sarah.

Vivian had said *The person responsible for everything would get away, and Sarah had to let it go*. She also said *a cop would kill another cop*.

If Roger Sterling was behind it all, he was dead, so that didn't add up because he didn't get away with it all. And was Ingrid's killing of Roger Sterling, the *cop will kill another cop* prophesy fulfilled? That didn't feel right, though, because it was a righteous kill. Vivian's prophesy gave Sarah the feeling that it would be an actual murder, as opposed to a self-defense killing.

Sarah had voiced her concerns to Ricigliano, and the detective had looked into several angles during the course of her investigation but had come up empty-handed.

Ricigliano couldn't join them for their celebratory dinner tonight as she was following up on one final lead but had said she'd call Sarah later to update her.

"I'd like to have a toast," Sarah said, holding up her glass of water.

Everyone set down their forks and grabbed their drinks.

"Thank you all for everything you've done for all these years."

Parkman and Daniel went to drink, but she stopped them with a raised hand.

"One more second."

They paused.

"I spoke with Vivian."

All eyes were on her now.

"We are taking some time off, and she will keep me shielded from more shit until the baby comes. Then Aaron and I will be busy with diapers, the dojo, and late-night feedings."

Daniel and Alex went to drink.

"Once more, thank you all for everything you've done, the risks you've all taken. This isn't over. I'm not done but calming down for the baby."

No one moved.

"Drink now."

A few of them chuckled as beverages were sipped.

"I truly hope this is all over, but Vivian did tell me one more thing."

Forks were set down as everyone faced her. Sarah waited a heartbeat, then glanced up.

"She said something will happen when the baby is born —"

"What?" Parkman snapped.

"Nothing will happen to the baby. She assured me."

"Oh, good." He placed a hand over his heart.

"She said something will happen, and I will be forced to make decisions."

"And?" Aaron prompted when she paused.

"I will be given an ultimatum, an impossible decision, and that Vivian couldn't tell me more. Just know that I'm having this baby, and she'll be healthy."

The room fell silent. Only the soft murmur of dishes and voices from outside the private room they'd commandeered for their dinner could be heard.

"She?" Alex whispered. "I heard she."

Sarah glanced his way, then placed a hand on his shoulder and nodded.

"I'm having a baby girl."

The room erupted in cheers as dinner was momentarily forgotten. They rose from their chairs to pat Aaron on the back and hug Sarah.

"Have you two chosen a name for her yet?" Parkman asked.

Sarah and Aaron exchanged a glance, then Sarah nodded.

"We have."

"And?" Darwin said, leaning closer. "Let's hear it."

Sarah shook her head. "No, we will wait. Let it sit with us for a few months."

"Oh, come on," Daniel protested.

Benjamin was nodding. "Sarah? Aaron? You can't do that to us."

Parkman laughed, and Darwin slapped him on the shoulder.

"You've known Sarah the longest, Parkman. Tell her to tell us."

Parkman snapped around to face Darwin. "If you think I can get Sarah to do anything she doesn't want to do, then you don't know her well enough."

More laughter erupted.

Sarah watched her friends and family and hoped they could always live in this moment, happy, alive, and safe.

But she knew that wouldn't be the case.

Vivian told her several other things that scared the shit out of her. Things about their future. Stuff nightmares were made of, and she just couldn't talk about that yet.

Everyone was too happy.

"Sarah," Alex muttered.

The room quieted again as everyone turned to Alex.

"Stop joking." Alex smiled. "You'll tell us. Right?"

Sarah stared at him, then nodded. "Of course, we'll tell you our baby's name. I was only kidding."

Then she told them the name of their baby girl.

Everyone loved it.

If only snapshots could be taken of a moment like this,

an emotional high, then Sarah's heart would be rich.

In the end, all we have are memories.

Those are what make it all worth it.

Life with such wonderful memories is a rich life indeed.

Chapter 36

Former Chief of Police Thomas Clark tossed another chunk of wood on the fire, then stood back to watch the flames rise higher.

He lowered himself slowly into his chair, lifted his glass of wine, and sipped it, staring into the flames, mesmerized by their calming nature and hypnotic qualities.

It was the head that confused things, the heart that saw through all the shit. If he'd listened to his heart all those years ago and taken a different career path, one less public, he would've found the love he always yearned for. But his head muddled his life into a chaotic mess.

Career, marriage, family life, house buying, and settling down. Follow in his father's footsteps and be a stand-up community man.

He could do all those things, but his heart suffered.

And he fell in love with Kevin Logan.

A torrid love affair, secrets that must remain locked away, and an unfair police brutality charge led to Kevin Logan facing serious time in jail, his career over.

Forced to expose their secret, choosing to do so in court that fateful Tuesday, offered Logan a jury who listened to his lawyer and Logan's plea for sympathy.

The media ran with it, the chief's wife moved out, divorce was imminent, and Clark's career was shot.

He should've listened to his heart in the first place and never got married. His wife didn't deserve the life he felt forced to live—neither one of them deserved it.

The fire crackled, a spark shooting out of the fireplace enclosure. Clark leaned forward to poke an outside chunk of wood, then contemplated adding more while he waited.

The clock above the mantle said Randy was late by several minutes.

Clark sipped more wine, his stomach in knots, and waited. That man had helped him so much over the past half a year that he didn't know what to do without him.

For tonight, Clark had set up two chairs with a small square table between them in front of the fireplace. As this was late October, his cabin near Huntsville cooled off in the evening.

Since his marriage had dissolved, he'd taken more time at the cottage so his wife could stay in their matrimonial home until other living arrangements could be implemented.

A car pulled up outside, gravel crunching under the tires.

Randy was here.

Clark set his glass down and strolled toward the door.

Outside, a car door closed with a solid thunk.

He waited by the door, listening for footsteps, his hand on the knob.

Someone rapped on the glass window behind him.

Clark jumped and spun around.

Randy waved at him through the window.

Clark scowled and swung open the door. "What are you trying to do? Give me a coronary?"

Randy stepped inside slowly, taking in the whole place. "Have to keep my wits about me, what with the current climate out there."

"What climate?" Clark asked as he closed the door.

"Everyone testifying, backstabbing, fucking each other over. One can never know what they're walking into."

"Come in," Clark said, gesturing toward the chairs. He closed the front door and locked it. "You're safe here. It's just us." Clark moved ahead of Randy and grabbed the bottle of wine. "A little red?"

Randy nodded. "Sure."

Clark poured some into Randy's glass, then topped up his own. He handed Randy his glass, and they clinked them together, then sipped. Randy's facial injuries had healed well. He was almost as good as new again.

"How was the drive?" Clark asked, taking his seat by the fire.

Randy eased down into the chair beside him. "Uneventful." He drank from his wine, then set the glass down on the table. "So much happening lately."

Clark nodded. "Yeah, too much."

"You okay?"

Clark poked a log in the fire, then sat back. "I'm as good as can be expected."

"Then why am I here?" Randy asked.

"To talk."

"About?"

"Everything."

"Can you be more specific?"

Clark cradled his glass of wine and stared into the fire. "You quit the force?" he asked.

"Yes, I quit."

"What are you going to do?"

"Who knows? Find work, get a job, and go into sales. What I do know is I can't be a cop anymore."

"Why's that?"

"Are you serious?" Randy asked, a look of disdain on his face. "You called me up here to ask about my future?"

Clark waited a moment, staring at Randy. "Just answer the question."

Randy stared back. "I can't be a cop anymore because everyone found out we had an affair, and through a series of unnecessary fuckups, my undercover gig was blown when my picture, name, and profession were blasted all over the newspapers in connection with you. The sort of men I've worked with before Silvio don't take kindly to that sort of thing."

Their eyes met momentarily, and Clark saw something he couldn't quite put his finger on. Sadness, regret, or perhaps it was resignation.

"I was there," Clark said.

"There?" Randy asked. "Where's there?"

"I was at that rooftop meeting with the deputy chief and Silvio. The one you were supposed to be at."

Randy crossed his legs, then uncrossed them. Was his longtime boyfriend nervous about something?

"If so, how did you get out? Detectives sealed the building shortly after Silvio was shot and tossed over, and Sterling came down to the lobby. We all know how that ended."

"I took the stairs the second Silvio was shot. Sterling took the elevator, which was faster, but while he got delayed in the lobby, I exited through the west side door and blended in with pedestrians."

"Why are we talking about this now?" Randy asked. "It's over."

"You were supposed to be at that meeting."

Clark felt his former lover glare at him sidelong.

"I was late," Randy said in an even tone.

"Silvio said some interesting things on that rooftop."

"Like what?" Randy crossed his legs again.

"That it was Sterling's idea to send Alex after me, to show me I wasn't above the law, that if someone wanted me dead, I'd be dead."

"Sure, it was Sterling."

"But he's dead now and can't defend himself."

Randy leaned forward and twisted around to look at Clark. "What are you getting at, man? That it was my idea?"

Clark faced him. "You want to know what I think?"

"Yeah, I do, without all this buildup. Just spit it out."

"I think you were behind this from the start. You knew Logan was a risk and wanted him silenced, so you went to

Silvio and told him you'd been in touch with someone who wanted to do a job. You called Sterling privately to get his support and tell him what was happening. Once you had planned everything with Sterling, you guys spoke with Silvio, and Sterling proposed the idea that Alex would try to kill me and be arrested, which would get him to the remand center and, ultimately, Kevin Logan. This served several purposes, but one, in particular, was Sterling would be at that speech at York University and could save the day."

"Wow," Randy said. "You've got this all figured out, don't you?"

"There's more. I suspect if Alex went ahead and killed Logan at the remand center, the information he leaked would still surface as his lawyer was in possession of it by then. The plan all along was to ruin my life and my career and possibly have me up on charges in connection with the hit on Logan, as that was obviously an attempt to shut him down. Ultimately, Sterling takes over the position I abandon due to the entire responsibility landing on my shoulders."

"You're crazy." Randy got to his feet. "You're insane."

Clark didn't look up at him. He steepled his fingers and stared into the fire. "But there's one thing I haven't figured out yet."

"Oh, yeah?" Randy crossed his arms in defiance. "What's that, Sherlock?"

"Who was the woman who called Silvio to take on the job?"

"How the fuck should I know?"

The fire crackled, causing Randy to jump.

"You okay? Nervous? Why don't you take a seat,

Randy?"

"I'm fine. I was just leaving. We done here?"

Clark placed his hands on his lap. "Are you sure you don't know the woman who hired Silvio?"

They glared at each other for a moment.

"You want to hear my thoughts?" Randy asked.

"By all means." Clark waved a hand for him to go ahead.

"I think you set this whole thing in motion."

Clark laughed. "Yeah, right. Kill Logan, a man I was in love with, and hire Silvio to get Alex to attempt to kill me, too. Now, why would I do something stupid like that?"

"To avoid detection if it all went to shit. Like a decoy, another version of sleight of hand."

Clark laughed again, this time louder.

"Laugh all you want, but this has your signature all over it, Thomas Clark."

Clark stopped laughing and tightened his fists at the formal use of his name. "Are you still employed, still working? Recording this conversation?"

"Suspended with pay pending investigation of my actions." Randy glared at him. "So, no, I'm not recording shit."

"Are you working right now? Investigating me?"

Randy's mouth dropped open. "You've lost your fucking mind."

"How about a wire? You wearing one?" Clark asked.

Randy smacked the back of the chair and started for the door. "Fuck you. I wasted my *fucking* time driving up here."

"Randy," Clark shouted, leaping up from his chair. "Stop."

Randy made it to the door, unlocked it, then turned back around. "What? Want to abuse me some more after all we've been through?"

"You worked for a lowlife like Silvio." Clark edged sideways around his chair. "What's the name of the lowlife you're working for now?"

"You've lost your fucking mind, Chief." Randy placed a hand on the doorknob. "Why don't you tell me who the woman was who called Silvio? I mean," Randy shrugged, "since you're the one who got this ball rolling."

"Do not open that door," Clark said. "Don't even jump or go for your weapon. I'm going to reach into my pocket and pull something out."

Randy frowned but nodded. "Go ahead."

Clark pulled out a small device and held it up for Randy to see.

"What is that?"

"It attaches to a phone and modifies the sound of your voice. It made me sound like a woman."

Their eyes met as understanding dawned on Randy's face.

"It was you," he whispered. "From day one, you set everything up, and now you get to walk away clean after all of Silvio's team are dead, and the deputy chief of police is dead. A cop died in the line of duty, Ingrid was shot, people were hospitalized, and charged with offenses they weren't guilty of." Randy's eyes watered. "How could you?"

The moment Randy had used his name, the moment Randy tried to bait him into admitting his guilt, he knew they had him. Randy came to the cabin to arrest him, and his backup was sitting outside the cabin. Otherwise, why else would Randy run for the door and unlock it, his hand on the knob. They were all listening, standing on the other side of that door.

Former Toronto Chief of Police Thomas Clark was sure of it and didn't care anymore.

It was over. Truly over.

There was nothing left to live for. He'd lost everything. His wife, career, money, reputation, and now the only person who mattered to him had betrayed him.

"I'm so sorry," Clark whispered and tossed the device at Randy, making him grab for it.

Clark withdrew the weapon at the back of his pants, brought it around, and fired twice into Randy's chest.

The surprised look on his former lover's face as he lowered to the ground, clutching at the blood bubbling from his chest, was enough to break Clark's heart, but some things needed to be done when dealing with a betrayal.

He was prepared to have Logan executed for not keeping their affair silent. So, he was sure as hell prepared to kill Randy, too.

Clark set the weapon on the table by the door and waited for Randy's backup to smash through the door and arrest him.

Randy whispered something Clark couldn't hear.

He dropped to his knees and leaned over the dying man.

"What was that?" Clark asked, all emotion gone for the man who would investigate him.

"I always ..." Randy coughed. "Loved you, sir." He gasped, blood bubbling out the side of his mouth. "I didn't ...

betray you."

Randy blinked once, averted his gaze to the cabin's ceiling, and then gasped his last breath.

Clark ran his hands over Randy's pockets, then around his shirt in search of a wire. No one had barged through the door yet. The gunfire had been loud, but Clark hadn't heard car doors or boots stomping up the front steps.

Where was Randy's backup?

After a full minute, he couldn't find anything on Randy that led him to believe he was wired.

"Did I just kill—" A sob choked him off.

Clark got to his feet, blood on his hands now, and retrieved the gun from the table.

He opened the front door of his cabin and stepped out onto the porch.

Only Clark's and Randy's cars were parked out front.

No one was waiting for him.

He'd lost everything by his own hand, and now he had lost his lover, his best friend. In a moment of madness, a momentary lapse of judgment brought on by the pressures of recent days, he had convinced himself Randy set him up.

But the man hadn't.

He came to the cabin because he still loved Clark.

The former chief of police brought the weapon up under his chin, held it there a moment as tears formed, slid over his eyelids, and then dropped down his cheeks.

Then he pulled the trigger, and the pain ended.

Chapter 37

Sarah's phone rang. She snapped it up while asking for everyone to be quiet.

"Detective Ricigliano, how are you this evening?"

"You sound happy, Sarah."

"We're all happy. Celebrating our health and that we're all still here."

"Well, prepare to get even happier."

Sarah waved for silence, then whispered, "It's the detective." Into the phone, she said, "Go ahead, but I'm going to put you on speaker so Aaron and Parkman and everyone else can listen in."

"Great. Hey guys."

There were muffled hellos offered back.

"I'm up north, in Huntsville. They called me when two bodies were found at a cabin registered to the former police chief. I can confirm the bodies were former Chief of Police Thomas Clark and that former undercover detective, Randy Wilson, the guy who worked with Silvio's team."

"Randy and Clark are dead?" Sarah said.

"Looks like a murder-suicide."

"Who killed who?"

"It appears the chief killed Randy, then stepped out onto the porch of his cabin and shot himself."

"Holy shit."

"I know. But there's more."

"Go ahead."

"The chief has a state-of-the-art security system in this cottage. Voice and movement-activated. We're going over the digital recordings now. We should be able to hear what they were talking about in their final moments very soon. I'm about to listen to the recordings."

"Okay, fill us in when you know more."

"I'll be in touch."

Sarah set her phone on the table and faced everyone. They sat in stunned silence.

"I guess that covers what Vivian had said."

"Remind us again," Parkman said.

"Vivian said the person responsible for everything would get away and to let them go and that a cop would commit murder."

"Didn't we think that was Sterling's murder?" Aaron asked.

Sarah nodded. "Could've been, but this is more likely. When Ingrid shot Sterling, it was self-defense, a righteous kill. This is a murder-suicide."

Several heads bobbed around the table as they nodded.

Darwin raised his glass. "Well, looks like it's finally over."

Everyone else raised their glasses.

"It would appear so," Daniel said.

They all drank as Sarah glanced at Alex. He had a smile forming on his lips.

"What?" Sarah asked him.

"Just happy."

"About what?"

"That it's truly over."

She placed a hand over his, then addressed everyone else. "Ricigliano said she'd be in touch. There's a chance their final conversation was recorded—"

Her phone rang. She snatched it off the table. "Sarah here." She hit the button for the speaker and held the phone up for everyone to listen in.

"It was the chief," Ricigliano said.

"What?"

"The chief confessed on tape. We even have an image of him pulling a device out of his pocket. When he called Silvio's team, he said the device modified his voice to sound like a woman. The chief wanted Logan dead to hide the affair, but everything got fucked up, and he couldn't live with it. Rumors are circulating that he was also having an affair with Randy."

"That all makes so much sense."

"I'll call you later in the week, Sarah. We'll get together. Fill you in more then."

"Talk then."

Sarah hung up again and stared at everyone.

"Anything more from Vivian?" Parkman asked.

Sarah shook her head. "Just that I'll face a decision in a year or two that I won't like. She keeps calling it *The Ultimatum*, but that's not for some time yet."

"Then let's relax, enjoy the rest of the evening, and look forward to March when the baby comes."

Sarah picked up her glass and smiled wide at the thought of the baby coming in March.

"To the baby," she said.

Glasses clinked around the room as a chorus of Sarah's words echoed.

It had been a long road to get where they all were, and they had the scars to prove it. Her dream of finally having a family was coming true. Even though she worried about miscarrying again, Vivian said this baby would be born and the baby would be healthy.

They had finally done it.

She clutched Aaron's hand as Darwin told a story about how the mafia came after him in Italy once and chased him to Florida years ago. He even told them about being deep in some canal where he thought he'd die as he clutched his wife and held her.

Sarah held Aaron's hand tight until he glanced at her and smiled.

Their baby was coming, and if anyone tried to hurt their baby … Sarah couldn't finish the thought.

She just hoped that *The Ultimatum* had nothing to do with her daughter.

Even though Vivian said, it had everything to do with the

baby.

Afterword

DEAR READER,

This was a delicate book for me to write as I had to consider Sarah's condition throughout it. Being four months pregnant, I didn't want her to endure too much punishment. Although this is called the Sarah Roberts Series for a reason, it must feature Sarah somehow.

While considering Sarah's condition, I wanted to feature Alex in a more unique role. He's always been a fun character to write about, so I wanted to show more depth of emotion with him as I've tried to do in this novel.

Also, since you've been reading the series up to this point, you'll notice Vivian has become less involved in Sarah's daily activities. There is a reason for this, which will be revealed in the next novel, *The Ultimatum*. Many things will make sense in the next novel.

I would love to thank author Rania Stone (my wife) for her brilliant help while discussing some of the twists in this storyline with me. Through several conversations where I talked about the plot out loud, Rania posed fabulous questions and even suggested a few things. She fired up my imagination and supported the story as it was written. After every day's writing session, I would email Rania the section I wrote that day for her to read. Since I write fast, and I write daily (every single day until the novel has been completed), Rania receives something to read on a routine basis. She would message me comments, support, and encouragement when she saw subtle plot twists coming together. This was the first novel I've ever written where someone read it as I wrote it, so thank you, Rania, for your help and understanding.

Rania Stone is a Greek author of several novels. Her first novel in English is called *The Unjustified*, and it was released on Amazon in September 2020.

I'd like to thank Ricigliano for using her name in this novel again (it was previously used in *The Delivery*).

And I'm so happy to thank Ingrid CK for allowing me to use her name as well. You're a great shot, Ingrid. Thanks for saving the day in the lobby of Sterling's building by taking him out.

I'm always writing the next novel, which means *The Ultimatum*, Sarah Roberts, book 25, is available wherever you get your ebooks. After that, *The Depraved*, Sarah Roberts, book 26, is ready for you.

Until then, take care of yourselves in this difficult time

and get caught reading.
Sarah and I are sending love your way,
Jonas Saul

About Jonas Saul

Jonas Saul is the bestselling author of the Sarah Roberts Series—more than two million sold!—and has written and published over sixty thrillers. After acquiring an agent, he signed several deals in Los Angeles, with MadRiver Pictures optioning his Sarah Roberts Series— over forty books!—(currently in development).

Jonas has often outranked Stephen King and Dean

Koontz on Amazon over the past decade. He's regularly invited to be a guest speaker, teacher, or workshop presenter at international writing conferences and film festivals worldwide. He hosts an annual writer's retreat in Greece, where he currently lives. He focuses his teaching on how to get tension and emotion in every scene, on every page, how he made it as a creator/writer, the path to success in this business, and the pitfalls to avoid. He also hosts a reading retreat in Greece with guest authors, yoga retreats, and hiking retreats. Visit the Imagine Greece Retreats website at www.imaginegreeceretreats.com, or email him directly to discuss an opportunity to join one of the retreats at jonas@imaginegreeceretreats.com.

Jonas is also a professional freelance editor. He works for several publishers and does private editing for clients, with many testimonials on his website at www.imaginepress.org, which details each author's response to Jonas's editing skills. Email Jonas directly for an editing quote at editor@imaginepress.org.

To book Jonas for a speaking engagement at a writer's conference/festival, to have him on your jury at a film festival, or even to say hello, email Jonas directly at jonassaul@icloud.com.

For updates on releases, hit the "Follow" button on Amazon or Bookbub, and join Jonas on Facebook, where he's most active.

Contact Jonas Saul

Linktree: Find me here

Email: jonassaul@icloud.com

www.ingramcontent.com/pod-product-compliance
Lightning Source LLC
Chambersburg PA
CBHW022014310726
48972CB00006B/1640